Figure of Eight

Figure of Eight

Ray Connolly has written several novels (including *Sunday Morning* and *Shadows On A Wall*), original screenplays (*That'll Be The Day* and *Stardust),* television films and series *(Lytton's Diary* and *Perfect Scoundrels*), radio plays, short stories, biographies (*Being Elvis* and *Being John Lennon*) and much journalism.

Kieron Connolly is a commissioning editor at Old Street Publishing. Previously he held editorial roles at Bloomsbury and Amber Books. As an author, his books include *Dark History of Hollywood* and *Abandoned Places*, as well as four books for children, including *Stories of the Constellations.* His books have been translated into ten languages. As a journalist he has written for *The Times* and *The Mail on Sunday*.

Figure of Eight

Ray Connolly

&

Kieron Connolly

Malignon Books

Copyright Ray Connolly and Kieron Connolly, 2025

The moral right of Ray Connolly and Kieron Connolly to be identified as the authors of this work has been asserted in accordance with the Copyright, Designs and Patents Act, 1988

All rights reserved. No part of this publication may be reproduced without the permission of the publisher.

An unfinished version of this book, titled Snakes & Ladders, was published in 2025. It has now been withdrawn.

Find out more about the authors at:
www.rayconnolly.co.uk
www.kieronconnolly.com

Cover design: James Nunn

Also by Ray Connolly

NOVELS
A Girl Who Came To Stay
That'll Be The Day
Stardust
Trick Or Treat?
Newsdeath
A Sunday Kind of Woman
Sunday Morning
Shadows On A Wall
Love Out Of Season
'Sorry, Boys, You Failed The Audition'

BIOGRAPHIES
Being Elvis – A Lonely Life
Being John Lennon – A Restless Life

ANTHOLOGIES OF JOURNALISM
Stardust Memories
In The Sixties (edited)
The Ray Connolly Beatles Archive

MEMOIR
Born At The Right Time

PLAYS AND SERIES FOR TELEVISION
Almost Tomorrow
Our Kid
A Day in the Life
Lytton's Diary (2 series)
Perfect Scoundrels (1 series)

SCREENPLAYS
That'll Be The Day
Stardust
Forever Young (For TV)
Defrosting The Fridge (For TV)

DOCUMENTARIES
James Dean – The First American Teenager
The Rhythm of Life (co-writer)

PLAYS FOR RADIO
An Easy Game to Play
Lost Fortnight
Unimaginable
Tim Merryman's Days of Clover (series)
God Bless Our Love
I Saw Her Standing There (short story)
'Sorry, Boys, You Failed the Audition'
Devoted

Also by Kieron Connolly

NON-FICTION
Dark History of Hollywood
Bloody History of America
Abandoned Places
Abandoned Castles
Abandoned Civilisations
Forests

FOR CHILDREN
Stories of the Constellations
Disasters
A-Z of Dinosaurs
World's Worst Monsters & Villains
Dragons (co-writer)

For Plum, Louise and Dominic

Prologue

Harry Culshaw wasn't shopping, not particularly, although he was carrying his green Harrods bag. He wasn't doing anything, really. Just mooching. Seeing what was about.

He was, he believed, a handsome man in his late forties, a neat man in an expensive, if ageing, second-hand suit. He had a friendly smile for everyone, soft hands, and thick, nicely cut, dark brown, wavy hair. Sometimes he would reflect that if his life had turned out differently, he could have been an actor and become a star. He always felt like a star, and he checked his look in a shop window as he passed.

Moving through the crowd, everyone seemed busier than he was. At a stall offering assorted roasted nuts a young woman held out her scoop for him and smiled.

People often smiled at Harry. He was that sort of man. Taking a couple of pecan nuts, he thanked her and moved on into a supermarket. Spotting an array of cans of soup, he casually took two and dropped them into the basket he had picked up. Then he wandered to the check-out.

A pretty, young cashier smiled at him, too, as she checked the bar code on the cans. 'So, you like tomato soup, do you?'

'Sorry?' Harry asked, slightly vacantly.

The cashier held up one of the cans as she was putting it into a supermarket bag. 'Tomato soup.'

'Oh, yes, of course. One never knows when they might come in handy.' He hesitated. 'Er, I wonder, d'you think you could double up…the bags, I mean.'

'No need to,' smiled the cashier. 'They are reinforced. Bags for life.'

'All the same.' Harry flashed her a smile.

Good naturedly, the girl reached for another bag and slipped it around the first. 'That should be all right.'

'Thank you,' Harry said and paid her. 'Doing anything exciting this summer?'

'Ten days in Portugal with my boyfriend.'

'Boyfriend! Lucky him!' Harry's eyes twinkled as he took his change. Then, for a second, he hesitated. 'While I'm here, you couldn't let me have another bag, could you. This old Harrods thing is looking a bit dodgy.'

'Sure.' The cashier laughed, as young women do to a man they consider a middle-aged flirt. Then she passed him another bag. 'It'll be thirty pence.'

Harry smiled and paid. 'I hope you have a lovely holiday. I know your boyfriend will.'

Then, carrying his supermarket bags, he wandered on out of the mall.

He was still smiling when he joined the people passing in the street outside.

1.

(i)

Jenny hadn't been looking for a place by the river. It was a sunny afternoon, and, after cycling around for hours, she'd just about accepted that she wasn't going to find anywhere around there that was within her budget. Then she saw it. It must have been a handsome villa once, but now with its stucco walls grey and peeling, it looked as if a wrong piece of an old jigsaw puzzle had been accidentally stuck on to another one showing a glossy, new-build riverside development.

Getting off her bike, she stepped closer to the house. There was a small estate agents' sign attached to the front garden gate. *'The River House - Flat to Let,'* it read.

'We have, of course, a couple of smaller apartments available,' the young woman estate agent said the next day as she led Jenny into the gloom of a two room, semi-basement flat. 'Bijou, I suppose you'd call them. But they would, of course, be more expensive.'

'Bijou!' Jenny repeated, smiling. 'Isn't that estate agent talk, meaning something small and pokey and maybe a bit posh?'

'Well…' The estate agent didn't know how to answer.

But Jenny didn't want to live in a 'bijou' apartment, even if she could have afforded one. So, she agreed a 36-month tenancy on the 'garden flat' of the River House.

'We don't do many fixed terms anymore,' the estate agent said the following day as Jenny signed the documents. 'They're rare nowadays. But the freeholder is getting on a bit and not really interested. Hence the house's general…well, tiredness…and the low rent.'

Jenny picked up the keys from a desk as the estate agent continued talking.

'There are four flats in the house, and, as it's a garden flat you're renting, there are two entrances. One is inside the house via the main staircase. And, if that doesn't suit, the flat has its own front door.'

Jenny liked the sound of that. Having her own front door gave her a feeling of independence. She couldn't remember when she'd last had her own front door.

(ii)

Two small boys were kicking a football about on the front lawn as Jenny climbed down from the Budget van she'd hired to bring her belongings to her new home. 'My neighbours,' she smiled to herself as she made her way up the garden path.

It was dark in the flat, and her footsteps echoed on the bare, old floorboards. But, when she opened the shutters and the afternoon sun came rushing in, she found herself smiling. This would make a terrific sitting room, she promised herself. Her bedroom would be in the other room at the back, where the window looked out on a little patch of brambles.

'It isn't much of a palace,' she murmured, as she studied the basic kitchen and tiny bathroom with its cracked black and white lino. 'But it's my palace.'

That morning she'd left the furnished room she'd been renting in Isleworth, loading up the hired van with books and clothes, and the bits and pieces of furniture that she'd accumulated throughout her adult life. After which had come a visit to Lidl to pick up her weekend groceries. She was excited. A new home meant a new start and her first act was to welcome the delivery men from John Lewis, who brought the new bed and desk to which she'd treated herself.

Her arrival at the River House hadn't gone unnoticed, and very soon an elderly couple introduced themselves and offered to help unload the van. They were the Morrisons, who lived on the first floor Spotting them, Sanjeev and Sarojini Ghelani, the parents of the footballing boys, whose flat on the ground floor, was directly above Jenny's, appeared next to carry Jenny's belongings down the front steps to the basement.

It didn't take very long, and, when they'd finished, Mrs Morrison brought a vase of pink roses from the conservatory that was on the back of her flat, together with a Sainsbury's 'Welcome' card.

'It's been lying in a drawer for ages waiting for someone to welcome,' she explained.

Budget wanted the van back by seven o'clock, so it was nearly nine when Jenny was able to return to tidying up her new home. She was putting Mrs Morrison's vase of flowers on to her sitting room window ledge, when she saw an old Volvo estate car draw up in the road outside. From behind the vase, she watched as a man got out and lifted a large antique, black and white rocking horse out of the back of the car.

He must be the 'quiet guy from the top attic flat', she mused as the man carried the rocking horse up the garden path to the front door.

'He's very nice,' Sarojini Ghelani had told her. 'He likes to go running.'

'He restores old things,' Angela Morrison had added.

'Perhaps he should have a go at restoring me.' That had been Ted Morrison.

'He's a restorer not a miracle worker,' his wife had teased.

It was a pleasant ride past the new riverside development when Jenny cycled to school on the Monday morning. She was in her first term as a Year Two teacher, which meant, she believed, that she got the children before life had scratched away their innocence. And she began this day by drawing on the whiteboard an outline of a square with a triangle on top.

'Who can tell me what this is?' she asked, as she began to add an oblong and squares.

'A house,' chorused some of the children.

'Yes, it is. But it isn't *any* house. It's *my* house. At least part of it is. That's my flat down there at the bottom.' She pointed to the basement. 'Above me, on the ground floor, is a family with two boys who play football a lot. On the next floor are a couple of older people who have a sort of little greenhouse. Then at the top of the house…here…!' She pointed again. 'There's a man who has a big rocking horse.'

'Are you allowed to ride the rocking horse?' a little boy asked.
'I don't know, Maxwell. Perhaps the man will let me, if I get to know him and ask very politely.'

She'd spent the weekend scrubbing and cleaning out her sitting room and kitchen, so she called at Asda on her way home from school to buy some Polyfilla and tins of paint, brushes and rollers.

Then, over the next few evenings, wearing a baseball cap and a pair of old overalls, she set about redecorating. It was satisfying to watch ribbons of sparkling white emerge from the rollers as they made their way across the dirty cream walls.

From the very beginning Jenny felt that the River House was her home. Sometimes in the mornings she would wave a 'hello' to the Ghelani boys as their father took them to school in the Uber he drove; and she would often see the Morrisons in the afternoon when they returned from shopping. But she scarcely saw the man from the top flat, other than when he came and went, usually carrying something.

She knew his name, though. She'd seen it by a bell next to the stained-glass window in the front door. He was Richard Hope. He obviously must have noticed her, too, but they hadn't yet spoken, which, Jenny knew, wasn't uncommon among neighbours in large cities.

Then, one evening, some weeks after she'd moved in, she was painting her window frames when a large globule of white gloss dripped on to a rug she'd bought. It was her own fault, but she'd run out of turpentine and the shops would now be closed. She was wondering what to do, when she saw the estate car arrive, and the man from the top floor make his way up the garden path. She hesitated. He would almost certainly have turpentine.

Climbing the internal three storeys of uncarpeted staircase that ran inside the house, she knocked on the attic door. 'I'm sorry to bother you,' she was saying the moment it opened, 'but I've moved into the basement and....'

The restorer smiled as she explained her problem. 'Of course. I'll just get a bottle.'

'You're sure you don't mind?'

'Not so long as you don't expect me to do the painting, too,' he replied. 'Come in.' And he went in search of the turpentine.

She glanced around. His attic home was the opposite of her basement. While she was aiming at a minimalist approach, mainly because she didn't have much more than the minimum with which to furnish it, every surface of the restorer's home was crammed with jars of restoring fluids and paints, tools, spatulas, brushes and chisels.

'Here we go,' the restorer smiled as he handed her a half full bottle of turpentine.

'Thank you so much. I'll bring it back tomorrow.'

'No need. I have other bottles. Tools of the trade.'

'Oh yes. You mend things, don't you. I mean, like the *Repair Shop* on TV.'

That amused him. 'Well, yes, sort of,' he said.

'Right, well...' Jenny said. Close to, she could now see that the restorer was younger than she'd thought - probably about fifty. His hair was receding and curly, and he was several days' unshaved. 'Anyway...' she continued. 'Better get back before the paint dries.'

As she was turning away, she noticed a cursor blinking on an old computer screen on which a chess set was laid out in mid-game. 'You play against a computer?' she inquired.

'Sometimes.'

'Do you ever win?'

'Yes.'

'And then what do you do?'

'Go to the next level,' he answered. There was a silence. They'd run out of conversation.

'Well, anyway, thank you again.' And, with that, she stepped back on to the landing. 'Good night.'

(iii)

He waited as he watched her go back down the stairs. He'd seen her several times from his window, cycling to and from school in her helmet and anorak. But tonight, with a baseball cap pulling her long, straw-coloured hair off her paint-smeared face, he realised that tough and sturdy as she'd seemed, she was, in fact, quite sunny. How old was she? Mid-forties? Something like that. And her accent? Probably somewhere near Liverpool.

Then he stepped back into his studio, stared at the screen on his computer chess set, made a move, and pressed 'Enter'.

(iv)

The turpentine did the trick and the rug was saved, so Jenny continued redecorating. She thought about the man upstairs as she worked, a single middle-aged man in his cluttered home. Then she forgot about him.

For the rest of the term, she spent every night and weekend building her home, rescuing odd pieces of furniture and carpet from car boot sales, lashing out on ready-made curtains and being choosy about the prints she stuck on the walls. Outside on the front lawn, the Ghelani boys never tired of their football, while at school the children learned to put a pea in a jar containing blotting paper and watch it grow into a little plant.

Her flat was the first place she'd lived that was completely her own. Never having had enough money to put down as a deposit on anywhere permanent, there'd always been a flatmate, sometimes several, or a boyfriend, a few of those, too, who'd had their own belongings and opinions. Here it would be only her opinion that counted. This house had been someone's home for over a hundred and fifty years. And now, part of it, was hers.

So, when, some weeks later she got a letter from the estate agents informing her, as a tenant, that the freehold of the River House had been sold, it didn't concern her, other than that, in future, her rent would go, via them, to another company, Jerricoe Properties.

2.

(i)

Richard Hope was standing by his attic window, getting the knots out of the rocking horse's mane, when he spotted the postwoman coming up the front garden. He was thinking that had the rocking horse been made today some kind of nylon fibre would have been used. But this was real horse's hair from two hundred years ago, and he wanted to preserve as much of it as possible.

So, he took his time, before going down to see if he had any mail. In the hall, Ted Morrison was holding a letter up to the light by the front door. 'Morning,' Richard nodded.

Engrossed in his letter, Mr Morrison didn't answer.

Wondering, vaguely, what could be so interesting, Richard was picking up an envelope from the old settle they all used for the post when a voice called from the open door of the ground floor flat.

'So, you have one, too!' Sanjeev Ghelani emerged holding a letter. 'They can't do this.' he was muttering. 'We have a lease. They can't demand that we leave our home.'

'What?' Richard turned to him.

Neither man answered, but, as one, their eyes fell on the post in Richard's hand. A name at the top of an envelope was written in red italics. *'JERRICOE PROPERTIES'*. Another letter from Jerricoe Properties lay waiting for the schoolteacher when she got home.

Work on the rocking horse was put aside. Jerricoe Properties were giving all the River House tenants four weeks' notice to vacate the premises, together with an offer of five thousand pounds to compensate 'for any inconvenience caused'.

It had to be a mistake. When he'd moved in two years earlier, Richard had signed a five-years fixed term lease. The Morrisons and the Ghelanis had similar agreements.

Richard wasn't perturbed. It was probably a paperwork cock-up. The letters must have been intended for the tenants of somewhere else, he said. Mr Morrison and Sanjeev were less sure.

'These new owners…' Sanjeev muttered. 'Jerricoe Properties! I knew when the house was sold things would change.'

'A change for the better, I'd imagined,' Angela Morrison answered, as she came down the stairs to join her husband in the hall. She was a rosy, capable woman in her late sixties with a billow of bright, white hair. 'Now we know why those surveyors spent all that time measuring and tapping the walls. I thought they were going to do something about the damp patch in our bathroom.'

Sanjeev Ghelani just looked worried. He and Sarojini had brought their two sons to London from Sri Lanka, but finding anything affordable for a pharmacist without the right UK qualifications had been difficult. He now worked shifts, driving a cab.

Going back up to his studio, Richard pulled out his lease and reread it, before looking briefly at the Jerricoe Properties' website which mainly showed a display of sparkling new buildings. There seemed to be nothing to worry about, but to please Ted Morrison, he agreed to accompany him to see a lawyer.

'I phoned Jerricoe Properties,' his neighbour said as they drove into Twickenham. 'But a fellow there said our leases aren't worth the paper they're written on. And that five thousand pounds was a very generous offer.'

'It's just a misunderstanding. You'll see,' Richard reassured.

George Lennox shook his shaved head. 'As I understand it, your previous landlord is sadly no longer with us, and his estate has been bought by Jerricoe Properties.'

'So?' Mr Morrison asked.

Lennox, a high street solicitor smiled. 'Well, it would appear that your new landlord doesn't like the arrangement you have.'

'So it *is* a misunderstanding?' Morrison asked

'No. I don't think it's a misunderstanding at all,' came back the solicitor. 'It's a try on.'

'Trying on what?'

'Putting it bluntly, I would say your new landlords, Jerricoe Properties, are trying on getting you out.'

'Despite us having…?' Richard began.

'Perfectly legal, watertight leases? Yes.'

'And that stuff about the leases "not being worth the paper they're written on"?' Morrison asked

'Huffing and puffing. It happens sometimes. A property company buys an old house to develop and then finds that the sitting tenants are a real nuisance.'

'But they must have known about the nuisance when they bought the house.' This was Richard.

'Of course, they did. That's why they're offering to pay you five thousand pounds to leave.'

'But…' Mr Morrison was becoming increasingly agitated. 'We don't want to leave. They're talking about our homes. They can't develop our homes, can they?'

Richard could hear the bleat of anxiety in the older man's voice.

'Not if you don't want them to,' Lennox smiled. 'Legally, the situation is that so long as you pay your rents for the full terms of your leases, which all seem to be about three further years, there's absolutely nothing Jerricoe Properties can do. They're just in a hurry to get started. These property companies always are. It's just a bluff.'

'A bluff,' echoed Morrison quietly. 'Just a bluff.'

Lennox stood up. 'Now, if you could ask Miss…Miss McKay, from the basement flat, and Mr and Mrs…Ghelani, to drop me a line confirming that they're in agreement, I'll reply to Jerricoe Properties on behalf of all four tenancies. Don't worry. You're all as safe as houses.' And he smiled at the old lawyers' joke.

Lawyers were always so cool, Richard thought, as he and Mr Morrison went out into the street. But it wasn't Lennox who was being bribed to leave his home.

(ii)

Jenny spotted Richard running along the towpath the following Saturday morning. He was in his shorts and fleece and she was on her bike, returning from buying some milk and a newspaper.

'Oh, hi,' she shouted.

He waved and kept on running.

'This Jerricoe Properties thing,' she said as she began to cycle alongside him. 'Do you have a minute for some coffee when you get back? I need to get it clear.'

'Yes, of course.'

'Good! I'll put the kettle on.' And she cycled ahead to read again the copy of the letter she'd received that Lennon, Khan and Partners had sent to Jerricoe Properties.

'So, what our lawyer is really saying to Jerricoe,' she said as she poured two mugs of coffee, is, "Push off, these tenants don't want your money and can't be evicted for the next three years".'

'Exactly,' Richard said.

'And he's quite certain of that?'

'Yes.'

She almost laughed in relief. 'Well, good for him!' Then, taking off her glasses, she folded the copy of the letter, and slipped it into a plastic folder. 'I never imagined being here for ever. I mean, three years will be longer than I've lived anywhere. But I love it here and I was worried.'

'Unnecessarily, I think,' Richard said.

'Well...' she began, and then stopped. Of course, she'd been worried.

'You're doing a brilliant job down here, you know,' he said looking around her sitting room.

'Oh...well... I've made a start,' she said. He was a restorer. The way things looked were probably more interesting to him than a lawyer's letter.

He was now studying the wooden floor that she'd sanded and re-varnished. 'You did this yourself?'

She nodded. She'd fretted when she'd been sanding because the dust from the machine had risen in clouds, and the noise had been mind-shavingly loud. But the other tenants hadn't complained. They were very tolerant.

'I remember what this flat was like before you arrived,' he said. 'Mrs Morrison used to be afraid that dossers would move in. I told her that it didn't seem likely. Even dossers have standards!'

It wasn't much of a joke, but she smiled out of politeness. 'I like to think it's a work in progress. I've spent a fortune…a fortune for me, anyway…doing the place up. So, when I got the letter from Jerricoe Properties…!'

He smiled. 'You never know, if they're as efficient as they are cheeky, they may now do something about the carpet in the hall….'

'Before it walks out by itself,' she laughed. 'They'll have to be quick.'

Then, as, once again, they'd run out of things to say, he left.

3.

Mark Jerricoe considered the letter from Lennox, Khan and Partners without expression. He was, he liked to tell himself, a smooth, clever, intuitive, and, above all, a speedy man of modern property. He understood property, and he understood London, bricks and mortar London, location-location-location London, buy-to-rent London, buy-to-develop London, buy, renovate and sell your way to millions in ever-inflation London.

London property was the modern Klondike. And the beauty of it was you didn't have to go prospecting for London's gold. It was all around you, if you had vision, if you could think and act quickly, super-quickly sometimes, if you could see the future, had the information, access to the money, and if you knew how to handle the right people. And the wrong people, too, when necessary.

Dick Whittington had been on the right track when he thought the streets of London were paved with gold, but, as Jerricoe liked to tell himself, he should be around now. It wasn't just the City or Knightsbridge or the Royal Borough of Kensington and Chelsea that were gold plated. There were millions to be made all over the place: in the former meat market in Smithfield which was being turned into advertising studios, in old churches in Hoxton that were being secularised into offices for software companies, and in the nineteenth century warehouses in Bermondsey that were being heritaged into apartments for City boys and girls. Even Cricklewood and Hornsey were coming up, with former banks and building societies being transformed into smart bakeries and coffee places on every high street. You didn't even have to let or sell some of the buildings you were throwing up! With property inflation it could pay to keep your new flats empty and just sit back and watch their values rise. Everywhere you looked in property there were more and more fortunes to be made. If you were smart…

He leant back in his chair. With his suit jacket on a hanger behind his office door, he was sitting at a large, black, circular graphite table. None of the other four directors' chairs was occupied. They never were. What did Jerricoe Properties want with four more directors apart from their names on a sheet of paper? He, Mark Jerricoe, was Jerricoe Properties, and he liked to sit here at the head of this empty table in his shirt sleeves, the all-powerful, portly 52-year-old property tycoon, with his thatch of blond, wavy hair, silk shirt and red braces.

He loved his hair and he loved his braces. Braces breathed self-confidence and old money. That was the image he wanted to project. Wealth. Wealth from property. Mark Twain had been right when he'd said: 'Buy land. They aren't making any more.' The only thing that puzzled Jerricoe was why everyone hadn't listened to him, why, with banks desperate to shovel money at you, there was still so much land, so much decrepit old property lying around just waiting to be transmuted into gold.

On the table in front of him was a scale model of a small block of offices. Greensleeves, he was calling it. Offices were useful investments, easy to raise mortgages on, easy to rent. But there'd been a hiccup. He was being messed around with this one. Some jobsworth functionaries didn't like the revised design of some of the Greensleeves units. They were, they'd said, 'aesthetically unappealing'. Jerricoe didn't like that. He'd have to deal with it, because, although it might not mean much to the jobsworths, without the redesign, the units would have been a bloody sight more expensive to build and that wouldn't have been very economic.

Putting the Greensleeves problem aside, his attention returned to the letter from some pesky little solicitors called Lennox, Khan and Partners. It concerned a dump called the River House, a place he'd picked up dead cheap for its location. Leaning forward, he pressed his intercom.

'Get Craig up here, will you!' he told Thelma, his secretary.

A minute later the one-man legal department of Jerricoe Properties, joined him. Thin and in his early fifties, he was Craig Hunt. 'Well, Mark? What do you think?' the lawyer asked.

Jerricoe shrugged. 'What do you think, I think? I think these River House tenants are taking advantage of our good nature. I think they're taking us for idiots. I think no more nicey-nicey for the River House. Cancel the offer we made them. They had their chance of a free five thousand easy pounds each and they've blown it. Tell them they're breaking the terms of their leases, let them know about the complaints we've had about the parties they throw, the loud music they play late at night, the drug dealing that we've been told goes on there, and the stinking litter they leave that's making the place a health hazard. The usual stuff. And, just to make sure they get the message, have Vincent give them a little hurry-up.'

'Right, Mark!' Hunt left the office.

Jerricoe looked again at the model of the Greensleeves development. What had those guys been talking about when they'd said, 'the revised design lacks aesthetic value'? What was it with these people? They were losers, all of them in their little, local government gerbil hutches. This world, this modern world of property and progress, wasn't about losers and little people. If all the Lefty losers of the world had their way, we'd still be living in caves.

4.

(i)

Jenny was laughing to herself as she cycled home from school. That afternoon she'd been telling her class about Noah's Ark, when one child had asked her if Noah had let the dinosaurs into the ark along with the other animals. About to explain a child's version of evolution, without offending anyone's religion, and that the story of Noah's Ark was only a legend, a very knowledgeable little girl had interrupted.

'No, he didn't,' she proclaimed. 'Dinosaurs were too big to fit in the ark. That was why they became eggstinct.'

Being a teacher of six-year-olds brought gems like that every day.

She reached the River House just as the Ghelani boys were just coming out to play. They went to a different school and sometimes got home earlier than she did. Pushing the gate open with the wheel of her bicycle, she was half-way to the front door when she saw their football bouncing on the path in front of her. Laying the bike down, she lined herself up for a free kick.

'All right! I'm Mo Salah! Top right-hand corner!' she shouted to them. And, stepping back a few paces, she ran ups and kicked the ball towards the outstretched arms of the elder boy. 'Great save!' she began to call. Then she stopped.

As the boy had caught the ball, blood had exploded across his replica white England shirt.

'Oh, my God!' Jenny raced to him.

In shock, the boy didn't move, then dropped the ball, blood now dripping from his hands. His younger brother began to cry, and ran back into the house, screaming for their mother.

'Are you alright?' Jenny put an arm desperately around the boy, searching for the wound.

The boy pulled the football shirt up to look at his body. There wasn't a wound. There wasn't even a mark.

Then she noticed that the toe of her right trainer was covered in blood, too.

'You're not hurt?' she asked.

'No.'

She looked back down at the football. Blood was leaking from a slit in its body, a man-made, knife-cut incision, four inches long.

(ii)

Richard and Jenny waited outside the Ghelanis' bathroom open door as Sarojini bathed her son. The bloodstained football shirt lay in a plastic bag on the floor. From the hall, they could hear Sanjeev talking to two policemen. In the boys' bedroom, Mrs Morrison was reading a story to the younger brother.

'Who would do this to a child?' sobbed Sarojini. 'What monster would terrify a little boy like this?'

Richard had no answer. He'd called Sanjeev's mobile phone when he'd heard, and then seen, the commotion in the garden. Sarojini had been close to hysterics.

The police officers had taken statements from everyone in the River House, but, after putting the football into a plastic bag 'for further examination', suggesting that it probably contained animal's blood from an abattoir, they'd left without further comment.

Richard had noticed that Jenny cringed on hearing that. Now, as Mrs Morrison returned, fretting, to her own flat, and Sarojini dried her son and took him and his brother to watch television, he and Jenny found themselves unsure of what to do.

'Well...' he began

Jenny looked worried. 'I'm starving. There's a gastro pub by the bridge... If you've nothing better to do...?'

(iii)

They ordered honey-fried lentils and sardines in the Stick and Carrot and waited to discover what that tasted like.

'Sanjeev is convinced that someone at Jerricoe Properties spiked the football to try to frighten us away,' Jenny said as they waited in a booth.

'Is that what you think?' Richard asked.

'It seems unlikely, but....'

He nodded. 'Why would a landlord do that? It doesn't make sense. Think of the bad publicity if he was found out. My bet is some idiot kids did it, thinking it was funny.'

'Idiot kids don't send eviction notices to law-abiding tenants, then, more letters withdrawing their offer and accusing them of breaking the terms of their leases by throwing parties with loud music late at night.' The latest letter from the lawyer at Jerricoe Properties had arrived that morning. 'It would be laughable, if it wasn't.'

'It would, and it isn't,' he agreed. 'But, because Jerricoe Properties are bullies, I'm not sure it follows that they would resort to frightening children.'

Jenny wasn't convinced, and his quiet confidence irritated her. But at that moment, a schoolgirl waitress brought their plates. It didn't taste anything like sardines.

'So, anyway...' Richard said, 'before you came to the River House, you were living...around here?'

'Isleworth. I had a bed-sitter. It was just an in-between thing when a teaching job came up.'

'In between?' he asked.

'In between one life and another.'

He looked at her. And waited.

She thought for a moment, then went on. 'I'm an actor.' She stopped herself. 'I mean, I *was* an actor, when I could be. Signing on when I couldn't. It's a tricky profession.'

'Might I ....er, have seen you in anything...I mean...?' He stopped awkwardly. 'I'm sorry... I mean...'

It was the question that Jenny, like all actors, hated, only asked of those whose careers had been unmemorable. She made it easy for him.

'Not if you blinked,' she joked. 'Bits here, bits there... Sometimes bigger, sometimes smaller. It was like a temporary life that went on for over twenty years, starting in Liverpool with a part in *Brookside*. Then there was *Casualty...Doctor Who,* a couple of parts as "the girl friend", then, when I got older, I graduated to being the "other woman" several times. I quite liked those parts.' She smiled at the memory.

'Then there were pantomimes, Scarborough…Dundee, some commercials, radio plays, more teles, some modelling now and then…that was also when I was younger. Summer seasons. Nothing grand or famous or West End, but it made for a convivial enough life for a single woman with no ties. A few weeks here, a few more there, always moving on to the next job, wherever it was. At the beginning I used to think that one day, if I kept trying, I'd be the next Scarlett Johansson. But… well, you reach thirty, then thirty-five, then forty, and, although actors always think they're younger than they are, you realise, "it's not going to happen, and that's half my life gone… So, what am I going to do with the other half?"'

She stopped. She'd told Richard more than she'd ever even told herself. This quiet man was easy to talk to. Now he was again waiting for her to answer her own question.

'No regrets. I loved the job of being an actor, when the work was good, but not the life in between. And I didn't fancy the look of the future. Then, a couple of years ago, I packed it in and went back to college. And I found that teaching was something I really enjoyed getting up in the morning for…'

He nodded.

'…the tears, the runny noses, someone's missing a mitten. And there I am to sort everything out. Julie Andrews one moment, Cruella de Vil the next.' She pulled a pretend stern face and then laughed. 'To be honest, I'm now wondering why it took me so long to realise how much fun I could have in a classroom.'

'So, you began again?' Richard said.

'I did. And from now on, it'll be just me for me.' She paused. 'What about you?'

'Well…' He stopped, as if wondering what to tell her.

She tried again. 'I mean, have you always been restoring old things?'

'No. I was in the City. Banking. Moving money around all day. Watching out for fraudsters most of the time, which could be quite illuminating. It was an odd thing to do for a guy with a history degree, but that was what I did.'

'So, what happened?'

He shook his head and stared at his plate. 'Things,' he said at last. 'Life. Then I realised I didn't enjoy banking. Probably never had done. So, I dropped out and, sort of like you, started again.'

'And you enjoy it?'

'Absolutely. Every day I come across something fascinating, some problem that needs working out and fixing.'

'And the running?'

He smiled. 'There's nothing like a long run to give the mind the opportunity to work things out … like how best to get nineteenth century varnish off a seventeenth century oak chest without damaging it.'

She understood that feeling. For a few moments they ate in silence. Then: 'Mrs Morrison said that you are…'

'Divorced?' he finished for her. 'Yes.'

'Do you have children?'

He hesitated. 'No,' he said, then looked across the bar. 'Have you ever played backgammon?'

She hadn't, but she was happy enough to be taught. So, with whatever it was partly eaten and partly left, Richard went to the bar to get more drinks and borrowed the board and pieces. Then, as she put the Jerricoe worry to the back of her mind, Richard quietly explained the rules of the game. 'The trick is plotting your assault without leaving yourself exposed,' he explained.

As in life, she thought, but didn't say, because she was trying hard to concentrate. She'd seen how he played chess against a computer and the keen interest he now took in plotting the curve of the play as they each brought their checkers home. He was unshaved again and he was wearing old blue jeans and a navy polo-neck jumper. If it hadn't been for his worn and scratched hands he might, behind those glasses, have been an academic.

The game went quickly, and, looking up from the board, she found herself watching him as he corralled her into a situation from which she couldn't fail to win.

'Hey, not bad,' he congratulated.

She pulled a face. He was patronising her. 'Not good either. You fixed it.'

'Well, maybe I helped. But you're really getting the hang of it.'

'So, let's play again. And this time don't let me win. Okay? I'm a teacher of six-year-olds, not six years old myself.'

He looked up at the sharpness in her tone. 'Sorry.'

She smiled a slight apology. Then together they laid out the board once more and began to play. It was fun. In his quiet, cerebral way, Richard was easy to get along with. She could see now why she'd told him about her life as an actor. He was one of life's listeners. And then she wondered why his marriage hadn't worked out.

5.

Holding the tin of dog food at arms' length, Craig Hunt emptied its contents into two trays, carefully keeping his nose away from the smell as the meat slid into the dishes. As lawyer for Jerricoe Properties, this was the most debasing of his functions, and his list of humiliations wasn't short. Jerricoe knew how much he hated the dogs, two mountainous Rhodesian ridgebacks, yet he insisted that it was Hunt, rather than his secretary, Thelma, or any of the other staff, who fed them. Quite why Jerricoe should enjoy watching him do something that clearly turned his lawyer's stomach, Hunt didn't know. Was it because Jerricoe knew he was afraid of the dogs? The dogs certainly sensed it. Or was it simply that Jerricoe got off on bullying?

'Craig, you're the only one I can trust with them,' Jerricoe would schmooze whenever Hunt suggested someone else feed the dogs. And then he would smile that row of white caps and bridges.

'Why do you take it?' Paula, Hunt's wife, would say, whenever he was unwise enough to voice his complaints at home. 'Why don't you take a walk and set up your own property business? You know you could!'

But if he'd told her once he'd told her twenty times why he didn't do that. Like him or loathe him, and none of the employees at Jerricoe House liked him, no-one could spot an opportunity quite like Jerricoe. He might be a reptile to work for, but he could see a good buy in a moment, and in another he would have acted on it. It might be a pain for Hunt to take all the abuse, but for the three percent of net profits which Hunt was given on top of his salary, he'd do whatever was thrown at him.

And, yes, there was something else. He might be only a lieutenant, but he was *the* lieutenant, the guy with the quiet advice when that was needed, and the one who got the difficult things done when other routes had to be taken. He was good at that. He had the contacts. He could make things happen with a phone call, no questions asked, no dirt on anyone's doorstep.

Jerricoe valued that. It meant that Jerricoe Properties always, just about, kept their hands clean; and that, although she didn't appreciate it, Paula could live in a very nice, four-bedroomed, detached house in Hendon.

Chucking the empty can into a waste bin, Hunt released the dogs from the pen at the back of the Jerricoe Properties office block and watched as they threw themselves at their breakfast.

Then, going back inside, he headed for the staff bathroom to wash any trace of dog food, or even dog, from his hands before Ella, his secretary, arrived. He didn't like to think he would be smelling of chunky jelly meat when she got there. Only when his hands were clean could he go to his office and begin his day's work.

And, in the expanding Jerricoe portfolio of properties, there was always work, always a problem to be resolved, arranging a little encouragement here, organising some discouragement there.

Turning on his computer, he opened the file on the River House.

6.

(i)

Richard had been out running, keeping to the pavements because it was now dark, and had been about to open the garden gate at the River House when the screaming started.

Ahead of him the house was in darkness, but he could see that the front door was open. The hysteria was coming from inside the hall. The Ghelani boys were coming out of the house on to the front steps, followed by their father who had his arms around their mother. Sarojini was sobbing uncontrollably.

'What's happening?' Richard asked as he approached them. 'What is it?'

Sanjeev could hardly speak. 'In her eyes…her hair…on her skin…'

'What…what?' Richard asked.

'She couldn't see.' Sanjeev pointed inside the house. 'No lights. It touched her lips. Blood on her mouth.'

Moving past the sobbing, frightened family, Richard stepped into the hall and tried the light switch. It didn't work. He peered into the darkness, then, taking his phone out of his fleece, he pointed its beam like a torch around the hall.

Only when he shone the beam towards the door to the Ghelanis' flat did he see it. Swinging backwards and forwards by its tail from the door frame was a large rat, its body now bloodied and leaking as it fought to escape from the hook and the length of wire holding it.

He stepped back in revulsion.

'She walked straight into it,' sobbed Sanjeev. 'Its claws, blood, tail, urine, everything! Vermin! Filth in her face! In her hair. On her lips!'

(ii)

'The electricity people say they received instructions from the landlord to disconnect the supply,' Ted Morrison was saying. 'They thought the house was unlived in. They apologised for any mistake.' He and his wife had been out all day doing some

Christmas shopping. 'That must be instructions from Jerricoe Properties.'

Richard didn't answer. The main junction box was in an outhouse around the back of the house. The engineers must have thought the house was empty and disconnected it.

Across the hall, in flickering candlelight, two vermin control officers, their hands clad in padded gloves, carefully cut the still wriggling animal down from the hook and dropped it into a thick sack. Its outline could be seen to be still moving, though more slowly now. Though the police had arrived quickly at the house, they hadn't been prepared to take the rat down. 'That's vermin: a council job,' they'd both insisted.

Richard looked back at the Ghelanis' door. It was stained with blood where the animal had battered itself nearly to death in its attempts to get free. The candles had been provided by Jenny. She'd arrived home from school shortly after the police had got there, and had immediately taken the still trembling Sarojini, and her sons, downstairs to her own flat.

At the front door, Sanjeev was still weeping in anger and frustration. 'This is the landlord's doing.'

The two police officers, one, a sergeant with a beard, the other pinker and younger, wouldn't be led. They'd heard Sanjeev say this several times already. 'Looks more like racist thugs to me,' the more senior one said, turning to Ted Morrison. 'You were out all day, right? And your neighbour upstairs was out running.' The beard indicated Richard.

'It could have been anyone,' chimed the boy policeman.

'It was Jerricoe Properties alright.' Ted Morrison insisted. 'They have keys to the house. They can just walk in at any time they like and do anything they want. They did this.'

'I'm sorry, sir, we'll look into it, but you have no evidence to support that. Perhaps Forensics will find something.' This was the sergeant.

Sanjeev was bubbling with emotion. 'For heaven's sake, we're being frightened, harassed, terrorised in our own homes…'

'We *know* who's behind it,' came in Ted Morrison.

'No, sir, you only *think* you know.' The younger officer was now scoring points.

His colleague frowned, not wanting to get into an argument.

'We know,' Sanjeev said dully.

'Yes, well, we'll be conducting enquiries. A report will be made.' The sergeant looked at his watch.

Richard stepped forward. 'Jerricoe Properties. Do you know anything about them?'

The policeman shook his head. 'A report will be made,' he repeated, and looked towards his younger colleague who was now taking a call on his radio about a traffic accident. 'But if I were you, I'd have a word with your landlord about the electricity. Obviously, someone slipped up there.' Then, glancing at the blood where the rat had been hanging, he added. 'And if anything like this happens again…' He didn't finish his sentence.

Sanjeev just looked at him. 'You can't help us, can you!'

There was no answer.

Sanjeev gave up. Then, as his wife and sons, followed by Jenny, arrived, back in the hall from the basement, he turned his back on the police, took his family into their flat and closed the door.

The police let themselves out.

Taking a damp cloth from a bucket held by his wife, Ted Morrison cleaned the traces of the rat from the door.

'Disgusting!' his wife shuddered. 'Jerricoe Properties are the real vermin.'

Jenny looked at Richard. 'So? Do you still think all this has nothing to do with Jerricoe Properties?' she asked.

Then, without waiting for an answer, she went back down the stairs to her own flat.

(iii)

Richard's politeness and ever-reasonable optimism had given Jenny false hope. There was every reason to worry. The Ghelanis' younger boy had been sick, throwing up over his school uniform. He'd been *that* frightened. It might not be Richard's fault, and up there in his studio with his artefacts, he might be as upset as she was. But he'd been wrong, and she couldn't help being angry with him.

Holding a candle, she considered her sitting room. It was looking better every time she came home. She'd nearly finished all the redecorating that she could presently afford. The rest would have to wait until the New Year when she'd have saved some more money. But would there be a New Year for her at the River House?

She stopped the thought. Going to her front door, she pushed the two solid mortise locks into place.

7.

The Ghelanis began to empty their flat as soon as Sanjeev had hired a white Ford Transit van the following morning. A cousin who lived near Heathrow Airport had promised them lodgings for a while.

'But, Sanjeev, we're in the right!' Richard protested, hurrying down the stairs as the family carried their belongings out to the van. 'See!' And he pointed through the window to an engineer who was reconnecting the electricity service.

'In the right, yes, but in the wrong place,' Sanjeev snapped.

Richard put a hand on his arm. 'Jerricoe Properties can't do this to us. We can't let them.'

Sanjeev shook his head. 'We can't stop them. Not me. Not you. The lawyer doesn't help. He just sends letters. They ignore him. Nor are the police of any assistance. I'm sorry. We've been happy in this house. Even after what happened last night my wife wanted to stay and fight them. Sarojini is a very brave woman. But we have our sons to think about.' And, picking up a packing case full of clothes, he pushed gently past, and went on down the path to the van.

At the foot of the stairs his two boys, the elder holding a new yellow football, watched in silence. Richard looked at them. Jerricoe Properties had chosen the right targets.

He'd phoned Lennox, Kahn and Partners earlier that morning only to be told once again that legally there was nothing Jerricoe Properties could do to them. Lennox had used the world 'legally' three times in a very short conversation, which, coming from a solicitor, perhaps particularly from a solicitor, sounded ominous.

'What about *illegally*?' Richard had inquired, but that hadn't been a conversation Lennox wanted to engage in.

From the front lawn he watched the final loading of the van. Then he tried calling Jerricoe Properties' lawyer once again.

A secretary was still blocking his way. 'Like I told you, Mr Hunt is in a meeting.'

'Actually, you told me he was out. I must speak to him.'

'He was out then and he's in a meeting now.'
'Can't you interrupt the meeting?'
'No.'
'What about Mr Jerricoe? Is he in?'
'He's in a meeting, too.'

He tried to keep his temper. 'Do you know that your company is driving a good and happy family from a home to which they are legally entitled?'

No answer.

'I must speak to either Mr Hunt or Mr Jerricoe.'
'Like I said…'
'I'm not getting off this phone until…'

There was a hesitation, a click and suddenly a man's voice. 'Hello?'

'Is that Mr Jerricoe?'

'No! It's your final warning. Get out of our house. All of you! D'you understand? You've broken the rules of your tenancy. You're trespassing.'

'We are not trespassing. We have every right …' Richard heard his voice rising.

The volume down the phone increased. 'You heard me! You're *trespassing!* Now get out!' The line went dead.

Richard felt his face redden. 'Bastards!'

'Excuse me! Richard?' He hadn't noticed Sarojini approach. She was holding two boxes that had been carefully wrapped in silver paper.

'Sarojini! I'm really sorry…' he began.

She stopped him. 'Yes, yes,' she tried to smile, but tears were too close. 'Perhaps it's for the best. Anyway, I wonder if you could give one of these to Jenny when she gets home from school today. I'm sorry to be leaving without saying goodbye to her. The other is for you.' And she passed the boxes to him.

He was surprised. 'Oh, thank you.'

'They're nothing really. Just little presents. They're supposed to bring good luck. If you're going to stay here at the River House you might need some good fortune.' And, with tears welling again, she hurried off across the lawn to collect her sons.

A few minutes later, standing on the steps of the River House, with the Morrisons at his side, silent and worried, Richard watched as the white van was driven away.

Going up to his flat, he looked inside the box that Sarojini had given him. It contained a ganesh, a tiny, brass, four-armed, elephant headed Hindu god. Then, sitting down at his computer, he wrote another letter to the head of the housing department at the London Borough of Riverside.

8.

'The rat trick! Beautiful. It never fails!' Mark Jerricoe chortled and sat down at his desk.

Standing opposite him, Craig Hunt was pleased, too. 'People have a deep-rooted psychological terror of rats. They associate rats with dirt and disease and death. So, they're very effective. And cheap.' He smiled. There would be no more whingeing calls from those River House tenants. Jerricoe never took those calls himself. He might be a callous bastard, but his voice was light and thin. Hunt's gravel bass did menace better.

'Yes, well, whatever. Thank Vincent and his pals for a nice, clean job.'

Hunt nodded. It was his policy to outsource and spread the workload when it came to persuasion. He'd learned early never to entrust any mercenaries with too much knowledge. In that way, if anyone ever got too nosey, there would be only so much they could be told. 'Yes. Vermin are a Vincent speciality,' he said.

'So, one down, three to go on. Keep after them. Now we've got rid of one lot, they'll all go if you push hard enough. And keep leaning on that letter-writing solicitor they've hired. Perhaps we can do him a favour. We need this thing settled.'

'No problem, Mark,' Hunt nodded. 'Plans are already in…'

Jerricoe cut him off. 'Just deal with it, Craig.'

Hunt left the room. Jerricoe had no right to speak to his lawyer so dismissively. One of these days he'd leave him to deal with the police himself when they came asking questions again, as they had that morning. It took skill and experience to keep putting the police off the scent.

9.

(i)

They were standing by the front door, sheltering together under a dripping umbrella, when Richard got back from the British Museum. Huddled there in the rain, they looked old and tired.

'Hello, what are you doing out here?' he asked as he was about to put his key into the door.

'We're locked out, aren't we!' Mrs Morrison smiled, fake jolly.

'You've lost your keys?'

'They've changed the locks. Jenny can't get in either.' And she indicated Jenny's bicycle propped against the wall. 'She's gone to get us a drink. Jerricoe's had different locks put in while we were all out. That's what comes of taking advantage of half-price matinee tickets.'

Richard took his key out of the lock. While Mrs Morrison was trying to make light of the situation, her husband was staring silently into space. 'And you've phoned Jerricoe Properties?' he asked.

Mrs Morrison smiled. 'Of course. We got the answering machine. Not to worry. The locksmith will be here shortly.'

Footsteps on the pavement alerted them to Jenny approaching with a tray of coffee from the Tesco service station on the main road. As Mr Morrison went to open the garden gate for her, his wife's cheery front dropped. 'I think this is the end for us', she said quietly. 'Ted can't go on like this. It's affecting his nerves.' She blinked back a tear. 'You know…I could kill that Jerricoe! I really could.'

It took two hours for the locksmith to arrive and get them back into the house, by which time they were all very wet and cold. No-one had said very much as they'd waited. Jenny hardly looked at Richard.

Back in his flat, Richard made himself a warm drink. Then, sitting down at his computer, he googled the name 'Mark Jerricoe', and set to work.

(ii)

Two hours later, Jenny stared in astonishment at the stack of paper on her desk. She'd been about to go to bed when Richard had phoned down to her. If it wasn't too late, he had something to show her, he'd said.

'Crikey! Where did you find all this?' she asked, sifting through scores of pages of printouts.

'Where I should have looked in the beginning. It's always thre somewhere online.'

'And you knew where to look?'

'Like I told you, when I was in banking, one of my jobs was digging into the financial backgrounds of some pretty big scallywags. Jerricoe is small time compared with them, but it took a while... It seems he's had quite a career.'

Jenny leafed through the pages of local newspaper cuttings, blogs, Companies House notifications and details of council meetings. 'So, does anyone ever win in disputes with Jerricoe Properties?' She could hear the dismay in her question.

'No tenant that I could find has ever won,' Richard said as he poured them both a glass of wine. 'Tenants complain to the police and their lawyers, just like we've done. But Jerricoe has a lawyer, too, this Craig Hunt guy, and somehow...'

He left the thought hanging. That morning, he had received a reply from the London Borough of Riverside telling him that disagreements between tenants and private landlords didn't concern them.

'What happens if the tenants don't do what Jerricoe wants them to?' Jenny asked.

'Well, according to one Twitter thread, a guy in Croydon tried that and a few weeks later he was involved in a hit and run. He changed his mind while he was in hospital.'

'They had him run over?' Jenny said aghast.

'It could have been a coincidence. No-one was ever charged.'

Jenny looked back at the printouts. Some were straightforward financial reports, and others were favourable profiles from glossy property magazines, charting the making of a new London company and its up-coming star in bricks and mortar. *'Multi-millionaire property genie who buys on instinct,'* she read aloud. Then another: *'Expanding empire of tycoon who just won't take "no" for an answer.'*

A couple of others, however, had a different perspective. *'Tenants complain over property tycoon's methods,'* read one. *'Landlord harassment charge dismissed: lack of evidence,'* bleated a court report.

She considered a photograph of Jerricoe from a magazine. He was middle-aged handsome, his blond hair coiffed and gelled, his nose slightly piggy. 'He's just a dandified spiv!' she exclaimed.

Richard nodded.

A headline caught her eye: 'What's this? *"Jerricoe to develop hi-tech leisure centre"'* she read. 'What's this all about?'

Richard looked awkward. 'Apparently us.'

'What?'

'We're sitting in it. Your landlord wants to convert the River House into an up-market health spa. He's taken a fancy to our mid- nineteenth century architecture.'

(iii)

For two weeks there was a quiet edginess around the River House as the Morrisons began putting their furniture into storage, saying goodbye to the plants they'd nursed, and looking around for a new home to rent. They would be out before Christmas, they said. There weren't any tears from them, just an angry bitterness.

As more demanding letters, which stopped just short of being threats, came from Jerricoe Properties, Richard gave up hope of doing much work, and concentrated instead on pleas for help to Lennox, Kahn and Partners, the Metropolitan Police, Citizens Advice and the local council. A letter to his

Member of Parliament resulted in a reply urging the MP's constituents to seek a meeting with their landlord to 'negotiate a settlement equitable to all parties'.

'How do we negotiate with someone who makes a point of refusing to take our calls?' Jenny asked as she'd read the MP's letter.

One evening Richard rerouted his regular run and jogged over to Acton to see the sort of place Jerricoe worked in. He was surprised. He'd expected something stylish and modern, but, as he passed the building, so unlikely did it appear he nearly missed it. A two-storey, square, yellow brick cubic blob on a practically deserted industrial trading estate, with window grills and CCTV cameras, Jerricoe Properties looked like a modern fort in a state of siege.

The following evening Mr Morrison took him for a goodbye drink. 'The thing is, Angela doesn't deserve this,' the old man wheezed, bleakly confessional, as they walked along the towpath towards the Fisherman's Rod, the only traditional pub left on this stretch of river. 'We owned a very nice semi when we had the business. Mock Tudor, late Twenties. You know the type. Good garden, too. Angela loved that garden. But when we gave up the business ...' He stopped talking. Then: 'Actually, we lost the business. We had to sell the house to repay the bank. I kept putting it off. Hoping that things would get better. They never did. We should have got out much earlier. By the time we did, we had hardly anything left...'

Richard had suspected something like this. The Morrisons had owned a small printing firm, but in an age when every office and every home had its own printer, it must have been a dying industry. Now he understood why a couple of the Morrisons' age and view of themselves didn't own their own home. They'd fallen off the property ladder and been unable to climb back on again.

'After that our pensions were enough to get by on, but not enough to buy another house. And getting a mortgage was impossible at my time of life. We rented various places, but they weren't right. So, when we found the River House, even with all its problems, we saw it as a sanctuary. We thought we had at least another three years or so. And then maybe an extension. Now we'll probably have to throw ourselves back on our daughter and her family for Christmas and hope that something turns up.'

Richard didn't say it, but the River House had become a sanctuary for him, too.

They'd reached the pub. Before the new apartments had been built it had been a cosy Victorian working man's relic. Now a group of young blades wearing expensively casual clothes talked loudly about cars and trading. Had he been like that when he'd worked in banking, Richard wondered. He hoped not.

Standing at a window with their beers, the two men watched reflected lights dappling on the river. Not everyone could be lucky in property, Richard thought, as Mr Morrison silently considered his regrets. For every winner, there had to be a corresponding loser, the unlucky person who bought or sold too soon, or too late. Or who could simply never afford to even get started. It was like a game, and it could be cruel. He knew a lot about games. And they were losing this one.

10

(i)

The Morrisons moved out the next day and Jenny and Richard found himself alone in the house. Every echo was now magnified in the bare rooms.

'It's strange how much bigger the house feels now that there are just the two of us here,' he told her as they met in the hall one afternoon. She was coming in from school and he was putting out his recycling.

She agreed. 'I miss the sound of the cartoons on television that the boys used to watch,' she said. 'They would wake me every morning.'

The following day was Saturday, and he had some books to return to the London Library. So, it was afternoon when he got back, and, letting himself into the River House, he was about to climb the stairs when he heard a door creak in the Ghelanis' former flat.

He stopped in alarm.

Should he investigate? He wasn't sure.

Then Jenny's head appeared around a door. 'Thank heavens it's you,' she said, relieved. 'I thought it might be the rat-man again.'

He smiled. 'Snap!'

She hesitated. 'I suppose it's all right to look around the rest of the house now, isn't it? The Morrisons left me their spare keys and the Ghelanis, too. But I feel as though I'm trespassing.'

'I don't see why you shouldn't look. I'll come, too, if you like.'

For the first time in weeks, she smiled at him. 'Thanks.'

So, he joined her, and they roamed together through the two middle, empty floors. With everywhere dutifully swept clean by their departed neighbours, they marvelled together at the spaciousness and elegance of the main rooms, the panels on the walls, and the cornices in the ceilings.

Their own two flats were in what would have originally been either the children's or servants' quarters, at the top and bottom of the house respectively, and they were, therefore, functional rather than grand. But in the middle floors, although the family rooms at some time, had been clumsily sub-divided, there was a memory of solid bourgeois aspirations where floor-to-ceiling windows looked out over the garden wall and across a patch of bushes towards the river.

'Can you imagine how it must have been to live here in Victorian times?' Jenny asked, as they watched the river from the Morrisons' old sitting room. 'I bet this was the wharf master's home, if there was such a job. At least it would have belonged to someone important like that. He'd have had a big, happy family living here, helping him in whatever he did.'

Richard smiled at the image of the Victorian idyll. 'Are you from a big, happy family?'

'Hardly,' she smiled, shaking her head and pulling a funny face of mock misfortune. 'My parents divorced when I was eight and both remarried quite quickly. My sister, Sue, and I spent most of our time going from one to the other, Mum and grandparents in Blundellsands, where we grew up, Dad and his family in Scotland. Not ideal.'

'Blundellsands?'

'Near Liverpool, where Antony Gormley put the figures on the beach.'

'Oh, yes! And your sister?'

'Sue's still in Liverpool. She's a nurse. I was the wanderer in the family. I always wanted to be somewhere else. Usually I was.'

'But your parents…?'

She shook her head. 'Mum died when I was at college. She was a nurse, too. My dad's been divorced a second time and is now living in New Zealand with some Australian bimbo called Marriette, who has a sexy gap between her teeth and a bottom the size of New South Wales.' She grinned when she said that.

'That's some bottom.'

'You should see it. She's my age and apparently took a shine to Dad when he was teaching the finer points of smuggling at a police college in Sydney. He was a customs officer before he retired.' Then, taking another look around the room, she added: 'If this place is to become a health spa it would suit Marriette. She's a keep-fit fanatic, despite the bottom…'

'Or perhaps because of it.'

She laughed at that, her eyes bright, and he thought, when she wasn't angry or disappointed, how attractive she was. And then he reflected that she'd had every reason to be angry and disappointed.

'What about your family?' she asked.

He shrugged. 'Retired now. They were both teachers. Happily married.'

'Lucky them!'

'I think so.'

'Or perhaps they made their own luck?' She looked closely at him when she said that, and it occurred that she might be enquiring about the failure of his own marriage. Had he made, or not made, his own luck? It was a question he'd asked himself many times.

He returned to working on the rocking horse that evening, having put it to one said while he'd had to re-carve part of one of its ears. Jenny would, he thought, probably be planning a lesson. They were hardly friends, only drawn together by a shared problem, but, as he worked, he realised, with some surprise, that he couldn't help but be aware of a slight, unspoken intimacy at their being alone together in this large empty house.

Whether Jenny noticed it, he didn't know.

(ii)

A week after the Morrisons left, Lennox, Khan and Partners, sent emails to the two remaining tenants, inviting them in for a meeting.

'Isn't this unusual?' Jenny demanded as they met outside the lawyers' office. She'd come straight from school and was wearing a red woollen hat, the flaps of which came down over her ears, and matching red mittens. 'He never calls us or takes any real interest apart from writing letters and sending bills. And now we're summoned.'

'Maybe he feels he should be doing more to help.'

Jenny looked at him coolly. 'You know, Richard, your generous view of the world might be considered admirable, even charitable, if we weren't bleeding in a sea of sharks.' Then she opened the door.

Sitting behind his teak desk there was, she thought, a change in Lennox's demeanour. Now, as he leafed once more through the River House file, wagging his head at the intransigence of Jerricoe Properties, his attitude seemed almost paternal towards them.

Eventually he pushed the file to one side. 'Of course, as your solicitor, I'll pursue every legal avenue open to you, and you do, as I've told you many times, have right on your side. But, if I can stop being a lawyer for a minute, it seems to me that there might be other things that you might wish to consider.'

For a second Jenny's eyes flickered towards Richard, but then they were summoned back, as Lennox directed his attention solely at her.

'Are you, Jenny, still happy in your home? Do you feel safe there?'

Suddenly they were on Christian name terms. Jenny seemed about to answer, but he didn't give her time.

'And you, Richard, can you work with all this going on? Whether or not we can prove that agents of Jerricoe Properties are responsible for the harassing of tenants, and, as you know, the police have no evidence to link Jerricoe with what's been happening. Is the River House as conducive a place for you to work as it used to be?'

'It would be if there were no more…incidents,' Richard said.

'I'm sure, I'm sure,' sympathised Lennox. 'But, sadly, neither you, nor I, nor the police, nor indeed anyone, seems to be in a position to guarantee that.'

Jenny now felt Richard looking at her, although she was staring out of the window at a flashing neon light over a betting shop across the street.

'What are you suggesting?' she heard Richard ask the lawyer.

Lennox wasn't to be drawn. 'Nothing. Nothing at all. Other than to say that, although the law may be on your side, can you afford the battle? Can you both really keep on fighting Jerricoe Properties?'

The door of Lennox, Kahn and Partners had hardly closed behind them before she came straight to the point. 'So, when will you go?'

They were walking back through the shoppers, past coloured fairy lights and Christmas trees in shop windows. The sound of Slade singing *Merry Xmas Everybody* was leaking from a jeans shop.

Richard frowned. 'God, I don't know. I don't know what to do. Maybe I'll wait until the New Year, then look around. I'm not sure. What about you?'

She'd guessed right. He hadn't admitted it in front of Lennox but the slump in his posture had betrayed him. He was giving in. She should have known. Anything for a quiet life so that he could get on with his work, that was Richard. She fixed her mind on the Slade record and walked on without answering. *'So here it is Merry Christmas, everybody's having fun...'* Noddy Holder was singing. Some lyrics, you could never forget.

'What about you?' he repeated. 'Any ideas?'

'I'm staying,' she said.

He frowned. 'I know how you feel, but I don't think that's …'

She exploded. 'I don't want another bloody home. I've got a home. A very nice home. I signed an agreement, and it's mine for the next three years. *Legally*, mine! So, I'm staying. You go if you want to…'

He stopped walking. 'You'll be alone in the house! By yourself!'

'Great! I'll be able to play my music as loud as I want to. Not Slade, mind you.'

'Jenny!'

'I can see why you should go. You have your studio, your clients, valuable objects. And, let's face it, you haven't been able to get much work done for weeks. I don't know why you've stayed as long as you have. I'm surprised you didn't go when Sanjeev and Sarojini went.'

'Oh, come on!'

'No, *you* come on. Honestly, it makes sense that you go somewhere where no-one will bother you and you can get quietly on mending things. But I love my home. I'm going to stay and fight the bastards for it.'

They walked on in an angry silence. It was beginning to rain.

Then, suddenly, as they passed a church doorway, she changed the subject. 'Richard, can you sing?'

'What?'

She nodded to herself. 'I bet you've got a lovely voice.'

Then, continuing on down the street, she turned away, lifting her face into the wind. If her eyes filled with tears of frustration, she'd be able to blame it on the cold.

11.

(i)

Whether it was charity fatigue, or maybe because passers-by didn't have much loose change in their pockets in these days of payment by card, Richard didn't know. What he did know, as they reached the end of *Little Town of Bethlehem,* was that as carol singers they weren't very successful at collecting money; and that he felt silly in the Father Christmas hat he'd been pressed into wearing.

Around his neck was an old accordion that he'd restored, and which, in the desolate months after his marriage had ended, he'd taught himself to play.

Yes, he could sing, he'd told Jenny. Then he'd mentioned the accordion, which had probably been a mistake. But it was too late now. It had been agreed that he would accompany her group of carol singers in their charity appearance for Age Gap.

'Are you all right?' Jenny asked at his side. She was wearing reindeer antlers that lit up, and all afternoon she'd been dashing about urging and cajoling.

'It's fun, isn't it!' he smiled back. 'Though we don't seem to be doing very well.'

Jenny considered the children collectors, dressed for the day in home-made Minions suits: 'Everybody's probably already spent up for Christmas.' Then, leaning forward, she put on her teacher's voice. 'Minions! Could you rattle your tins a little more loudly...' And she indicated by vigorously waving her wrist.

A couple of the children, probably from her own form, followed her example, but without much enthusiasm.

Christina, the buxom head teacher at Jenny's school, was smiling at him across a huddle of sweaters and anoraks, 'I wonder, Richard... *Good King Wenceslas?* Everyone likes that.'

Dutifully Richard found the page on his laminated collection of hymn sheets and played the introductory chords.

*'Good King Wenceslas looked out on the feast of Stephen,
As the snow lay round about, deep and crisp and even...'*

Alongside him Jenny was now laughing as she sang. A natural performer, she was enjoying it. So was he, in truth. It was nice to be doing something with her and getting along. There might not be another opportunity. After much soul-searching, he would be moving out of the River House after Christmas. It just wasn't worth the aggravation that Jerricoe was throwing at them; he'd already missed a lot of work.

(ii)

Walking through the Christmas market, Harry Culshaw was carrying his Harrods bag when he heard the singing and saw the little choir of carol singers. Moving towards them, he listened to the singing for a couple of minutes.

Then, turning into Sainsburys, he selected a small tray of mince pies, before, leaving the supermarket, he walked on towards the carol singers.

Where, joining them, he began to sing.

(iii)

For a chess-playing, semi-recluse, Richard was being a good sport, Jenny was thinking as she watched him at his accordion. Her suggestion that he join the group had been on impulse, but she should have known he wasn't the sort of person to do anything by half. Now he was singing as loudly as any of them.

It was a pity the collectors weren't showing much spirit, she was thinking, when, almost in front of her, a good-looking man in a navy-blue overcoat produced a £20 note from his wallet and dropped it into a tin being held by one of the Minions.

'Gloria in excelsis deo!' Jenny laughed as she sang, as Richard, who had also noticed the size of the donation, almost stopped playing in surprise. A couple of the other carol singers exchanged glances and nodded thanks to the newcomer.

He smiled back. Then, apparently wanting to enjoy himself, instead of moving on with the other Christmas shoppers, he joined in. Throwing his head back, he sang loudly along with the choir: *'Glor-or-or-or-or-or-or-or-oria in excelsis de-eo...'*

A grateful amusement rippled across the faces of the choir as they welcomed their latest recruit. At Jenny's side, Richard smiled at the newcomer's enthusiasm.

Suddenly, however, he was more than a singer. Pulling off his overcoat, he dropped it and his bags on top of the mountain of coats.

'Could you just keep an eye on my stuff...?' he asked Jenny.

She smiled an agreement.

Then, grabbing a spare collecting tin, he turned towards the passing shoppers. 'Happy Christmas everybody,' he called over the singing. 'Happy Christmas from...' He glanced at the name on his tin. '...Age Gap.'

The choir watched in bemusement. But now there was a new accompaniment to their singing. The sound of coins rattling into tins.

Still playing his accordion, Richard looked towards Jenny. She grinned. Whoever this fellow was, he was brilliant at working the shoppers, as off he went through the choir, smiling, thanking and charming the silver from those he passed.

(iv)

They'd sung *We Wish You a Merry Christmas* for the final time, and, as Richard took off his accordion, Jenny thanked the newcomer. 'I think you've found your vocation.'

'I'm sorry?'

'Getting people to give you their money,' Richard grinned. 'You're brilliant at it.'

'Oh *that*.' The man shrugged, as if unable to explain it. 'By the way, what's Age Gap? A dress shop for old people?'

'Try sheltered housing for the elderly,' Jenny beamed, taking off her reindeer antlers.

'Oh, right! Excellent!'

'Yes, *excellent!* Thank you so much...erm?' It was Christina parting the choir with her bosom. She'd just sung the descant to *Silent Night* in German.

'Harry!' The newcomer put out his hand.

'Well, thank you so much, Harry. Some elderly people will be very grateful to you today.'

'Nonsense. What else is Christmas for?'

As Harry deflected the thanks, Richard watched the melee of congratulations around him, Jenny seeming to be particularly animated.

'Er, Jenny!' It was Christina again, now laden with bags. 'Sophie and I have some last-minute shopping to do. I've forgotten Gordon's mother. You couldn't do me one more favour could you, and bring the collecting tins?'

'Oh. Yes, of course.'

'You're an angel. See you back at The Ridge for the count. Number 27.' And, with that, the leader of the choir put a hand on the back of her teenage daughter and guided her quickly away.

Jenny sighed. 'It must be something in the way I look.'

'We'll manage,' Richard said, and pulled on his coat.

Picking up his own bags, Harry stopped as he was about to leave. 'Are you sure you can handle all that?'

'We only have to get to the car park,' Richard explained.

'Ah!' Harry turned away, then hesitated again as he watched them. 'I tell you what...' he began, and, quickly taking his tray of mince pies from his supermarket bag, he put them in his Harrods carrier. 'There you go. Put the collecting tins in this and I'll carry the accordion. It'll be easier for you.' And passing Richard the supermarket bag he picked up the accordion.

'If you're sure you don't mind,' Richard thanked, slipping the collecting tins into the extra bag.

'Not at all.'

Heavily laden, the three now made their way on to the escalator.

Looking around at the last-minute rush of present buying, Harry shook his head. 'Nice to think that Jesus was born for all this, isn't it?'

Both Richard and Jenny had to smile.

'If you give me the ticket, I'll go and pay the machine,' Jenny offered as they reached the rooftop car park.

Thanking her, Richard passed over the ticket and she hurried away. 'We're just over here,' he pointed as he and Harry continued between the cars. 'It's the Volvo.' Then he frowned. Another vehicle had parked very close to it.

'That isn't very friendly, is it,' sympathised Harry.

'Not really. Er, do you think you could just hold this for a second while I squeeze between the two...?' Richard said, holding the supermarket bag out to Harry.

'Of course.' Harry took it from him and put it down by the passenger's door alongside his Harrods bag and the accordion.

'Thank you.' Edging towards the driver's door, Richard felt in his pocket for the car keys.

'It isn't snowing, is it?' Harry suddenly asked, looking up.

Richard was surprised. 'Is it cold enough?'

'I thought I saw a snowflake.'

Richard stared hard at the sky. It was already dark. 'No. It's too warm, surely.' Then unlocking the driver's door, he squeezed into the car and leant across to open the front passenger door.

'Here you go,' Harry said, and passed him the supermarket bag.

Richard swung it on to the back seat. 'Thank you.' Then, stretching, he opened the back door for Harry to put the accordion on the seat.

Trotting back across the car park, Jenny now rejoined them with the endorsed ticket. 'Can we give you a lift anywhere, Harry?' she asked.

He shook his head. 'Actually. I'm just around the corner. Quicker to walk. But thank you, anyway. And thanks for the singsong. I enjoyed it. Same time next year! Merry Christmas!'

'And you.' Jenny replied, and, smiling goodbye, she joined Richard in the car.

'Yes, thanks, Harry,' Richard called as Harry politely closed the door after Jenny.

Then, picking up his Harrods bag, he walked away across the car park.

'Nice guy,' Jenny said, watching him go.
'Very nice,' Richard agreed, and started the car.

The drive to Christina's house didn't take long. She lived in a pleasant, semi-detached house in a quiet avenue. Fairy lights sparkled on a fat Christmas tree in the front garden.

Jenny grimaced to Richard as they entered the house. 'We needn't stay long,' she whispered. The smell of cinnamon and cloves greeted them in the living room.

'It's so kind of you to bring the tins, Jenny! You, too, Richard. Mulled wine?' Christina was already filling their glasses, as the few carol singers, who'd come back for the count, began to clear the table. 'Now, let's see how it went.'

'Best year ever, thanks to…whatever his name was,' someone said.

'His name was Harry,' offered Jenny.

At her side, Richard lifted the supermarket bag on to the table and looked inside. Suddenly his face knotted in surprise. 'Oh, no!'

'What?' Jenny leant forward to look.

'We've only driven off with Harry's mince pies.'

'Oh, God! After all he did.'

'Ah, well, can't be helped.' Christina was business-like. 'Now come on, show me the money, as they say.' And she scooped the tray of mince pies out of the bag.

Richard looked into the bag again. And stopped. He didn't understand.

'Richard?' This was Jenny.

He put his hand inside the bag and felt the contents.

'Richard?' Christina was staring anxiously at him. Then leaning forward, she pulled the bag wide open. 'Oh, my God!'

Where there should have been six collecting tins for Age Gap, there were two tins of tomato soup.

(v)

Richard didn't speak as they drove home. He'd blushed quite scarlet when the soup tins had been discovered. His mouth had opened, but words hadn't come. He'd looked, Jenny thought, quite broken, almost guilty, although no one had suggested he'd done anything dishonest.

As they entered the silent River House through the front door, he made immediately for the stairs, as if wanting nothing more than to be by himself.

Jenny stopped in the hall. 'It wasn't your fault, Richard,' she called after him. 'You couldn't have known.'

He looked back down at her. 'You were right when you said I was too trusting. I always have been. Goodnight.' And, with that, he continued up the stairs.

There was nothing more she could say. But it was such a shame. It had been kind of him to help with the choir.

Going down to her basement flat, she went into her bedroom and pulled a suitcase out from under her bed. She would be leaving early the following morning to spend Christmas with her sister in Liverpool.

She thought about Harry as she packed, picturing his easy smile, confident charm and glib jokes. And she hated herself for having been charmed by him.

(vi)

He'd let everyone down and he'd felt like a thief. Immediately he'd offered to give Age Gap the money that had been stolen. But, of course, Christina wouldn't hear of it. He'd meant it, though. Worst of all had been Jenny's expression, as first shock, merged into embarrassment and then pity. He didn't want pity.

Taking off his overcoat, he flopped down on his Chesterfield. How could he have been so stupid?

At first, he'd felt nothing but humiliation. Anger had followed. But slowly, as he went over the events of the afternoon, another part of his brain began to engage. He'd been taken for a fool, but how? He'd been conned. There'd been a switch. Yes! Obviously. But when? How had it been done?

He was a games player. He was good at working out puzzles. They were his subject. He ought to be able to figure this out.

Getting up, he found two large carrier bags in the kitchen and set them alongside each other on his worktop. Then, facing them, he ran his mind over the events of the afternoon, recalling how Harry had joined in the singing and asked Jenny to keep an eye on his shopping; how he'd been a brilliant collector as he'd worked the mall; and how generous he'd been with his £20 contribution.

Everything had seemed so genuine.

Or had it? 'Is it snowing?' Harry had asked.

Of course, it hadn't been snowing. It was nowhere nearly cold enough for snow.

Richard had been slightly puzzled at the time, looked at the sky, and then let it pass. At that moment Harry had been on the far side of the car from him, holding the two carrier bags, his own from Harrods and the other, the one containing the Age Gap money, from the supermarket.

Was that when the switch had taken place? It had to have been.

But how would it have been possible to take the tins of money from one bag and replace them with cans of soup from the other in so few seconds? What was he missing?

The answer didn't come immediately. But it came. Going back into the kitchen, he found two more carrier bags, put a jar of jam in one and a packet of tortellini in the other. Then, returning to his worktop, he put each of the two new bags inside the two empty ones already there. Tortellini bag in one, jam bag in the other.

'Is it snowing?' he said aloud to himself, and, as he did, he lifted both inside bags simultaneously and swapped them over, so that the bags containing the tortellini and the jam were now in opposite outer bags, just as the soup and the money had been. At first, he was clumsy and knocked a bag over. But after a couple of attempts it worked well enough.

Four bags and a couple of seconds' and distraction by a professional. It had been that simple.

Now he found himself thinking about Jenny, how attractive and funny and eccentric she'd looked in the shopping mall with her toy antlers; and then how stunned at Christina's house, where the mulled wine had gone cold as despondency had filled the room. He'd wanted to perhaps impress her tonight. The opposite had occurred.

For a moment he thought of going downstairs to tell her he'd worked out how they'd been conned.

He didn't. It might have made him sound pathetic.

12.

'It's obvious, isn't it! Just because it's Christmas everyone thinks we're some sort of charity, like a housing trust that doesn't notice if the rents don't come in. Right?'

No-one answered. They weren't expected to.

Jerricoe continued. 'How else do you explain these late payments?'

No-one tried to.

It was the morning after Boxing Day and the monthly rentals meeting, with Jerricoe, his ever-silent secretary, Thelma, a solid woman he'd chosen for that very quality, lawyer Hunt, and the rents manager Choudhrai.

Jerricoe enjoyed these sessions. When he went to meetings on the building, planning and development side, all of which he outsourced, he had to balance his outbursts because there was always someone, an architect, designer or builder who would answer back. But in the rentals department, though renting only brought in peanuts, just enough to pay the office staff, while the values of the freeholds went on increasing, nobody ever crossed him.

Still glaring, he scrolled down the pages on his computer. There they were, the lazy, late-paying freeloaders who thought the world owed them a living: two in Islington, three more in Lambeth, and a Bangladeshi convenience store in New Cross that was three months behind.

'What's this? Convenience store! *Convenience?* I'll say. Convenient for them, all right. Not paying the rent is very convenient. Get someone to pop in on them, set them straight.'

'I believe the tenants there may be having some family problems....' Choudhrai, a tall, thin, timid man began, but his voice faded under Jerricoe's stare.

'Did you hear me?'

'I mean, perhaps we should give them a little more time...'

Jerricoe turned theatrically to Hunt. '*You* heard me, didn't you, Craig!'

'I heard you, Mark,' Hunt chimed back.

Choudhrai looked at the pattern of the rug on the wooden floor.

Jerricoe felt his lips tighten in satisfaction. Choudhrai was scrupulous at his books and as honest as a Sunday morning, but he had to be watched. He was soft. All the same, the guy wasn't going to risk his job on account of some poxy convenience store in New Cross. Biting into the pastry that Thelma had brought him, Jerricoe turned back to his computer. 'Ah yes…and what about the River House? We're not there yet, are we?'

'The rents are always paid on time,' Choudhrai offered. 'By standing order.'

'I wasn't talking to you,' Jerricoe snapped.

It was now Hunt's turn to be discomfited. 'The word from their lawyer is, two gone… one going in the New Year…to be confirmed, and, er, one to go…'

'*One to go!!!!* Plans drawn up, schedules agreed and *one to go?*'

'Apparently the tenant there is a schoolteacher. A single woman. She's very determined, very difficult, and…'

'*Determined?* I'll show her what determined is! I want her out. Now! Do you understand? Keep after her. Keep upping the pressure. She'll crack in the end. They always do.'

13.

(i)

Richard was watching *Local Hero* on television when Jenny got back from her Christmas in Liverpool. He'd seen it before; several times. But he loved the innocence of the story and the characters in it.

By family tradition he'd celebrated the festivities at his parents' house in Bristol, where he'd managed to lose his River House problems among the three grandchildren his brother and sister children had produced. There was a ten-year age gap between his sister and himself, twelve years in the case of his brother. So, as they'd been practically teenagers by the time he'd got to know them, he'd never felt particularly close to either. And, although Christmas lunch had been cosy, he'd long since realised that, even before his divorce, he felt semi-detached from his family. So, he'd returned to London in the evening.

Back in the empty River House, he'd been surprised to find that he was uneasy at being alone there and had looked out on a couple of occasions to see if anyone was watching. So, he was pleased to hear Jenny's footsteps thumping up the stairs four nights later.

'God, it was freezing on Merseyside,' she said as she came bursting into his studio. 'Is that a new cardigan?'

'Er…yes. Christmas present.' He was already turning off the TV. 'How was your sister?'

'Busy. I hardly saw her. Everyone's off with 'flu so she was called in. She's a got a new man, though.'

'Ah! Is that good?'

'I think so. He's a doctor. Egyptian guy. Dr Kamel. Honestly, that's his name. Very nice. Long eyelashes, she said. Camels have long eyelashes, too, don't they. Probably to protect their eyes from the sand or something, I suppose, Anyway, she's sorted. For now, anyway. I think she even mentioned the "love" word.' She paused for breath and going to the window pulled up the blind and peered at the lights across the river. 'Wow, it's good to be home!'

Home! He felt a blade of guilt.

'And how's our fiend of a landlord?'

'Unfiendishly quiet this week.'

'That's festive of him.' She smiled. 'He'll be sending mistletoe and wine round next. But he won't get a snog.'

She was speaking more quickly than he'd ever heard her, and it occurred to him that they were both now nervous with each other. Neither mentioned the carol singing.

'Anyway... I've got a Christmas present for you...' Almost awkwardly, she pushed a soft packet into his hand.

He was surprised. 'Thank you. Actually... I've got something for you, too.'

'Really!'

He'd bought it just before the carol singing and had then not known how to give it to her in the mess of the day. Going to his desk, he pulled a similar sized packet from a drawer. They began opening their gifts together.

'A scarf! Lovely!' he said, laughing.

For a moment, she looked quite hurt. 'It's real Scottish lambswool. I thought navy blue would suit you.'

'Oh, yes. It does. Thank you.'

He was still smiling as she pulled the tissue paper from her present. She realised at once why he'd laughed. 'A *scarf*!' she hooted. 'We both bought scarves. Also blue! It's beautiful!' And she threw the Liberty's cashmere around her neck. 'Thank you. It's lovely!'

He thought she might have been tired after her journey, but 'home again' she was in a giddy mood. 'You know, we should have a Christmas party,' she said as Richard opened a bottle of wine. 'This is a perfect house for parties.'

'Isn't it a bit late to arrange one?'

She nodded. 'I suppose so. Everybody else will already have things to do.'

He poured the wine. 'We could still have one, though.'

'Yes?'

'A little one.'

She looked slightly comical. 'You mean, just you and me?'

'Why not?'

She hesitated. 'We could think of it as a farewell party for you, I suppose.'

He blinked in embarrassment. He'd found another flat to rent in Putney and would be leaving the River House at the end of the week. The new flat wasn't as big or as light as his present studio, but it would suffice, and he would be able to get on with his work without interruption.

'Well, I'm not going quite yet,' he said lamely.

She touched his arm and then withdrew her hand. 'I'm sorry. That was unfair. But yes! Let's have our own party.' She got up. 'What have you got to eat? I have some nuts and stuff like that. Don't go away.'

He stared after her. Her eagerness was infectious.

(ii)

Jenny was only downstairs for a few minutes but by the time she got back the studio was almost festive. Candles were now burning on saucers, tangerines were in a fruit dish, more wine had been joined by cheese and crackers and a blues singer on the CD was singing *'Merry, merry Christmas, baby, you sure did treat me right.'*

'I suppose,' Richard said, as she opened a box of Christmas chocolates that one of the parents had given her at school, 'if it's a party we should have a sort of theme.'

'Such as?'

'Well, if it was Hallowe'en we could tell ghost stories.'

'So, thank God it isn't. After Jerricoe's swinging rats and a football full of blood, the last thing I want to hear in this empty, old, creaking house is a ghost story.'

'Ah, right! Bad idea! Your turn.'

'Let's play a game.'

'Fine. Take your choice. I've got a few. What about Monopoly?'

Jenny frowned. 'Come on, Richard. It's Christmas. Can't we forget houses for tonight?'

'Oh, sorry.' He tried again. 'We used to play Scrabble when I was little.'

'I'm sure you did. And I bet you were brilliant at it.'

'Not particularly.'

'That usually means "yes". I was useless at it. So, we aren't playing Scrabble.' She took a large gulp of wine. 'What about that game where I tell you the name of the title of a film and you have to think up the title of another one using a word from the title, but not including prepositions, conjunctions or definite and indefinite articles?'

He grinned. 'I can see why you became a teacher.'

She ignored that. 'So, if I say *Gone With The Wind,* you say…'

'*Whistle Down The Wind.*'

She was surprised that he'd replied so quickly. 'Very good. And then I think of a title with another word from your title, which in this case could be 'whistle' or 'down', until it becomes a chain. The first one who can't think of a title breaks the chain and loses the round. Okay?'

'Got it.'

She nodded. 'Right. I'll start.' Her eyes fell on an old cushion showing a photo of Jack Lemmon dressed as a woman lying on a sofa. 'I know. *Some Like It Hot.* Now you think of…'

'…a title that includes "some", "like" or "hot"?'

'Yes.'

'Okay. *Hot Fuzz.*'

'*Hot Fuzz?*' She pulled a face. '*Hot Fuzz!*...Fuzz? Fuzz? Was that a film?'

'Yes. It was very popular. Round one to me?'

'You bastard!'

'Probably.'

'You start this time,' she said.

'Okay… *Raiders of the Lost Ark?*'

'Er… "lost". I know. *Lost Horizon,*' she came back.

'Very good. "Horizon!" Is there a film just called *Horizon?* He wasn't sure.'

'Probably. But the rules also insist that you must be able to name at least one star who was in it. And I bet you can't, can you?' She was gleeful.

'Can I phone a friend?'

'No. You're already with a friend. And I'm not telling you.'

He looked at her for a second.

Aware of the moment, she was embarrassed. Had she meant to use the word 'friend', she wondered. Yes, she had. Drawn together by Jerricoe, they'd progressed from being uneasy housemates to being, sometimes awkward, friends. It might be a friendship based only on a shared problem, but, yes, they were friends, as friendly as either of them wanted it to be, anyway.

She took that round of the game, and they began again, moving swiftly through *The Great Escape, Escape from Alcatraz, Birdman of Alcatraz, To Kill a Mockingbird,* until they got stuck after *Licence To Kill*. Neither of them could think of another film with the word 'licence' in the title, so they began again with *Double Indemnity*.

They played until the candles were almost gone, with Jenny mainly winning. 'Sorry, about that. Actors do tend to watch a lot of films when they're out of work…which they usually are.'

He smiled and then told her how he'd worked out how Harry had pulled off the scam at the Christmas carols, but she didn't want to think about Harry and that terrible day.

They said goodnight at four in the morning, both pretty drunk. As she went downstairs to her own flat, she felt a sudden chill of loneliness when she remembered that Richard would soon be leaving the River House.

And it wasn't just that she was afraid of being left alone there.

14.

(i)

He began packing the following day. Wrapping his tools and valuables carefully, he cosseted them in old shirts and torn sheets; then unplugging and boxing his computer, he opened his safe. Usually, it kept small items of jewellery that he was restoring, but, since the problems with Jerricoe had begun, it was almost empty. Then, making up another packing case, he began to sort through his books, puzzled as to why he'd bought so many, yet read so few.

He was into his fourth packing case when he heard the quiet thump of a downstairs door. He looked at his watch. It wasn't yet three. Jenny had gone out to give some holiday catch-up lessons to a couple of pupils. She must be back earlier than he'd expected.

He returned to his packing. The familiar sound of gurgling pipes and water running from the main tank on the roof now accompanied his work. Jenny must have turned on the washing machine in the basement, he conjectured. And he thought about the fun they'd had the previous night: and the hangover that morning. It was a long time since he'd had a hangover.

Four more boxes were filled. When he'd been married and he'd had more space, there'd been some order to his books: Byzantine, Vikings and European all neatly classified. Now there was no shape to his library. In his next place he'd do something about…

Something was troubling him. He stopped and listened. Then getting up from the floor he opened his door and went out on to the landing. No washing machine should last this long. Puzzled by the sound he went down the stairs. He couldn't hear the pipes when he reached the hall, but there was still the sound of running water.

He hurried on towards the basement. Halfway down the bottom stairs, he saw the source of the noise. Water was flooding out of Jenny's flat and into the basement hall. The door was open, the door frame splintered.

'Jesus! Jenny! Jenny!' The large house echoed his alarm. He was nervous. Was someone in there?

He pushed on. Inside Jenny's door her entire flat was an inch deep in water. He splashed into the bathroom. Water was cascading down the sides of the tub. Pushing his arm into the bath, he snatched out the plug. The overflow had been blocked with a pair of socks.

He paddled back into the living room. So recently redecorated, it was now a lake, rugs floating on the newly varnished floor, children's paintings lying sodden in the water.

'You bastards!' he shouted. 'You bloody bastards!' His anger echoed up the stairs and through the empty rooms.

(ii)

'What was it our lawyer said about our leases?' Jenny asked as she rang the mop out into the bucket.

'Watertight!' Richard came back.

'That's all right then. For a moment I thought I might have a problem.'

There was a hesitation from Richard who was hanging one of her rugs over a clothes horse. 'We have,' he said at last.

'Er, sorry. I have the problem. Not you. You're leaving.'

He hesitated, 'Actually, I'm not. I'm staying.'

She stopped work.

'I've changed my mind. I like it here, too.' He avoided looking her in the eye.

'But you *want* to go.'

'Not anymore.'

'But what about all the stuff you have? What if something happened to it? Jerricoe could ruin you.'

He smiled. 'Only if I let him.'

For a moment neither said anything. Then: 'Is it because of me ... because I won't leave? I don't want to be the reason that...'

He stopped her. 'No, it isn't because of you. It's because of them. Jerricoe Properties. And all the other bullying monsters. We can't let them win. You were right.'

She didn't reply. She needed time to think about this, so she returned to squeezing out the mop. Finally, she nodded: 'Okay. We'll fight them together.'

She hadn't been sure of him at first. With his shy, anything-for-a-quiet-life attitude, he'd seemed weak.

She'd been wrong.

(iii)

He cancelled the lease on his new flat the following morning. It was an expensive change of mind, the Putney estate agents insisting upon three months' rent. He didn't argue. He was relieved by his decision to stay.

Then he wrote a letter to Jerricoe Properties telling them that he would be staying for the duration of his lease as agreed with the previous landlord. He smiled to himself as he posted it.

It was a good feeling.

The New Year's Eve dinner was a last-minute thing, and Jenny's invitation to him so backhanded that he took it that she didn't necessarily care how he answered.

'I don't know whether you've got anything planned,' she said casually, as they met in the hall, 'but, if you haven't, some colleagues from school have booked a room in an Italian restaurant and I know you'd be very welcome…'

It was very late when they reached the restaurant, Jenny now in a velvet burgundy dress with lace collars and cuffs that she said she'd bought for five pounds in an Oxfam shop. She was wearing make-up, too, at least more than he'd ever noticed her wear before. She looked, he thought, 'bohemian-glitzy'.

Already the other partygoers, mainly a collection of teachers and their partners, were merry, talking shop and getting rowdy. So, seated together at the end of the table, they raced into the Pinot Noir to catch up with the mood, while negotiating the carre d'agnello.

They hadn't meant to talk about Jerricoe, but then, Sally, who taught Owls at Jenny's school, and whom Richard had met one Sunday when she'd come to see the River House, enquired how the battle with the landlord was going.

'Sadly, there hasn't been much in the way of a Christmas truce, but we're still fighting,' he replied.

'Anything I can do to help, just let me know,' Sally came back as she continued an uncertain way back to her place.

At the other end of the room another teacher had begun to sing a karaoke version of *Sweet Caroline*.

Jenny turned to Richard: 'The trouble is the people who want to help can't, and those who could and should…'

'Won't,' he finished for her. 'So, we have to help ourselves.'

'How?' she asked. 'Barricade ourselves in…go on a hunger strike and protest that an unscrupulous property developer is menacing us? We might even get on TV.'

'More likely we'd starve to death before anyone noticed!'

At that, they fell silent.

A television at the end of the room was soon showing the minute hand on Big Ben. It was almost midnight.

'I've got it,' Jenny said at last. 'Let's just murder the bastard.'

Richard had to smile. 'Is that what you teach the children these days?'

'No. They teach us.' Suddenly tears washed Jenny's eyes.

Richard rested his hand on the sleeve of her dress. 'We'll find a way to fight them. We'll think of something.'

Whether she believed him, he couldn't tell. But, wiping her face with a Christmas paper napkin, she was trying to smile when the volume on the television was turned up as the last seconds of the year ticked away.

'Five, four, three, two, one…' the party chanted. And, as Big Ben chimed midnight, an ensemble rejoicing of 'Happy New Year, everybody' erupted.

'Happy New Year,' Richard smiled across at Jenny as everyone stood up.

Through still shining eyes she smiled back, her lips mouthing the greeting in return.

Suddenly, all around them couples were kissing. He looked at her. She was watching him. Was she waiting? He couldn't tell.

Then, as a boyish young teacher came up behind her and planted a platonic kiss on the side of her neck, he saw her drawn away from him into a circular chain of crossed arms as the party broke into *Auld Lang Syne* around the long table.

From the other side of the table, he watched as they sang, their arms pumping goodwill up and down, their voices ragged, joining in with the fireworks and televised multitudes below Edinburgh Castle.

For a moment she looked back at him, her eyes were saying...what? Was it a message of regret that they'd been separated when the kissing had started. He didn't know.

Then, uncertain, he looked away from her, and the New Year began. If it had been a moment, he'd missed it.

(iv)

She couldn't sleep. What would have happened, she wondered, if she'd been next to Richard when the New Year was being rung in and the kissing had started? Would they have kissed?

Yes.

Really kissed?

Possibly.

Was that what she'd wanted at that moment?

Yes.

And then what? Would they have walked home together, arm in arm?

Probably.

And, perhaps, after another drink and some uncertainty, would they have ended up in bed together?

She mulled that over. Would it be a probably or a yes?

Yes, probably, yes, she decided.

But what next? What about tomorrow and the next day? Was that what she wanted? What Richard wanted? What if he or she discovered it wasn't and they had to continue to live in the same house, regretful and awkward?

All in all, perhaps it was better that they hadn't kissed. But at four in the morning, on a cold winter's night, she rather wished they had.

15.

It snowed on New Year's Day and Jenny watched from her basement window as the flakes bled what little colour there was from the garden. It was no longer damp in her flat, the rugs having now been dried on her old Dimplex or by the ancient, rudimentary heating system which slightly warmed the house. But it was cold, so she kept both bars of her electric fire turned on as she polished the apple green Victorian tiles in her living room fireplace.

In the afternoon she wandered around the little overgrown lawn beyond the brambles at the back of the house, enjoying the squeak of her walking boots in the new snow. Looking back at the building, monochrome against the dark sky, she allowed herself to imagine how beautiful the River House might look if its stucco were restored, its window frames painted, and a new conservatory, in keeping with the building's period, erected to replace the cheap, ramshackle one that the Morrisons had tended.

Then glancing at the new apartment blocks down the lane, she wondered if the people who lived in them really wanted the last remaining house on this stretch of river to become just another body pampering emporium.

She was turning back to the house when she caught a wave behind Richard's top floor window. He'd been watching her. She beckoned him down, and a few minutes later they were walking around the garden together. With their faces bright in the reflected snow, he showed her where a fox had raised her family under a crumbling potting shed two summers ago, and where a branch had been cut from a magnolia tree when it had begun to blow against the Morrisons' bedroom window.

And then he took her to where the bluebells came out at the end of the garden at Easter. It wasn't a very big garden, but it looked wider and longer when covered in snow.

Before long, they found themselves walking along the towpath, ignoring the new development, and watching the river as it danced in the blizzard. As they strolled, they discussed the trade that had once made it London's main thoroughfare, and of the people who'd worked it. 'It must have been a hard life,' Richard said,

'For sure,' she agreed. 'But at least the people living along here then were members of a community and probably helped each other. We've lost that.'

In a gap between some flashy cliffs of apartments, they approached a square, steepled, eighteenth century church. Surrounded by a walled graveyard, it looked, Jenny thought, like a little cove of politeness, with its modest scale and classically columned porch.

Unhurried, they wandered between the gravestones, reading the names and inscriptions of those who had known the area over a century and a half earlier.

'The river would have probably looked the same to them as it does to us now,' Jenny mused. 'It's just that everything else has changed, on it and around it. Everything is different apart from the water.'

An old sandstone gravestone caught Richard's eyes. On top of it stood a statue of an angel, its arms open in welcome. 'Elspeth Worsley, 1806–1892,' he read. 'I wonder who she was.'

'No family mentioned, nothing even to tell us who mourned her. That's sad,' Jenny said.

The church was locked so they sheltered under the portico for a while and watched a family pass by, the father pushing a baby in a buggy, as two older children enjoyed making tracks in the snow.

The afternoon ended as, with their noses pink from the cold, they went home again and toasted some crumpets that Jenny had bought at Sainsburys. After which she returned to polishing her fireplace and Richard went back upstairs. He'd fallen behind with his work on the rocking horse. The client would be wondering where it was.

16.

(i)

The snow was already melting by the following morning, leaving puddles and banks of slush as Richard made his way to the borough town hall, a large Victorian building that was across a narrow atrium from a matching library. Seeking directions in the lofty marble hall, he found the planning department on the first floor. Quite what he was seeking, as he asked the assistant for anything relating to the River House, he wasn't sure. But any information might help.

'It would be better if you had a planning application reference number,' the young man behind the desk grumbled, but it didn't take him long to find the file. 'Here we are.' Then, putting the documents down on a table, he returned to his tasks.

Richard studied the plans. He wasn't an architect, but they were straightforward enough, preliminary designs for a health club to be put before the council's planning committee.

Taking them back to the desk, he asked if he might have a printout and then followed as the assistant crossed to a large architect's copier overlooking the atrium. 'It's three pounds a page,' he was warned as the machine warmed up.

Agreeing, Richard waited as the machine set to work, his gaze wandering through the window and out across the atrium towards a window in the library opposite.

Suddenly, he found himself focusing. In the library window a familiar figure was standing at a lectern examining a large book.

'That'll be fifteen pounds.' The assistant had finished the photocopying and was rolling up the plans. 'Would you like a rubber band to hold them?'

'No. That's fine. Thank you.,' Richard said. And, pushing a tenner and a fiver into the young man's hand, he grabbed the plans and was off, running back down the stairs and across the atrium.

(ii)

Harry Culshaw sensed the approaching problem even before he heard it. He'd only stepped into the library to keep warm and take a look through *Who's Who*. But now he could tell from the expression on the face of the old guy facing him, who'd been reading an Australian cricket report in the *Daily Telegraph,* that someone was about to be rudely interrupted.

He didn't wait. As the sound of approaching footsteps grew louder, he set off down the library, out through the swing doors at the far end and down the back staircase. It was best not to run in these situations, because it only drew even more unwelcome attention. But he could walk very quickly.

'Harry! Harry!' A voice yelled behind him as he clattered down the stone steps.

He kept going, out into the atrium and off towards the High Street, dodging between cars and behind a van. A horn blew angrily at someone behind him, but he didn't look back. In his game it didn't do to look back. Slipping through an alleyway, he hurried out into the crowds of shoppers on the High Street.

(iii)

The car with the blaring horn had only just missed Richard, who, still holding his roll of plans, slipped in the slush. Then he was off again. Reaching the end of the alley, he peered through the multitude of shoppers, everybody out for the New Year sales. There was no sign of Harry.

Moving through the crowds, he gazed up and down the length of the street. Then he stopped. He shouldn't have been this far behind. This was a game of hide and seek. If *he'd* been pursued, what would he have done?

Gone to ground, came the answer, and after peering in Tesco, he retraced his steps. No open-plan shop would have offered a good hiding place. An arcade was a better bet.

He'd guessed right. 'Hello, Harry!' he said quietly to the man in dark rimmed reading glasses who was studying a photograph of *The Forbidden City* in a second-hand bookshop.

Harry's handsome face was a friendly, open blank. 'I'm sorry! I don't think…?'

'Age Gap mean nothing to you either, I suppose,' Richard's voice rose.

A sales assistant glanced up from a book she was reading.

Harry looked puzzled, dismissive, as though dealing with a nutty pest whom he'd never seen before. 'I wouldn't have thought there was much between us…actually. Now, I'm sorry, but I must be off.' He began to leave.

Richard blocked his way. 'How about the money you stole from me just before Christmas then?'

The sales assistant nudged a colleague.

Harry noticed. In an instant his expression changed. 'Richard! How are you! Good to see you again,' his face lighting into a happy shine of recognition. 'Anywhere round here we can get a cup of tea, d'you think?' And, putting a friendly arm around his pursuer, he led him past the puzzled assistant and out of the shop.

Surprised by the sudden change of attitude, Richard didn't resist.

'Not much along here. I don't know what the world's coming to. Can't get a cup of tea anywhere anymore! Have a good Christmas, did you?' Harry was still talking, denying Richard the chance to interrupt, as they moved along the arcade. A Starbucks stood on the corner. 'This should be okay.' And, putting his hand on the door he held it open for Richard to enter ahead of him, 'After you,' he said, before holding it open a little longer as a couple of middle-aged women, laden with shopping bags, followed Richard inside.

Then he was gone.

Pushing past the women, Richard raced back out and on to the High Street, where Harry was already getting into a taxi. Grabbing the door as Harry was about to slam it, he clambered in and sat down.

'Drop you anywhere, can I?' Harry asked calmly as the cab made a U-turn in the street.

Richard stared at him. 'How could you do it? Carol singers! Of all people. There must have been five hundred pounds in those tins.'

Harry practically snorted. 'What? There wasn't a penny more than three hundred, and half of that was in some very dodgy currencies.'

'Three hundred then. The morality's the same.'

After a second's reflection Harry smiled. 'You're absolutely right. It is.'

Richard didn't know how to answer him. 'You're despicable, you know that?' he said limply at last.

'Thank you,' said Harry, then he shook a world-weary head. 'Come on, you know as well as I do, ninety percent of anything given to charity goes in admin charges. Right?' Putting his hand into his inside pocket he withdrew his wallet. 'So, here you are. Thirty quid. Give this to the first old lady you see, and you'll both be up on the deal. She'll be thrilled, you'll have sealed your place in heaven and we'll have cut out the middleman.' And he pushed some notes into Richard's hand.

Richard looked at the money. 'There's only twenty here.'

Harry sighed and gave him a further ten pounds. 'Happy now?'

'Not really.'

'Ah, well.'

This was how bastards like Jerricoe got on, Richard was thinking.

'People like you…you just don't care, do you!' he said. 'Hurting people, walking right over them, wrecking their lives.'

Harry pulled a face. 'Eh, steady on! It was only a couple of verses of *Hark the Herald Angels*.'

'You just go around taking advantage of those too trusting or too weak to stop you. And it isn't fair!'

For a moment, he thought Harry wasn't listening as the taxi made its way past a row of large Victorian semi-detached houses on a tree-lined road.

'Anywhere at the end will do!' Harry called to the driver through the intercom. Then, as the taxi began to slow, he turned back to Richard. 'The truth is, old man, life isn't fair. It isn't my fault. That's just the way it is. Sometimes we have to bend the rules a little if we're to survive. Think about it! Been good catching up. Say hello to er...Whatshername Pretty Woman! Bye.' And, as the taxi stopped, he climbed out, slammed the door, and strode swiftly away down the street.

The cab driver turned to Richard. 'I take it that you're paying this fare.'

'What, er...oh yes!' Richard almost had to smile. Harry had cheated him again. 'Can you drop me off round the corner, please.'

The taxi turned into a side street.

Getting out, Richard paid the fare and hurried back to where he'd last seen Harry. Already he was a hundred yards away. For a fellow who went around robbing charities, he appeared to live in a very smart area, Richard thought, as, keeping a distance, he followed him past some obviously valuable houses.

But then a surprise. Turning a corner, Harry made his way around the backs of the big houses towards a row of ugly little modern shops. Then, hanging back, Richard watched as Harry went down some steps into a basement flat.

'Well now,' Richard said to himself.

(iv)

Jenny peered at the Town Hall's plans for the River House, spread now across her kitchen table. 'It looks like pedicures in your place, consultations on the first floor and a locker room and a steam bath down here. And what's this?'

Richard leaned forward. 'A jacuzzi.'

'In my bedroom?'

'Well, yes. En suite. Quite handy I would have thought.'

'It isn't funny!' Jenny frowned. For some reason, Richard was in a very skittish mood tonight.

'No. We'll appeal, of course. The borough planning committee will never agree to it. We'll get it stopped.'

'You're certain?'

'No.' Then he smiled again. 'But our luck might be changing.' And feeling inside his jacket he pulled out three £10 notes. 'Thirty pounds for the Age Gap carol singers. And Harry says "Happy New Year" to you…Well, sort of.'

'Harry? That thieving bastard?'

'Yes. That's the chap.'

'You've seen him?'

'I have and I view it as a very good omen.'

'You mean, he isn't a complete rat!'

'Oh, I think he might be that all right.'

After Richard had left, Jenny wrote protesting about Jerricoe's plans to the chairman of the London Borough of Riverside's planning committee. It was her fourth approach. Then, going to her laptop, she took her turn at research. Was there anything Richard might have missed, she wondered, as she clicked around through the London glossy property magazines. *'I always read local obituary notices says tycoon'*, was one thing; and a small account of a dispute with the National Trust was another: *'Developer sneezes over Pepperdome building as National Trust drags feet,'* it read. So not everyone had lost when they took on Jerricoe.

'Multi-millionaire with head for hair,' said a headline in an online shopping magazine over an article about a hairdressing salon that boasted about cutting Mark Jerricoe's hair every Friday morning. Cutting Jerricoe's hair wasn't much for them to brag about, she thought. But…might it be useful?

It was already late, and she knew Richard was working, so, instead of interrupting him, she drew a little cartoon of Mark Jerricoe having his hair cut. Then, clipping the cartoon to the new printouts, she crept upstairs and slid them into the sliver of light under his door.

17.

(i)

The drilling began with a crack, immediately followed by a grating whine of metal on brick, loud and harsh.

Richard, who'd been giving the rocking horse a final polish, put his hands to his ears. It got worse. The roar got louder. Racing down the stairs, he threw open the front door. This time he'd catch his tormentors in the act. A ladder was propped against the front of the house. A man in a hardhat and blue gilet had his foot against the bottom rung, while above him a colleague was drilling into the stucco, releasing a cloud of grey-red dust.

'What the hell do you think you're doing?' Richard shouted over the noise.

'What?' The man at the foot of the ladder put a hand to his ear. The one up the ladder stopped drilling.

Richard approached them. 'This is my home. Now just take that bloody ladder down. And you can tell Jerricoe he can't frighten us.'

'All right there, William?' The man with the drill was coming down the ladder.

The hardhat man looked puzzled. 'You mean, you don't want a blue plaque on your wall?'

'What?' Richard stopped.

Taking a sealed package from a cardboard box, the hardhat opened it and produced a blue metal plaque. *'London Heritage,'* he began to read. *'H. L. Arnold, chemist, lived here. 1890-1924.'*

Richard's face froze. 'London Heritage? You mean you're not from Jerricoe Properties?'

'Who?'

'Oh God, I'm sorry! I thought the landlord sent you.'

The second workman now began pulling paperwork from the pocket of his jean jacket. '1 Wharf Road, right?'

'But no. This is Wharf Lane'.

'Wharf *Lane!* Oh! Sorry, mate. Wrong house!' And turning to his colleague the hard hat repeated it. 'Wrong house, Sean!'

'That's all right.' Richard could feel himself blushing.

The workmen began to collect their tools. 'You had a lucky escape there,' said the hard hat.

'I did?'

'Oh yes. You'll still be able to build that kitchen extension you thought about. Not like Wharf Road.'

The driller joined in. 'That's right. London Heritage listed, blue plaqued, and you're frozen in time. Can't change a thing. See. It's all here.' And, shoving a London Heritage flyer into Richard's hand, he put away his tools.

'Sorry about the hole in the wall,' his colleague said as they took the ladder down. 'I'd put some filler in, but we haven't got any on the van.'

Richard went back into the house as the workmen drove off. He was embarrassed about his outburst. Was he becoming irrational? That morning's post had brought new demands from Jerricoe Properties, a bill from Lennox, Khan and Partners, although with no suggestion of further help. There's been a reply, too, from the Department For Levelling Up, Housing & Communities saying that, as this case involved a private rental agreement, it was of no concern of theirs. The police had gone quiet as well. There was no help anywhere.

It was a day of brusque white clouds as, with the rocking horse in the back of the car, he drove out of London along the M40 and then headed west into the Cotswolds. Passing through mellow little villages, where slabs of snow still lay against tall hedges, and with everywhere so beautifully kept, he found himself contrasting Jerricoe's modernising England with everything organisations like London Heritage were trying to preserve. But then, an art restorer would think like that, he chided himself.

He'd been visiting Creswell Manor for two years, each time taking a vase or a piece of furniture home to work on. And as he drove past the tall iron gates of the estate and down the long drive towards the house, he marvelled as always at the elegance that only history could bestow on a building. Creswell Manor wasn't vast or palatial, but, built and rebuilt in a variety of styles over the past five hundred years, it seemed perfect in its colour and shape. Only the weathering of centuries could do that.

Ignoring the heavy oak front doors of the house, he continued around the side of the building, and drove through an archway into a small, cobbled courtyard.

An empty hearse, with its tailgate open, was standing at one side of the door.

Thoughtful now, he parked his car and made for the kitchen door.

'Richard!' A thin, elderly man with dyed, chestnut hair, and dressed almost wholly in grey smiled at him as the door opened. Then, seeing Richard looking at the hearse, he said: 'It was very peaceful. She didn't suffer.'

'I'm so sorry, Maurice. I wouldn't have come had I known.' Richard didn't quite know what to say.

'Of course, you had to come,' came the reply. 'She'll be gone soon when the girls have decided what she should wear to meet her Maker.' He nodded to the hearse. 'They've come to take her to the funeral parlour.' Then, patting Richard on the hand, he gushed: 'Come on now, no sad faces. What about this rocking horse of ours? Let's see what you've done with him.'

They kept a couple of dry sherries waiting while Maurice helped him to return the rocking horse to its usual position at the farthest side of the panelled hall. 'If we tether him there, there'll be no fear of children being thrown and ending up in the fire,' Maurice joked gently, before adding: 'Though I don't believe there's been a fire in this room since the war, the First War, let alone any children. Sadly, the Creswells weren't great breeders, not in recent centuries anyway.' A kind, practical man who'd run the house for nearly thirty years, he was, Richard always thought, an employee from a gentler time.

'So, let's drink to the old lady,' Maurice said at last. And he held up his glass.

Richard didn't much like sherry, but he never had the heart to admit that to Maurice who did, and who was now stroking the rocking horse's wooden nose.

'He's beautiful, Richard. She would have been so delighted. It's such a pity she missed seeing what you've done.

She always looked forward to you coming down and having one of your long chats. Sorry if she bored you sometimes with her stories about how life used to be here.'

'Not at all! She was always interested in what I do, which is more than I can say for some clients.' And Richard looked down the hall at a small marble Hanoverian statue of two cherubs that he'd worked on. 'I'm going to miss coming here.'

Maurice looked surprised. 'What do you mean? Not coming here?'

'Well...' Richard indicated the waiting hearse through the mullioned window. 'I would imagine my work's finished now.'

'Good Lord, no. There's much more to do. The doll's house, for instance...' And, carrying his glass, Maurice led the way across the hall to a seventeenth century dolls house in a small anteroom. 'There! Wouldn't you say she could do with a little bit of redecorating?'

'Well, yes, but surely the house and its belongings will be sold now. Wasn't she the last of the Creswell line?'

Maurice smiled and finished his sherry. 'That depends on which line you mean.'

'I'm sorry, I don't follow?'

'Well...' Maurice dropped his voice. 'I don't suppose there's any harm in you knowing, not now, anyway. But the fact is, her ladyship was a tenant here, just like the rest of us.'

Richard looked at him. 'But it was *her* house. *Her* family's house, the Creswells, right back to the Reformation...'

Maurice gently shook his head. 'She was very proud, and, as you know, very secretive when she wanted to be. She liked people to think the Creswell family still owned the house. She never corrected that impression. The staff here played along with her, the few of us who knew the truth. We were the nearest she had to friends at the end, you see. We didn't want to upset her. But the fact is, the Creswells haven't owned this place for donkeys' years?'

Richard stared in surprise. 'So, who does own it?'

The undertakers in the hearse didn't notice him as they drove out through the gates of the house, the coffin in the back. He'd parked his car down a side lane, beneath some overhanging cedars. He hadn't particularly wanted to see the hearse again. He just needed time to think.

Next to him on the passenger seat lay the flyer he'd been given by the London Heritage workers earlier that morning. He picked it up and read it again. Then he remembered the old lady, and thought about other less fortunate old people, and that terrible day singing carols on behalf of Age Gap, and how he'd been taken in. In her way, Lady Alice had been conning people, too.

He would never know exactly when the idea came to him. But the seed was planted that morning, sitting outside the gates of Creswell Manor, as the body of an old lady was carried away to a funeral parlour.

And, when he started the Volvo, it wasn't towards London that he drove, but to Oxford and the county records offices.

18.

(i)

For the following week, Jenny hardly saw Richard. Teaching her class of 30 six-year-olds, kept her more than busy, but she'd taken on extra work, too. Children developed at such different speeds. The Maxwells of this world, the little boy who had enquired about riding the rocking horse, needed her extra attention after school, which, she'd come to realise, was the part of teaching she found most rewarding.

As for Richard, when he wasn't out running, he was always working. She messaged him one evening suggesting that as housemates they go to see a film and have a pizza, but he excused himself saying that he had something to finish, asking if they could make it another night. She was puzzled and it crossed her mind that he might be seeing someone, although he'd never mentioned anyone. Would she mind if there was a girlfriend, she thought, as she cycled to and from school? Why should she? But, with his quiet intensity, he was an attractive man.

(ii)

Since boyhood, Richard had enjoyed solving puzzles created by others. Now, as he pounded the towpath, parks and lanes of south-west London, he found himself creating a puzzle from a problem and then attempting to come up with a solution to it. As he ran, he mentally tried out one scenario after another. Then, when he got home, he drew patterns and scenarios on a large sketchbook and worked at his computer.

His objective was simple: to find a way that he and Jenny could stay in the River House for the length of their leases without harassment. Ideally, Jerricoe would have backed down, but, as that wasn't going to happen, an alternative had to be found.

The planning was all consuming. Was there anything he could take from the London Heritage flyer he'd been given, which was now pinned to a cork board over his worktop? And was there something else from the lifelong duplicity of the old lady at Creswell Manor? Did the two fit together in some way? The Oxfordshire County Council records office had been a treasure trove of information on Creswell Manor. How much of it might be useful? And, most importantly, how much might his years in banking help him? Piece by piece, as he ran, the first threads of a scheme began to emerge.

He thought about Jenny often, and wondered what she was doing in the basement, hoping that she hadn't found herself a boyfriend. But he resisted the temptation to see her. He had to work out his plan first.

(iii)

He surfaced on a Sunday evening. Jenny, who was taking her class swimming the following day, had been thinking of an early night, when, at just after ten, she heard Richard's footsteps on the stairs and his quiet tap on her door.

Never one for regular shaving, he was now wearing days of stubble, but the oddest thing about him was that he was smiling. Carrying a large folder, he crossed to her living room table and set it down. 'It'll never work, but I think I've done it,' he said, as he pulled a bottle of red wine from his jacket pocket.

She reached for glasses and a corkscrew. 'Done what?'

'Found a way to beat Jerricoe,' he answered, and, opening the folder, he took out a large, reinforced sheet of folded cardboard and spread it on the table.

She looked at the cardboard. It looked like an elaborate sketching of a variation of Snakes & Ladders, with ladders climbing up the board, and drainpipes winding down. In the bottom left-hand corner, there was a drawing of what seemed to be an old manor house. While, in the top right-hand corner, a small photograph of the River House had been stuck down.

'So, do you want to play a game or something?' she asked.

'It is a game, of sorts, but not one between you and me. We're on the same side.'

'That's nice.'

'And it seems to me, that if Jerricoe won't let us live in the River House in peace as honest tenants, there's only one thing we can do.'

'Which is?'

'We'll just have to buy the house off him.'

She blinked.

'We've no other option.'

'But this place will cost more than a million.'

'Much more.'

'Yes,' she agreed. 'So where are we going to find a million plus pounds?'

'From him. From Jerricoe. He's going to give us the money.'

She wanted to laugh. 'And how are we going to get him to give it to us?'

'By selling him a house called Creswell Manor.' Richard rested his forefinger on the drawing of the big old house at the bottom of the board.

'That's the place the rocking horse came from?'

He nodded.

'A place we don't own.'

'Correct.'

'Which is inconvenient.'

'Not necessarily.'

She looked at him. 'Richard... it's too late for jokes.'

'I'm not joking. Anyway, that's the easy part.'

Now she did laugh. 'And the tricky bit?'

'Doing it all without him ever knowing that you and I are involved.'

This was too much. 'You don't think you might be going a bit doo-lally, do you? Cracking under the tension?

'Thank you.' Richard laughed. He looked so boyish, so pleased with himself. The studious, shy, man she'd first met was gone.

She began again. 'Jerricoe Properties have only just bought this house. Why would they want to sell it to us?'

'Because...' Dipping once more into his box, Richard produced his London Heritage flyer and began to read.

'*London Heritage lists buildings on grounds of age, rarity and architectural merit and, or occasionally, one that has...*'

Jenny took the flyer from him and continued reading... '*"played a part in the life of a distinguished person."* So?'

'So! What do you think he'll do when he discovers that he can't turn this place into a money-spinning health spa because London Heritage have slapped a preservation order on it, having discovered that someone very famous lived here?'

'But no one famous did live here...did they?'

'I don't know. It doesn't really matter.'

'Well, okay. But in all probability, they didn't. So why would London Heritage stick a preservation order on the house?'

'They won't. What's important isn't what London Heritage do, it's what Jerricoe *thinks* they'll do. If you believe something to be true, you act accordingly.'

'Well, yes...' she conceded.

He turned back to his sheet of cardboard. 'As you said, it's like a board game. A figure of eight. We start here at the River House, then we move on to Creswell Manor, which we sell to Jerricoe, after which we use his money to buy the River House from him. It's simple, really!'

Jenny shook her head. 'It isn't simple. And, anyway, it's just a game. As you said, it can't work in real life.'

'Probably not. But if Jerricoe keeps on menacing us, and the lawyer can't stop him, the police still can't find any evidence, and nobody else wants to know...?'

She didn't answer. Richard had come up with an outrageous, crazy, fairy tale scheme of a world in which bullies didn't always have to win, where ordinary people could have their day, too. It was an attractive fantasy.

He hadn't eaten properly for days, and although she'd already had dinner, she made him an omelette and salad while he went over his scheme again. It still sounded totally mad, but, because she wanted to believe, she began to fantasise what it would be like to actually own the River House, to decorate and restore it, and give it back its former elegance.

Then came Richard's pin prick back to reality. 'There is one thing that we should perhaps consider.'

'Which is?'

'By doing this, by even trying to do this, we'll both become criminals.'

'Criminals!' Her smile disappeared.

'I'm afraid so.'

The fun had gone out of her fantasy. 'Richard, every day I teach small children right and wrong. I can't be a criminal.'

'No. I knew you'd say that,' he replied. 'It was just a silly, crazy thought. Sorry.' And he folded up his board game.

He was right, of course. It was just a mad, lunatic, desperate, criminal idea which would almost certainly never have come off. But perhaps it had been a romantic one, too.

19.

(i)

Four days later, sitting in the dark in the back seat of his BMW, as it made its way around London, Mark Jerricoe was angry. Nothing ever went quickly enough. He was an impetuous man. 'One look is all it took', was his personal motto. That was how he beat the competition. But there was always someone who wanted to put his foot on the brake and slow everybody down. That afternoon he'd learned that, after all the money and hospitality he'd thrown at it, his revised plan for the Greensleeves Estate had been turned down again.

He'd find a way. He bloody would. But why did everything have to be so hard?

He wasn't being driven anywhere in particular, just doing his regular tour of some of his smaller properties, cruising around London at night, checking the neighbourhoods in which he'd invested. Neighbourhoods could change quickly, especially at night. And if any did, he wanted to know. Change affected perceptions; and perceptions altered property values.

At that moment they were cruising near the canyons of new apartment blocks along the river.

'A bit slower, Angel. It's just along here, where the road turns back on itself,' Craig Hunt, sitting in the front passenger seat, muttered to the young driver.

Hunt knew the location of every Jerricoe stick and stone.

The BMW slowed and Jerricoe found himself looking at the River House as the car drove past. 'The old guy who'd owned that place might not have realised it, but he was shrewd to hang on to it for so long,' he murmured to himself, while not quite saying, 'but not as shrewd as the smooth-talking fellow who'd got those who'd inherited the house to sell it'.

'What about those last two tenants?' he asked, registering the lights in the front basement window and on the top floor of the house.

Hunt shook his head. 'We'll get there…'

Jerricoe exploded. 'For Christ's sake! What's going on? Get someone to give those scumbags a little taste of what their future might look like. All right!'

Without replying, Hunt took out his mobile and tapped a number.

'Come on, Angel!' Jerricoe snapped. 'What are we waiting for?'

The BMW drove on.

(ii)

In her basement flat Jenny was dreaming up ways of holding the attention of the most easily distracted children. Richard would be good at this, she mused, as she devised a simple addition and subtraction puzzle involving different fruits. He would have invented a game for them. He was clever like that.

At ten, she put on her pyjamas and got into bed to watch on her laptop a *Call My Agent* episode that she'd missed. It was nearly eleven when she turned out the light. She was tired, but she couldn't sleep, her mind fluttering from school to Richard. Her bedroom was at the back of the house, and, because she hadn't yet got around to lining her curtains, the room was always partly lit by the lights further down the river. Normally, she slept facing away from the window, but tonight, as sleep evaded her, she turned and tossed, this way and that.

It must have been after three when she heard the crack of a twig in the back garden, the crushing perhaps of a fragment of a plane tree branch that had been brought down by the New Year's snow. She opened her eyes and peered at the thin curtains.

Was something out there? Probably a fox. Every district of London had its nightly patrols of urban foxes rummaging in the bins.

She turned towards the wall.

Another twig snapped. Then another. That wasn't a fox. Something heavy was moving immediately outside her window.

She opened her eyes again and swivelled her head on the pillow. There was nothing to see. But then another sound and a looming silhouette appeared, a figure which seemed to inflate as it drew closer to the window. She wanted to scream, but, as if in a dream, no sound would come.

With a crash, the window shattered into shards of glass. Almost simultaneously she was gasping for breath as smoke billowed around the room, filling her eyes, blinding her, suffocating her.

(iii)

Richard had been awoken by the sound of the crash and had almost reached the basement when Jenny emerged from her flat, coughing and gulping in a cloud of smoke.

Pulling her away from her door, and slapping his arm over his face, he pushed into the bedroom. In the light from the stairs, he could see a metal canister lying in a field of broken glass beneath the window. It was still belching fumes. Grabbing hold of the canister, he pulled back the curtain and threw it back outside.

When he rejoined her, Jenny was sitting at the top of the stairs. She wasn't quite crying, but, huddled there, in her pale blue winter pyjamas, she was shaking.

Crouching next to her, he put an arm around her shoulders. She leaned into him for comfort. A single warm tear bled on to his neck. 'It's all right,' he murmured.

(iv)

'You can have my bed,' Richard said as, sitting in her dressing gown in his studio flat she sipped a cup of tea. She was no longer trembling, but with her window smashed, he'd insisted that she spend the night in his studio.

'I'll be fine here on the couch,' she said.

'No, take the bed,' he insisted. 'After what you've been through, you need somewhere comfortable.'

She wouldn't be moved. 'Here will be perfect. Thank you.' And, to show him that she meant what she said, she finished her drink, pushed a cushion under her head, pulled the blankets around her, and stretched out.

For a moment Richard looked as though he didn't quite know what to do.

'You were right,' she said. 'If you'd moved out, it would have been crazy of me to stay in the house by myself. I'd have been terrified. Thank you for staying.'

'I'm glad I did.' There was another hesitation, before he said: 'Well, anyway. Good night.' And he went into his bedroom and closed the door. Soon she heard his light go out and turned off the lamp that was beside the sofa.

She was too shaken to sleep immediately. The figure at her window and the crashing of the glass replayed in her imagination when she closed her eyes. Opening them, she looked at the outline of the Creswell Manor doll's house on the worktop, aware of the slight smell of the acrylic paints that Richard had been using to redecorate it. And she remembered how as a little girl she'd imagined that she would one day have a home like a doll's house.

Life hadn't worked out like that.

20.

okJenny showed the two police officers the broken glass lying inside her bedroom window The police sergeant, a sturdy, mid-career woman who was accompanied by a young male constable, were sympathetic, and noted that the room still smelled sulphurous. The smoke canister, they suggested, looked like something a film studio might use to simulate the effect of a blaze: harmless but frightening.

'Bloody frightening,' the constable agreed.

Then, as he put the canister into a plastic bag for forensic examination, Jenny made a statement, leaving no doubt as to whom she thought was responsible.

Neither officer commented on that. It wasn't their place to guess, they said.

They didn't spend very long in the garden looking for clues. She hardly expected them to. It wasn't as though anyone had been killed or even badly hurt in the incident. She hadn't reported it, until that morning when, creeping downstairs from Richard's flat while he was still sleeping, she'd surveyed the damage to her home.

'You should have phoned us as soon as the vandalism took place,' the sergeant said as she walked them to the garden gate.

'Why call the police out in the middle of the night, when the guy who did it would be miles away by the time you got here?' she answered.

'I know,' smiled the sergeant. 'Any idea who might have been behind this? Anyone with a grudge against you?'

'Apart from the landlord you, mean?' Jenny said, and once again explained the regular harassment.

The sergeant looked sympathetic but unconvinced. 'We'll be making a report,' she said

'Yet another report, when we all know who ordered it and why.'

'Unless there's a positive identification...'

'I know... The landlord can have me murdered in my bed.'

'Well...' Both police officers looked uncomfortable.

'Anyway, it was good of you to call round.' And, leaving them, she walked back inside her flat and began to sweep up the fragments of glass.

Her home had been invaded. Not just the house she lived in, but her home. That changed everything.

A glazier came to the River House and repaired her window when she got home from school that afternoon. Richard came down to see her after he'd left.

'Thank you for last night,' she said as he examined the new window. 'I was so …well…terrified, actually.'

He nodded. 'I don't blame you.'

'And grateful that you were there. Thanks again.' She paused. 'God, I was scared.'

He nodded bleakly. 'Which would have been Jerricoe's intention, wouldn't it.'

She smiled ruefully. 'He certainly succeeded in doing that. But…' Spotting an overlooked shard of glass on the carpet, she broke off and very carefully picked it up, before dropping it into a waste bin. '…it isn't going to work,' she continued.

Richard looked at her.

'Jerricoe has been fighting dirty all along. Now, it seems to me, it's our turn to fight dirty, too.'

He appeared not to follow. 'I'm not sure…?'

'That crazy, mad, insane Figure of Eight idea you had…'

'Yes?'

'I think we should give it a try.'

His expression spelled astonishment. 'Jenny, we've been through this. As you said, it would make us criminals.'

'Jerricoe's the criminal, intimidating us, frightening me, forcing the Ghelanis and the Morrisons out.'

'Well, yes. Obviously. Morally, you're right. But in the eyes of the law…'

She stopped him. 'Bugger the law.' She looked around her room. 'I love my home. I want to stay in it. I've spent all my savings on it and it's where I want to begin the second half of my life.'

'But, Jenny…'

She wouldn't let him in. 'Richard! We've asked and pleaded and got no help from anyone. No-one at all. We just keep being fobbed off although we're in the *right*. If we wait for the law to help us, we'll be sleeping in the Mersey Tunnel by Easter.'

Richard smiled at that, and she realised that she'd suddenly sounded very Liverpudlian. 'But you know,' he said, 'if Jerricoe had honoured our leases, it would only have kept us here for another three years. We'd all have had to move on then.'

'Yes, I know. But he should have waited. And been honest. And decent. But he didn't want to wait. And he wouldn't know honesty if it had a halo around it. He's a greedy bastard who's been treating us, not like honest tenants, but like worthless nuisances. To him the River House is just another toy, a piece of property to be bartered for profit. But to me, and to you and to all of us, it's our home. And the way I see it, greedy people like Jerricoe should be punished by having their toys taken away from them. So, let's do it and see what happens.'

'We could go to jail, you know. Think about it. It could ruin your career as…'

She stared at him. 'My *second* career. And, I have been thinking about it. All day.'

For several seconds he was silent. Then, suddenly, he smiled. 'All right. If Jerricoe won't play fair, nor will we. It probably won't work. Almost certainly it won't work. We must both be crackers for even thinking about it. But…let's give it a try. We're going to need some help though.'

She smiled brilliantly. 'Well, I could ask my sister and maybe one of the…'

'No, no,' he stopped her. 'Someone who knows about these things…'

'What do you mean?'

'Well, you know, someone whose…'

'What? Dodgy?' she asked.

'Yes.'

'Like who?'

'Like a conman.'

21.

(i)

'You're out of your mind.' Harry Culshaw shook his head in derision. He'd heard of some foolish long cons in his career, but this do-gooding idiot was the worst. He was kicking himself for allowing the chap into his home. He'd just been settling down to watch *Antiques Roadshow,* which he'd always thought was the sort of programme he would have been presenting had he gone into television, when, there was Richard the Accordion Playing Carol Singer, ringing his bell with a smile bigger than Salisbury Cathedral. Not many people smiled when you'd conned them. That should have been a warning.

'Good to see you, old man,' Harry had said, because politeness never hurt anyone. 'Bad timing, though! I'm just on my way out.' And he'd automatically reached for his overcoat which he kept on a peg behind the door.

'Five minutes. It could change your life,' the madman had insisted, foot in door.

For a moment Harry had hesitated. That had been a mistake, too. Because now here he was, stuck with a guy who was spouting some scheme which sounded as though it had been specifically designed to feed them both into a concrete mixer. And the fellow just wouldn't take goodbye for an answer.

'Just to recap...' Harry sighed, as Richard paused for breath. 'This chap Jerricoe is powerful, greedy and apparently untouchable.'

'He's also very rich.'

'Yes. You said. And you want me to con him?'

'Wrong. I want *us* to con him.'

This amused Harry. 'Sorry. Don't think I'm not flattered and all that. But you're an amateur.'

Richard looked dismissively around the flat. 'Nice here, isn't it!'

Harry felt that. All right, so the place, a barely furnished couple of rented rooms in what some might flatteringly describe as a mixed terrace, wasn't the best he'd had. But it had been a thin time, hence the carol singing blunder. To pull a stunt so close to home had been sloppy: unprofessional. But he'd been tempted. It had looked so simple. It was Christmas. Now, here he was, stuck with a nutter.

'Or is it that you can only con children and old people?' Richard pursued.

'What was it you said you do for a living?' Harry jibed back. In truth he'd never been told, nor even wanted to know.

'Perhaps it's too tricky for you…nailing a big-time guy like Jerricoe. Is that it?'

Harry grinned. 'That's another thing. It's personal with you. That can be dangerous.'

'It could be your chance of redemption. Robbing the rich property baron to help the poor. Just like Robin Hood.'

Harry shrugged. What did he want with redemption? He wished he was a property baron.

Quickly, as if realising that appealing to Harry's better nature was the wrong approach, the idiot tried another tack. '*And* you could make a million. Maybe more. Maybe a lot more.'

'How?' Harry tried not to laugh. He hadn't envisaged a figure anywhere near that ever being dangled.

'By combining our talents.' Richard was watching him closely.

'Which are?'

'You're crooked and I'm clever.'

In the background the signature tune denoting the end of *Antiques Roadshow* was playing.

It was Richard's idea that they take a drive out to Jerricoe House. It was evening. The place would be deserted now. Harry knew that Richard was attempting to reel him in. He'd made his own career by tempting his victims ever closer; he knew the tricks. All the same, he was prepared to go, if only to see just how far-fetched the fellow's plan was.

At first, they drove past the dismal Jerricoe Properties office on the industrial estate. Then, parking some distance away, they approached it on foot. 'Before we get any closer, perhaps you'd better pull your coat collar up to your face and wear this,' Richard told him, withdrawing a red striped, woollen football hat from his pocket. 'There's a CCTV-camera over the front door. You never know who might check the tapes.'

Harry shrugged. But he put on the hat and hid his face just the same.

Unbuttoning a hood from inside the collar of his anorak, Richard pulled it over his head, and together, they walked past the front of the building, moving swiftly as if on their way to somewhere else.

'Jerricoe House,' Harry murmured, reading the embossed platinum sign over the front door. 'Pentonville is more welcoming.'

'This guy didn't get rich by being hospitable,' Richard returned.

At the corner of the building was an alleyway. 'What's down there?' Harry asked.

Richard shook his head.

Harry smiled. 'No recce's complete without a look around the back.' And he walked a dozen paces down the alley to a high, iron gateway, along the top of which ran a length of barbed wire.

Richard stayed on the street, watching.

Harry hadn't expected to see anything in the alley. And he didn't, until, pushing his face to the iron bars, there was a sudden scampering and a snarling erupted from the blackness as two huge dogs, tongues spitting, teeth bared, hurled themselves, one after the other at his face.

He jumped back, the heat of the dogs' breath on his skin. 'Jesus!' Then, as the dogs continued to throw themselves at the gate, he hurried away.

Richard was waiting. 'Good recce?'

'I just wanted to see what you were up against.'

'And?'

'If this Jerricoe guy is anything like his dogs, he's too big and too dangerous.'

'There you go again. Small time.'

Then, keeping their heads turned away from the CCTV camera, they walked back to the car.

'This doesn't mean I'm in, you know,' Harry said as Richard turned the ignition.

''Course not! Come and see Jenny. She can't wait to tell you how much she detests you.'

He wasn't exaggerating. 'The man's a reptile,' Jenny had argued when Richard had first suggested Harry. 'We'll be putting ourselves in the hands of a crook. What's to stop him fiddling us again if it suits him?'

'Nothing,' Richard had agreed. '*If* it suits him. But he won't do that if he's smart enough to understand that he's better off working *with* us rather than against us. We don't have to like him if he can be useful to us.'

(ii)

Thirty minutes later, Harry was lolling on Jenny's sofa. Indolent and confident, his hair was longer and wavier than she'd remembered, his features softer. He was certainly handsome. So, no one knows that this old bird didn't actually own her folks' ancestral home?' he was saying.

'It won't become public knowledge until her will's published,' Richard explained. 'And that won't be for months. People believe what they're told.'

'And she told lies. Like you!' Jenny needled, facing Harry across the fireplace.

'Ouch!' Harry flashed her a smile.

Richard, on an upright chair, ignored the intervention and shuffled through a handful of printouts. 'Mark Jerricoe made his first fortune by reading the death notices in local newspapers, then bullying or cajoling the relatives of the dead to sell him their homes at knock-down prices.'

'Not bad,' Harry murmured admiringly.

Jenny winced.

'Which is what we're going to get him to do with Creswell Manor. Buy it!' Richard indicated the Figure of Eight board game that he'd made.

'And how do you know he'll want to buy the place? He may not like it.'

'He'll like the price. Jerricoe's a businessman. There's no way he won't like it when he's offered a twelve or fourteen million pounds house for eight or nine million.'

'Would you say no?' Jenny asked quietly.

Harry leant forward. 'Maybe not.'

Greed is shameless, Jenny thought as she watched him. But, as he pulled on a pair of horn-rimmed glasses, she couldn't help noticing the blue of his eyes.

Richard had registered Harry's sudden interest. 'If something is cheap enough, it's virtually impossible to turn down. Right?'

'He'll know the place isn't yours to sell as soon as he sees the name on the title deeds.'

Jenny looked at Richard. Had he overlooked something?

He was smiling. 'There won't be a name on the deeds. Land registry wasn't made compulsory in Britain until 1925. All buildings older than that aren't registered until they're sold.'

'You're sure about that?' Harry was surprised.

'I spend my life renovating what's old. Believe me, I know about old.' Richard paused. 'And, as an ex-banker, I know about moving money around, too.'

'Interesting!' Harry took a gingerbread man from a plate that Jenny had put on a sawn-off table she'd rescued from a skip she'd passed near her school. 'But what you didn't say is, if the old lady didn't own the house, who does own it?'

Richard met his gaze. 'I can't tell you that.'

'What?' Harry was surprised. 'Why not?'

'I promised not to tell anyone.'

'Hang on!' Harry was indignant. 'You expect me to join in this insane scheme without knowing all the details.'

'Without knowing just this one detail.'

'Why can't you tell me?'

'I made a promise. And I keep my promises.'

Jenny glanced at Richard. Why the ownership of Creswell Manor should be a secret she didn't know. He hadn't told her either.

Harry got to his feet, looking both puzzled and thoughtful, as though he'd just encountered a kind of species new to him: a would-be colleague who said he kept his word.

For a second, Jenny thought Harry might be about to leave. Then suddenly he became serious. 'Scams like this are expensive to set up, you know.'

'How expensive?' Richard asked.

'A few thousand. Professionals expect something up front as well as a cut. And you'll need professionals to help.'

'Okay.'

Jenny looked at Richard but didn't say anything.

Harry now became energised. 'Then there's stuff you need to know.'

'So, teach us,' Jenny said.

He hesitated. 'How much did you say Jerricoe's worth?'

Richard consulted his papers again. 'According to the *Sunday* last count, and the figure rises every year.'

'And what does he do with it all?'

'Nothing much. He lives alone in a penthouse flat overlooking Kensington Gardens. He owns the building, and he has a boat down at Lymington, but doesn't sail much. He just sits on it and gets a tan.'

'He likes to wear expensive suits, too,' Jenny came in. 'And he has his cut every other week at some place in Chelsea. He's very keen on his hair. Probably dyes it blonder than it really is. You know the type. Other than that, he just likes making money for the sake of it. No gambling, no regular woman, so to speak, and no real hobbies. In fact, he seems to be a mean, selfish bugger all round… Just like you, really.'

Harry took another gingerbread man. He'd now cleared almost the entire plate.

Of course, he had, Jenny thought. They were free.

'Actually, I'm very generous with other people's money. As for women…well…' Harry smiled at her, leaving the thought hanging, and bit the head off his biscuit. 'These are *very* good, Jenny. Shame about the legs.' And he held up a very short legged gingerbread man.

She was immediately defensive. 'The children made them at school. They muddled the measurements.'

'Bless 'em!' And he dazzled his smile at her.

She ignored it.

'Anyway,' Richard was saying, 'it seems to me, for this to work we're going to need…'

'A team. Specialists! A top lawyer…a good forger…and some bit part players…' Harry was now striding around the room.

Make it attractive enough and Harry will help us, Richard had told Jenny earlier. He'd never had any doubts.

'Do you know any other conmen?' Jenny asked.

'Oh, loads.' Again, that smile. 'I just don't know if I can trust them.'

'Get us those you distrust least,' Richard said. 'Can you find a lawyer who would be interested?'

'Probably. But you'll need a conveyancing specialist. Forgers are easier.' Then, as though not wanting to appear too keen, Harry applied a gentle brake. 'Let me think about it.' And he got up to go.

Jenny stood at the front door as he left.

'Great seeing you again, Jenny. Thrilling to know that we might soon be colleagues!' Then he was gone, off down the garden path after Richard.

'Colleagues!' I should count the spoons now, Jenny told herself as she watched the car drive away. As for Richard, she'd never seen him so sure of himself.

But what about her? What was she? A schoolteacher who taught six-year-olds to read and write by day…and helped plan a multi-million-pound property scam by night?

She forced the thought aside. It wouldn't work anyway.

But if it did?

Jerricoe had it coming.

(iii)

'Well?' Richard asked, as he pulled his Volvo into the kerb outside Harry's flat.

'Fifty-fifty if we get Creswell Manor,' said Harry. 'Your share to cover all expenses and anyone else involved. A two thousand pounds advance before we begin and I'm to be paid first when any money comes through.'

'Fine,' Richard replied. 'But the advance will be paid in three hundred pounds a week instalments.'

Harry was surprised. He'd expected more of an argument. He would have accepted a smaller share. This madman might be clever, but in a business sense he was naïve. 'Let's shake on it,' he said quickly before Richard had chance to reconsider

Richard put out a hand. 'Does that mean I can trust you now?'

'Of course!' Harry smiled. 'We're partners. Good night.' And, climbing out of the car, he crossed the pavement and went into his home.

Maybe the likelihood of success was negligible, Harry thought, as he heard the Volvo drive away. But a two thousand pounds advance would be two thousand pounds. All things considered it had been a more entertaining evening than watching *Antiques Roadshow*.

22.

(i)

The Morrisons' conservatory came down in a brief series of prolonged crashes, as a demolition man went along the wall at the back of the house with a sledgehammer knocking off those pieces of timber and glass which clung on. Meanwhile a yellow excavator was ploughing across the lawn.

Richard watched from the front steps. He'd tried remonstrating with the workmen when they'd arrived at eight that morning just as Jenny had been cycling off to school, glaring at them as she went. But they were Bulgarian contract workers, who'd never even met anyone from Jerricoe Properties, so a disagreement with a landlord was no concern of theirs. Besides, the conservatory had indeed been unsafe. The Morrisons had asked the previous landlord to repair it on several occasions but without success. Now it was gone, leaving smashed terracotta pots, damaged geraniums and a skip full of glass, metal and wood.

It was a new tactic, Richard reflected as he went back up the stairs to his studio. Jerricoe Properties were now behaving as though the house was already empty and he and Jenny no longer lived there.

(ii)

Jenny messaged him in late morning. A colleague was doing her lunchtime playground duty, she told him. Did he have time for a pizza?

He did.

She was sitting at a corner table for two in the Pizza Express, just down the road from her school, when he arrived.

'I already ordered,' she said as he sat down. 'A margherita for you. Is that all right?'

He smiled.

'Unadorned. As usual.'

He looked puzzled. 'What's going on?'

'Before things got complicated,' she said, 'I thought we should have a business meeting. And this seemed as neutral a place as any.'

'A business meeting? Is that really necessary?'

'As development money is going to be involved, I think it is. Harry said it would cost thousands for us to pull this thing off. So, if you give me your bank details I want to chip in with three thousand pounds. There'll be more later.'

'You can't afford three thousand pounds,' he said.

'You can't afford to fund this thing by yourself.'

'Actually, I can,' Richard countered. 'Nobody ever got rich being an art restorer but I have enough to start this thing off.'

'So do I. And I want to be involved.'

'You *are* involved.' His voice had risen, and he glanced around anxiously.

At that moment two pizzas, balanced on the arm of a waitress, appeared in front of them.

'Involved as an *equal* partner,' Jenny said as the waitress left. 'Involved in everything, every step of the way.'

Richard looked unhappy and she regretted telling him that she'd pushed herself as far as she could to furnish her flat. 'If you trust Harry with any of your money you may never see it again,' he said.

'I know. Isn't that the risk all venture capitalists take?' She grinned. 'I thought an ex-banker like you would know that.'

He didn't smile. 'It could be dangerous. There's no telling what Jerricoe might do if…'

'Richard, it's *already* dangerous. You must have noticed!' She was teasing now, and, taking a mouthful of pizza, she pulled a strand of elasticated cheese from her mouth. 'Sorry about that!' And she wiped her lips with a paper napkin.

'Jenny, listen…'

'No! You listen! I've told you. You're not doing it without me. I've been messed around enough during my life. Can you imagine the humiliations of twenty years' being told that I'm not quite what they're looking for. Too old for this, too young for that? Not pretty enough, too pretty. Too tall, too small, not posh enough, not famous enough. Can you?'

He didn't answer.

'Well, all that's behind me now, and no-one's going to tell me what to do or what not to do. This may be your plan, but I'm going to be involved and doing my bit all the way. So...sort code and account number, please. And let's make sure Harry doesn't con us again!'

Richard smiled and felt in the inside pocket of his jacket for a pen and his bank details.

She smiled as he wrote them out. 'Good. Now, come on. Eat your pizza before it goes cold. This is a treat for me. I usually have school dinners.'

(iii)

Jenny stayed behind in her classroom after the children had gone home from school that afternoon. Sitting at her desk she studied her calculator. She'd borrowed three thousand pounds at 7.5 per cent over three years. Richard was right. She couldn't afford it. But that was no longer the point.

(iv)

Harry turned the pages of the glossy property magazines slowly. He'd always known that the price of a London flat was beyond his reach, but since it *was* impossible, he'd never taken the trouble to discover just how far beyond that might be. Now, sitting up in bed and wearing his dressing gown to stay warm, he was beginning to realise the nature of the impossibility.

A two bedroomed flat in Chelsea was going for £3 million: a 'tired' five bedroomed house in South Kensington was on the market for six million pounds. Property: how could he have missed it? That was what he should have gone into. He would have been brilliant at it.

It had been Richard's idea that he study the property magazines. 'They make everyone who owns a home feel richer,' he'd said, 'and the rest of us feel poorer. And if you're going to be playing someone in the property business, you're going to have to learn a bit about it.'

As if he wouldn't, Harry had thought, irritated at being taught his job by an amateur. That was the trouble with

Richard. All right, so he was a clever bugger, though he'd hidden it well at Christmas. But did he have any idea of the chances of success involved in the long con, a job that, if successful, which was very unlikely, would take months to pull off. In fact, a couple of mates he'd sounded out had immediately backed away when Harry had begun to outline it. Impossible, they'd reckoned.

He looked at his watch. Richard would be calling for him soon. Getting up, he went into his tiny bathroom to wash. He shivered as he did. Poverty was always so bloody cold.

He thought about Richard as he studied his face in the mirror while he shaved. What did he think about the guy?

Well, he didn't dislike him.

Then another thought. What about her? What about Jenny? And not for the first time he imagined the two of them, Richard and Jenny, alone together in that big, empty house. Sexy.

Finishing shaving, he dabbed his cheeks with some aftershave that he'd been given as a free sample in Selfridges and then went in search of a clean shirt and his good charity shop suit.

It was almost time to take the first step. He was excited, as he was at the beginning of every job. One never knew where it might lead.

23

(i)

From the other side of the street Richard watched as Harry approached the estate agents' office and perused the *For Sale* houses in the window. Then, seeming to have decided, he went inside.

They'd selected the agency carefully, eventually choosing the head offices of Heyes & Heys on Kensington High Street because it marketed both town and country properties. Proudly old school and staffed with chaps with privately educated accents and elegant girls with names like Candida and Lucinda, it suggested property snobbery.

'You'd fit in there perfectly,' Richard had said when they'd chosen it, and had then been amused when Harry had taken a moment to realise that it hadn't been a compliment. This was the first working day of the partnership, and, though his plan was still only half formed, a first payment had already gone Harry's way.

After a minute or two the door of Heyes & Heys opened. Harry emerged and strolled down the pavement, a brochure in his hand.

Richard followed him. 'Okay?' he asked as, rounding a corner, they reached the parked Volvo,

Harry nodded. Then, as they climbed into the car, he opened the brochure and took a Heyes & Heys business card from the four little slits that held it.

It was a short drive to North Kensington, where, pulling on to some waste ground, Richard followed Harry along a row of nineteenth century railway arches, newly fashioned as workshops and storerooms. The last door bore no name

'Hello, Inky! It's Michaelangelo!' Harry called into an intercom.

The door clicked open.

Holding his arm out, Harry let Richard enter first. Then he closed and locked the door behind them.

A thin, morose little man with a shaved head peered at them through the gloom. He was standing at an old table, lit by a bright spotlight, and had, it seemed, been writing some Arabic script on a sheet of parchment with a finely sharpened feather nib. Scattered around were drawings, sketches, cameras on tripods, lenses, paints and brushes.

Richard felt almost at home. It was an artist's studio, though no artist he knew worked in a place without windows.

'Inky meet Richard. He's the genius who's going to make us rich. Richard, Inky's the genius who's going to help.'

Richard nodded a greeting.

Inky's reply wasn't to him. 'What have you got?' he asked Harry.

From the breast pocket of his suit Harry passed him the business card from Heyes & Heys. 'This is just the start.'

Picking up a magnifying glass, Inky examined the card carefully. 'All right. That's easy enough,' he said after a moment. 'How many do you want?'

'Just the one for my purpose,' Harry said. 'And maybe a few copies for insurance. But there's only going to be one client.'

Very carefully, Inky put the business card into an envelope which he slid into a drawer. 'And the rest?'

'All kinds of documents, old property deeds, birth certificates…it's a long con. There'll be…'

Inky cut him off. 'What's my cut?'

Harry turned to Richard.

'Four per cent off the top …' Richard said. 'And a thousand down.'

Done.' Satisfied, Inky turned back to his lettering.

Richard's eyes had now become accustomed to the semi-darkness and had found a painting on an easel behind Inky's desk. It was a Modigliani nude. He moved closer to examine it. 'Isn't that in the National Gallery?' he asked.

Inky didn't even look up. 'It will be.'

Harry grinned. 'Inky's in a similar business to you, Richard. If opposites can be similar. You make old things look new. He makes new ones look old.' And he laughed.

Richard wasn't laughing. This was the moment he crossed the border he thought. He was among thieves now. And he was about to become one himself. It was something he was going to have to get used to.

'Can I ask you something?' Richard asked.

'Can I stop you?'

He and Harry were sitting in the Volvo. Parked fifty yards from Jerricoe House. In the shadow of some vacant warehouses, they were keeping watch to see who came and went. Richard had done it several times in the past few weeks, usually in a hired car or van, always parking in different parts of the street, so as not to be noticed. 'Well, I worked out how you did it, when you stole from the carol singers at Christmas,' he began, 'but…'

'Oh, not that again… The old stand-by can of soup trick.'

'Yes…seriously, I want to know. When you ripped us off, how could you be certain I'd be the one left carrying the money?'

Harry shrugged. 'I couldn't. Most of this job is coming up with a plausible persona, then watching and waiting for an opportunity, just as we're doing now. It's a percentage game. If that bossy woman with the pink bosom had taken the tins, I'd have suggested helping her instead of you and then looked for an opportunity. I might never have got one. She looked formidable. Eight or nine times out of ten I don't get a chance, and, if I hadn't, you'd all have still been thinking what a great guy I was, and I would have been twenty pounds worse off. But you agreed to carry the money. And you, I'm afraid, were a doddle…' He suddenly stopped talking and, leaning forward in his seat, stared down the road. 'Unlike this guy. He'll be a tougher prospect altogether.'

A black BMW was approaching from the opposite direction. As it pulled on to the concrete apron in front of Jerricoe House, the blond chief executive of Jerricoe Properties was quickly out and heading towards the door.

'That's him, Mark Jerricoe. And the guy with him…' Richard leafed through his printouts to a local newspaper photograph. It showed Jerricoe and a thin faced colleague, both smiling, as they'd left a magistrates' court after having a harassment charge thrown out. 'That'll be his lawyer, Craig Hunt.'

Taking the file, Harry began to read Richard's notes. 'Craig Hunt. "Four years studying law…five years appealing against his conviction".' He grinned. 'Sounds like a man after my own heart.'

'You wouldn't say that if he was after your home,' Richard murmured.

A plump, dowdy, heavy legged woman wearing a brown raincoat and carrying a shopping bag now emerged from Jerricoe House and began walking towards them on the opposite side of the street.

'That's Jerricoe's secretary,' Richard said, looking at his watch. 'Exactly the same time every day.'

They waited as, reaching a post box, the secretary opened her bag, took out a wad of white envelopes and dropped them inside. Then, turning a corner, she made her way towards a bus stop.

Richard made a note. *'Secretary with post - 5.30 daily.'*

Considering the secretary, Harry was shaking his head. 'She must have a very tidy mind.'

Richard wasn't listening. He was wondering where this information might fit into his plan, then scribbled a reminder to himself: 'Find out what time post arrives.'

(ii)

It wasn't much of a space, and it had taken some effort pulling out the weeds and clearing the brambles. But, having bought some secateurs and a fork, Jenny had turned over the soil, and the daffodils and tulips that she'd planted were already close to flowering.

Having her own little garden had always been one of her daydreams. And, as she put her back into planting the hollyhocks, foxgloves and polyanthus that she'd bought from the garden centre behind Homebase, she smiled to herself. All being well, this summer there would be quite a show outside her bedroom window.

(iii)

'Have you two never thought about moving out until…you know…?' Harry was standing at Richard's window, looking down on the garden.

Richard knew that he was watching Jenny at work, and it irritated him. 'If we did move out, we'd probably never get back in,' he replied.

'Good point.'

Richard had asked Harry to come over so that they might go through some last-minute preparations, but he was now finding it difficult to get his companion to concentrate. He turned to his Figure of Eight board. 'See. Jerricoe is here.' He pointed at the square with the photograph of the River House. 'And he's going here. The hairdressers.' And he moved his finger along a few places to a square in which he'd drawn a comb and a pair of scissors.

Harry took his gaze from Jenny and looked at the board. 'Mmm.'

'And when we get him *here*…' Reaching for the one subject that was sure to concentrate Harry's thoughts, Richard slid his finger quickly down a succession of drainpipes to the bottom square that represented Creswell Manor. 'We collect millions of pounds.'

Harry was amused. 'You should patent this, you know. When we've finished, you should turn it into a game. Call it "Property Scam". It could make you a fortune.'

'But I'll already have a fortune. So will you.'

'Attractive, isn't she!' Harry was watching Jenny again.

Richard began to put away the board.

'Very attractive, I'd say.'

Richard changed the subject. 'Do you ever get nervous before a job?'

Harry left the window. 'That's half the fun of it.'

(iv)

Jenny had been aware of Harry's eyes on her as she'd raked over the soil. She'd felt self-conscious. Yet, despite herself, flattered, too.

24.

(i)

'It's grown quickly,' the Lithuanian hair stylist commented, her expression a lilt of pleasantry.

From the seat next to him Harry was aware of a spasm of irritation.

'Do me a favour. Just cut it, will you!' Mark Jerricoe snapped, his eyes never leaving his own reflection.

The stylist hesitated for a moment at the rebuff. Then, concentrating on her comb and scissors, she continued her work.

Harry watched her through the mirror. Such a beautiful girl! How could any man be rude to someone who looked like that! Who could tell what delights might follow from a little friendliness?

So far things were going well. He'd waited next door in Gail's until the black BMW had arrived, smack on 11.30, just as Richard, who'd staked out the hairdressers twice before, had predicted. Then he'd watched as Jerricoe had entered the small salon.

Five minutes later he'd followed him in. Once again, he was wearing his decent suit. The tricky bit had come next when he'd been shown to a seat by the window. But a complaint about an imaginary draft had soon fixed it.

'Is there nothing closer to the back?' He'd said to the junior who'd washed his hair. 'What about over there?' And he'd gestured vaguely in the direction of the blond on grey streaks of Jerricoe.

'Of course,' the junior had replied, and, leading him to the seat next to Jerricoe, had tucked a gown around his neck and gone to fetch him a lemon tea. Jerricoe hadn't even looked up.

Reaching for a copy of *Country Life* on the shelf in front of him, Harry began to casually flip through its pages. At that moment his mobile phone rang. With a sigh of mild embarrassment, he pulled it out from under his gown.

'Hello! Ah, yes! How are you? Good to hear from you, again. But…look, I can't talk now…I'll call you back…'

About to hang up, he suddenly stopped and listened. 'Really? What period are we talking here? And acreage? And value?' He listened again. 'Well now…' And then: 'Hello? Hello?'

(ii)

Mark Jerricoe glared into the mirror. It had been bad enough that his regular stylist was off on her honeymoon and he'd been fobbed off with this Baltic doll, but now the oaf who was sitting next to him was carrying on his business as if he was in his office. They should ban mobile phones in public places, he thought. In future he'd get the stylist to come to him at Jerricoe House. He should have done it before, but he'd wanted to keep his highlights secret from the staff. But who gave a monkey's what they thought? The mobile phone alongside him rang again. Jesus!

'Ah. You're back! Yes. I know, bloody hills! Well, that's the Cotswolds.'

The buffoon was chuntering into his phone again. Jerricoe closed his eyes.

'Anyway, you were saying… How many acres? And cottages? How old? My word! That's something. 'A former monastery! Perhaps it could be converted into a mosque for the right client. Ha Ha! Er, look…who else knows about this?'

The fellow's voice had suddenly dropped. Standing behind Jerricoe, the beautiful Lithuanian stylist clipped minutely away.

'Because, you know, if my bosses… Well, you know… Curtains!' Then he fell silent, as he listened. 'You're certain? Very good. Look….' His voice went even quieter.

Jerricoe opened his eyes. The guy had now turned completely away, his voice hushed to virtual inaudibility.

'Look, I really can't speak now. I'll call you later. But, yes, I'm definitely interested. And thank you very much. Bye.'

From the next chair, Jerricoe watched him through the mirror.

(iii)

Richard ended the call and slipped his phone into the door compartment of the Volvo. His mouth was dry. It had been the first time in his life he'd pretended to be something he wasn't.

(iv)

Harry swung around in his chair. 'Sorry,' he smiled an apology to Jerricoe. 'I should have turned it off. But...some work just can't be done in the office....'

Jerricoe made no response.

'I'm Raphael. And how are you today?' A muscular ponytailed stylist approached Harry.

'Busy, busy...you know how it is,' Harry beamed, glancing towards Jerricoe.

But he'd now closed his eyes again as his hair was blow dried. Raphael ran a comb through Harry's wet hair. 'How would you like it?'

'Oh, long, long.' Inwardly Harry was cursing. Jerricoe hadn't bitten. For a moment he thought of calling Richard back, then rejected the idea. That would have been pushing it too far.

Becoming impatient to be off, Jerricoe got up to leave.

'Blast!' Harry swore to himself. The scheme had stumbled at the first fence. He should have known Jerricoe wouldn't have been so easy. There would have to be another way.

Then, suddenly, Jerricoe turned back to him: 'If you want to talk to me, why don't you just make an appointment like everybody else?'

Harry jumped. 'I'm sorry?'

Jerricoe's eyes stared down at Harry. 'Have you got a card?'

Indicating that Raphael should wait a moment, Harry reached under his gown. 'Yes, of course. But perhaps it would be better if you called me on my mobile. The number's on here, too.'

Jerricoe took the card. 'Harry Culshaw, valuer and negotiator, Heyes and Heys,' he read, his voice laced with mockery. 'I might be in touch.' And turning, he walked swiftly from the salon.

25

(i)

There was nothing to do now but wait. So, Jenny went to school, Richard got on with the doll's house, and Harry did whatever Harry did when he wasn't with them, about which he was never forthcoming.

To say that she was distracted wouldn't have been true. No teacher can ever be distracted, and she spent a lot of happy time reading an abridged junior edition of *The Wind In The Willows* to her class. The children loved hearing how Mole invited Ratty and Badger to Mole End. They understood the importance of a place of their own.

With no immediate threat from Jerricoe Properties, she found herself sifting through old DVDs for conmen movies on a market stall one day. And, on another, watching them with Richard. *The Sting* and *The Spanish Prisoner* were the favourites.

'Of course, it's only a movie,' she mused after they'd both savoured the twist at the end of *The Sting*. 'What we don't know is whether normal, honest straight people like us can actually pull off a con.'

'You're beginning to have doubts?' Richard asked.

'No more than I ever had,' she smiled. 'And it's the doubts that will stop us making a mistake. Right?'

The next Saturday morning she was pushing her bicycle out of the school gates, after she'd been giving Maxwell and a couple of other children an extra reading lesson, when she found Richard's car waiting. He and Harry were standing by it.

'He, what about this!' she exclaimed laughing. 'A nice sunny afternoon and a couple of swindlers are meeting me out of school. My mother warned me about days like this.'

Taking her bicycle, Harry opened the back of the estate car and lifted it inside. 'Richard thought a ride in the country might do us good,' he said.

'So where are we going?' Jenny asked Richard as they all got into the car.

'The Cotswolds.'

'Ah-ha!' And she settled back in her seat.

For weeks, Richard had been urging Harry to give them hints on the practicalities of conning, but, so far, few clues had been proffered. 'It's as though he wants to preserve the mysteries of his profession, the way magicians do,' he'd told Jenny. 'But we need to know what he knows.'

'Let me try,' she'd replied.

Now, as the Volvo sped down the motorway, the teacher, in the passenger seat, became an eager student. 'What I don't get,' she asked Harry who was sitting in the back, 'is how you ever get a con started.'

'Well, it's smoke and mirrors, really,' Harry explained. 'In that the person you're conning doesn't have to see that much. A glimpse can often convince.'

'You mean, he'll think he's seen more than he has?'

'Exactly.'

'But how far will a glimpse take us before difficult questions arise?'

Harry smiled at her. 'That's when it gets exciting.'

(ii)

Leaving the motorway behind, they were soon driving through the narrow Cotswold lanes. Then, dropping through a gap in the small, close hills, they rounded a corner and slowed down.

'Wow!' Jenny gasped as the main gates of Creswell Manor came into view,

'Wow indeed,' agreed Harry,

'This is the place you're going to sell to Jerricoe,' Richard said as the car drew up and they gazed down the long private avenue of leafless oak trees to the house. Then, pulling a book from the door compartment he turned and pushed it into his Harry's hand. 'Better read about the place. Page 72.'

Harry looked at the book's title: '*Historic Houses of the Cotswolds,*' he read. 'Splendid! Thank you, Richard. An early birthday present.' Then, casually passing the book to Jenny, he climbed out of the car and made his way up to the gates of the estate.

Richard and Jenny, who was now opening the book, followed.

'"*Creswell Manor…sixteenth century…lived in by generations of Dukes and Duchesses of Creswell*"', Jenny read as she walked.

'Lucky them,' Harry murmured, staring at a couple of fallow deer eyeing them from an enclosure behind the mansion's gates. 'You know, if I'd been born in a place like this, I wouldn't have had to con people for a living.'

She looked at him coyly. 'Are you sure?'

Digging her playfully in the ribs with his elbow, Harry took the book back.

Richard returned to the car. Jenny's antipathy towards Harry was thawing. It was understandable. Harry was an amusing, good looking man. But he'd preferred it when she'd hated him.

26.

(i)

The call from Jerricoe came via Hunt three days later. Harry was watching afternoon television, learning how to make the perfect lemon soufflé. Had he had the chance, he was sure he would have made an excellent TV chef. He turned the television's volume off before answering.

'Mr Culshaw? Mr Jerricoe would like a meeting.'

'Ah…' A slightly vague hesitation, as though trying to recall the name. 'Er, ah yes. Very good…'

'We'll pick you up outside your office. Nine o'clock tonight.' Click.

Still holding his phone, Harry watched the silent television as a perfect soufflé rose in the bowl. He didn't like the idea of being picked up. Things happened to people when they were taken for a drive, especially when people weren't what they claimed to be.

The BMW was late. Sheltering from the rain in the porch outside the Heyes and Heys office, hoping he looked as though he'd only just finished work, Harry had been about to give up and go home when the black car splashed to a halt in a kerbside puddle in front of him. A ripple of water spread across the pavement. A rear door of the car opened.

With a black leather attaché case under his arm, Harry stepped forward and looked inside. A very large dog lay dribbling in the middle of the back seat, its jaw hanging open. Beyond it sat Jerricoe. Hunt was in the front with a shaven-headed young driver. 'Good to see you again, Mr Jerricoe,' Harry breezed.

Jerricoe didn't answer but moved his head in a silent indication that Harry should join him.

Slipping into the car, Harry sat down next to the dog. It didn't move.

'Filthy night, eh!' Harry tried again as the car slid forward.

There was no reply: the silence menaced.

At least Jerricoe picked me up himself, Harry was thinking. His dirty work was always supposed to be contracted out. He certainly hoped so.

They'd been driving for a full five minutes before Jerricoe spoke. 'What have you got for me?' he said at last.

Opening his attaché case, Harry passed over a large brown envelop and watched as Jerricoe withdrew a ten-by-eight inch colour photograph that Richard had taken. 'Creswell Manor,' he explained.

Jerricoe looked at the photograph without expression. 'And?'

Harry raised an eyebrow. 'You didn't see it in *The Times*? The old lady who owned it died. Very sad.'

'I'm breaking my heart.'

'The point is there's no heir. She was the last of the line.'

'Go on.'

'The house has been in trust for generations. The trustees now want a quick sale.' Harry paused. 'Well, shall we say, one of them does.'

'What's his hurry?'

'I imagine he's rather hoping there might be something in it for him. He's seen the will, you see, and he's not in it, which comes as something of a disappointment as he's been running the place for years.'

'And the other trustees?'

'There are two of them. One is abroad. The Congo. Doing God's work. A very unworldly sort, by all accounts. He doesn't ask questions. The other one's out to lunch most of the time. He's getting on a bit. Neither of them has the foggiest idea about today's property prices. Not interested. Which means…'

'They can be led by someone who does.' Jerricoe's eyes hadn't left Harry's since their conversation had started.

'Well…' Harry began with a little smile.

Jerricoe cut him off. 'What's do you think it's worth?'

'A fair price, in this market…fifteen million.'

Jerricoe sniffed. 'What'll he take, this trustee?'

'Ten.'

Jerricoe stared out of the car window.

They'd now left fashionable London and were heading towards the back streets of Tower Hamlets. Never once had Jerricoe suggested where they might be going. 'So, why have I got so lucky?' he now asked.

'If I could raise the ten million myself, you wouldn't have done.'

Jerricoe considered that for a moment. And then: 'How did you come across this place?'

'The trustee, the chap I've been dealing with...I helped him out over the sale of a cottage just off the estate a few years ago. Found him some buyers. Young couple. City people. Very grateful. Anyway, when it came to the main house, he thought he might do better if he avoided a public sale.'

'And what's in it for you?'

'A finder's fee. Three hundred and fifty thousand. Two hundred for the trustee.'

Jerricoe smiled. 'Don't you think you're being a little bit greedy?'

'I'm risking my career. The place is a steal at ten million.' He nodded towards the photograph which Jerricoe was still holding.

Jerricoe smirked. 'As the man said, "all property is theft"'.

'Well, yes...in a manner of speaking.'

Jerricoe turned away. The dog next to him shifted its position, closer to Harry.

The BMW was now rolling almost silently along a dark street. On one side was what appeared to be a disused warehouse; on the other, an area of waste ground, presumably where other warehouses had been pulled down to provide space for more development. Bumping on to the pavement, the car splashed its way into the mud and blackness of the wasteland.

'Stop here, Angel,' Hunt instructed.

Harry looked out at the rain. This was as desolate a spot as you were likely to find in London. Had Richard got this badly wrong? Did Jerricoe sometimes like to do his own dirty work? 'We're visiting someone?' he asked airily, aware that his voice had risen an anxious half tone.

Nobody answered. He waited.

Then: 'You're a conman, aren't you?' Jerricoe's voice was flat.

Harry felt his belt tighten. Jerricoe had realised.

In the front seat Hunt turned and, without expression, examined him.

Jerricoe's eyes never left Harry's. 'Isn't that right?'

Harry's mouth was dry. He swallowed. 'I'm an estate agent, if that's what you mean.'

Jerricoe's expression didn't change. 'You're conning this estate manager. Does he know how much you want for yourself?'

Harry could almost hear his own sigh of relief. Jerricoe had only half seen through the set-up.

'Well...' he shrugged, hoping he was displaying more nonchalance than he was feeling. 'One has one's modus operandi.'

Jerricoe didn't answer.

'It's time,' said Hunt.

Jerricoe checked his watch. Then, abruptly turning away from Harry, he peered into the darkness at the silhouette of a couple of semi-derelict houses in the middle distance.

For two or three minutes nothing happened, other than the rattle of rain on the roof of the car and the panting of the dog.

Then a flame exploded in a ground floor window of one of the houses.

'Jesus!' Harry exclaimed.

No-one else spoke.

Quickly the flames soared upwards. A light came on in an upper window. Screams and shouts could be heard. The fire was spreading.

'Shouldn't we call...?' Harry began.

'Bloody squatters!' Jerricoe spat, as the dog, excited by the fire, got to its feet and began whining. 'They were told not to mess with us. They wouldn't listen. They will now!'

In the glow from the fire, Harry could see figures running out of the house.

'All right, Angel. Let's go.' Jerricoe tapped his driver on the shoulder.

The BMW bounced wildly as it turned across the wasteland and bounced on to the road.

Resting his hand on the dog to calm it, Jerricoe settled back in his seat and stared at Harry. 'Look and learn!'

This time it was Harry's turn not to answer.

27.

Jenny considered Richard. She was sitting in his studio. In her lap was a pile of small children's paintings about the seasons. She should have been writing some encouraging words on each of them, but tonight she couldn't concentrate. Waiting for Harry to call, they were both edgy, with Richard even quieter than usual as he jotted notes in his artists' sketchbook.

Was this how he'd been when he'd been married, she wondered. Lost in a world of his own? Or had this wall around him been built afterwards? He was a strange housemate. While both helpful and generous, sometimes almost cozy, there was an innate privacy about him. He'd still never talked to her about his divorce, or about what had gone wrong with his marriage, never mentioning the wife he'd once had. Even tonight he'd dodged the subject when she'd told him she thought she'd seen an old boyfriend at a bus stop.

'The thing was,' she'd said as she'd watched Richard boil some pasta in his tiny kitchen, 'when I first spotted him, I felt a thrill like the way I used to feel when we first got together. He was an actor, too. But then, almost immediately, I was hoping that he wouldn't see me cycling past, because I wouldn't have known what to say if he called after me and I would have had to stop and talk to him. And then, when I realised it wasn't him after all, and he was probably still in Wakefield, I was relieved, but, at the same time, disappointed, although I really didn't want to see him again. It's stupid but there's still this residue lurking, mainly about my old life, I suppose. Although I've never wanted it back.'

At that moment Richard got up from his notebook to drain the pasta through a colander. The space between them filled with steam.

'Do you ever get those contradictory thoughts?' she asked. 'About you, and…I mean, about when you were married?'

'Not really,' he'd said quietly, and looked at his watch. 'Jerricoe should be picking Harry up about now. Fingers crossed.' And the subject was closed.

Putting the paintings to one side, Jenny leant over the notes Richard had been making in his artists' sketchbook. 'Can I see?' she asked.

'There's not much more to see yet,' he said, showing her his plans. 'We've only really got the bones of the scam so far. It'll be step by step from now on.'

'For instance?' she pursued.

'Well, if, and when, we get Jerricoe to view Creswell Manor. How do we get the staff there out of house while he's looking round it?'

She nodded. 'Let me think about it.'

It was after eleven when Richard's mobile rang. It was Harry, 'Just so that you know,' he began, 'if we have any sense, we'll get out now.'

'We've got nothing but sense. Which is why we're going to win,' Richard countered, putting the phone on speaker so that Jenny could listen to the conversation.

'The guy's a psychopath. If he suspects anything he'll probably have us all chopped up.'

Richard smiled. 'But he's on the hook. Right?'

'Just about.'

'You're sure?'

'Richard, if I say he's virtually there, he's virtually there.'

'Fair enough.' He changed the subject. 'Jenny and I have been wondering how you're getting on with a lawyer and bit part players?'

'The lawyer's coming along. He's a good man.'

'And the bit parts?'

'Well…there's still a little way to go with them.' There was a flicker of uncertainty in Harry's voice.

Richard sensed it and glanced at Jenny. 'But you *will* get them?'

'Of course. It's just that one or two are on other jobs.'

'Can't they get out of them? Just for one day?' chipped in Jenny.

'Hard to say. I like one guy very much… But he's doing jury service. Some long-running fraud case.'

Richard winced. The scam he was planning needed a team.

'Harry…!'

'Don't worry. I'll have a team there on the day. How's the lovely Jenny, by the way. Any chance of saying close-up "hello"?'

Richard held out the phone to Jenny.

She took it, smiling.

Harry could now always make her smile.

28.

Craig Hunt wasn't happy. He and Jerricoe knew London. They knew about London prices, London rents, and the difference in value between adjacent London postcodes; and how to play local building regulations and local council members to their advantage. In London they knew what they were doing. But now Jerricoe was mooning over a photo of some old ruin of a place in the middle of nowhere, because some twat of an estate agent reckoned he could get him a deal on the sly.

Hunt had hated Harry Culshaw on sight. The casual superiority of all those public school bastards who worked for firms like Heyes and Heys got right up his nose. They despised people like him. He could tell that by the way they looked at him when he sometimes collided with them on what they thought was their patch. Everything about them said they thought he had no right to be in the smart end of town.

If Jerricoe was aware of how they viewed his lawyer, he obviously didn't care. He might talk tough with them, but he liked their style and suits. He felt comfortable with people with toff accents. Of course, he did. That was how he saw himself. He liked a bit of posh tottie to swank around with now and again, too, though the birds he pulled and took back to Notting Hill Gate never lasted long.

Being Jerricoe, he hadn't, of course, said anything much about the country pile he'd been pitched. But anyone could see he was distracted by the idea. Taking the fop with the old-fashioned suit along as a witness to the bonfire party in Bermondsey had been as good as an admission. It might have looked like just a little squirt of Jerricoe testosterone, a guy showing off his muscle, but it was more than that. It was a message to let the guy know that, provided he understood the rules, Jerricoe might be interested. Hence the grandstand seat.

On another day, Hunt might have tried some gentle persuasion and reminded his boss where his real business expertise lay. But Rakesh Choudhrai had been bollocked again that morning about some late rents, and Whiley, the accountant, had caught it in the neck over an income tax refund he'd failed to deliver. So, maybe, Hunt decided, he'd leave out the friendly advice for the time being. There were, at least, another dozen problems to be sorted, and he began to mentally scroll down the portfolio of Jerricoe Properties.

He stopped at the River House. No change there. He had to hand it to those two remaining tenants: they were stubborn bastards. All the same.

He picked up his phone.

29.

(i)

Jenny discovered the scaffolding when she got home from school. She gasped when she saw it. It wasn't just that the entire River House had been clad in interlocking steel poles. Every door and window had been boarded up, too. There was no way in.

Locking her bicycle as usual in the tumbledown outhouse around the back of the house, where trampling feet and scaffolding poles had now wrecked her newly planted little garden, she messaged Richard. She felt surprisingly calm. She would replant the garden. Whatever Jerricoe did, their revenge would be sweeter.

She was sitting on the front garden wall sketching the nearby new apartment blocks Richard got back. He'd been doing some temporary repairs to a clock face at Greenwich Observatory that had cracked in the winter frost.

'No need for us to worry about burglars anymore,' she joked as he saw the scaffolding. 'They'll never get in now.'

Richard didn't answer. Going up the front path, he examined the boarding covering the front door. Then, returning to his car, he came back with a wheel jack and tyre jemmy. Delicately, he pushed the jemmy into a crack between the boards covering the front door. Then, lifting the wheel jack, he slammed it hard against the jemmy. Nothing happened. He hit it again. Still nothing. And again. This time the crack widened a fraction. Again, he hit the jemmy. And again.

Jenny watched his determination in admiration. Then she went to help.

Twenty minutes later they had pulled enough board away from the door to get inside. Within a further hour the windows in their two flats had been uncovered, not completely, but enough to let in the daylight.

'Whatever they do, we'll undo it. Whatever move they make, we'll counter it,' Richard grinned as together they looked out from his studio at the mist on the river.

Just then, his phone rang. It was Harry. 'What is it? Good news?' he asked.

(ii)

'Well...sort of good news. I've just had a call from Hunt. Jerricoe's biting. He wants to see Creswell Manor.' Harry was smiling into the phone. He always felt more confident when he smiled.

'That *is* good news. When?'

Harry cleared his voice. He was standing in his overcoat because it was so cold in his flat. 'Er...very soon. But...I'm afraid, we might have a problem with the bit part players...'

There was a silence from the other end of the phone. Then: 'How many have you managed to find?'

'Well, actually... Bad time. Everyone's away. I did mention it.'

'How many?'

'None.'

'None?' Richard repeated flatly. 'Not one?' His voice neither rose nor fell.

'Terribly sorry.'

'You mean, you don't know *anyone*...?'

'We've already got Inky. Our forger. He's very keen. And I've got an excellent lawyer on stand-by.'

'That isn't the point, Harry. We need the walk-on players, and a good decoy to even start the con. You told me yourself. The plan won't work without them.'

Harry didn't answer.

'Right. We'll speak later,' said Richard, and abruptly ended the conversation.

Harry clicked off his phone. He'd never attempted anything on this scale before. No-one, apart from a very dubious Inky, had thought they could pull it off. So much for the romantic, movie image of a fraternity among conmen. The reality was that the guys he knew weren't Paul Newman and Robert Redford, they were just cheap little crooks, looking for the easy hit. Like him.

He sat down on the edge of his bed and considered his dreary room. Nothing here was his, apart from a few clothes. Not much to show for a career. What had Richard called him? 'Small time.'

(iii)

Richard stared at his Figure of Eight board. Just as at the carol singing, he'd fallen for the halo of confidence that Harry projected.

Jenny was looking anxious. 'We're not giving up, Richard,' she said. 'No way.'

'When we started, Harry said that my trouble was that it was personal with me. That you and I were amateurs.'

Jenny nodded forcefully. 'He's right. It *is* real with us. That's our advantage.'

30.

(i)

A Boeing 747 was roaring overhead coming into land as Jenny pressed one of a cluster of Entryphone bells on a tower block half a mile east of Heathrow Airport.

'Hello?' asked a woman's voice.

'Er...is that Sarojini...Sarojini Ghelani,' Jenny shouted into the Entryphone above the sound of the plane. 'Is that you?'

'Jenny!' There was a squeal of delight. 'Stay there. I'm coming down.'

Jenny had chosen the moment carefully. Sanjeev's cousin and his new wife would both be working night shifts at the airport, Sanjeev would be out driving his Uber and the boys would be doing their homework. She hadn't lived below the Ghelanis without getting some idea of the real balance of power among them. Sarojini had been the one to approach.

Two minutes later Sarojini appeared at the door. 'Tell me, what is it?'

Jenny smiled as they hugged. 'You remember how when you were leaving the River House, you gave Richard and me a ganesh each for good luck?'

'Oh, yes.'

'Well, I think the ganeshes may need a little help.'

(ii)

He thought at first that he must have the wrong address as, stopping his car, Richard peered along the graffiti smeared terrace of Edwardian villas. Along the pavement empty bottles and used tea bags were spreading from a split plastic bag. It was a rough area.

This would once have been a pleasant part of town, he reflected, as he found a place to park the Volvo. But transport planners had decided to build an elevated motorway over the top of it and local pride had fallen. Now the thudding hammer of traffic from above provided a continuous, rhythmic accompaniment as he reached the last house on the strip. Beyond it, the motorway dropped down to ground level, blowing fumes back over those who lived here.

The front garden of the house was short, with scarcely enough space for the six bins congregated there, although he noticed that someone had recently planted a couple of rose bushes, with their labels still attached. To the side of the front door there were, as on every other house on the street, a collection of different bells, some labelled, some hanging off. Peering at the names, he rang one and waited.

No answer.

He rang again.

At last, a light came on in the hall. The door opened. A woman's face peered nervously round it. 'Yes?'

Richard smiled. 'Mrs Morrison, do you remember how you once said you could kill Mark Jerricoe. Well, what would you say to helping us do the next best thing…?'

31.

(i)

The courtyard door to Creswell Manor swung open. 'Richard! We didn't know you were coming today!' Maurice, the estate manager exclaimed in surprise. He was wearing a black overcoat.

'You didn't? Oh, God! I'm sorry. You didn't get my email? I've brought the doll's house back.' And Richard gestured towards his car. 'It's all finished.'

'Ah, splendid!' Maurice looked quickly at his watch. 'But actually, you nearly missed us. We're just on our way out.'

'Oh dear! Look, I'll just bring the doll's house inside, if that's all right. It's still in parts. It was a more delicate piece than I realised, and I didn't want to risk damaging it on the way back here.' Already Richard was opening the rear door of the Volvo.

'Ah, right! I'll give you a hand. But…we'll have to be quick. We're all off to church.'

'Church…?' Richard began, then watched anxiously as he passed Maurice the rear section of the doll's house. 'Er…if you could just hold it at the corner by the chimney. That's it.' Then, picking up a wing of the house, he followed Maurice inside.

A couple of minutes later the half dozen pieces of the doll's house were spread across the floor of the library.

'I'm sorry,' Richard turned to Maurice as the older man looked again at his watch. 'Did you say you were going to church? On a Wednesday?'

'Yes, and I'm afraid I really must join the others.' As he spoke, Maurice glanced through the window to where several members of the Creswell Manor staff were assembling in their best suits and coats. 'It's the old lady, you see. A distant relative of hers turned up the other day. From Australia, would you believe!' His face dimpled at the thought that anyone related to the former mistress of Creswell Manor should live in such a place.

'*Australia!*' Obediently Richard's eyebrows arched.

'Exactly. The poor lady missed the funeral...' Maurice dropped his voice. 'Not invited, to be honest. None of us even knew she existed. It just shows. Every family has its little secrets.' He brightened. 'So, anyway, she's arranged a special service for her and the staff.'

'That's very nice. And you're all going?'

'She insisted. All of us.'

'I see! In that case I'd better come back some other time to put the doll's house back together... I'm not quite sure when, though...'

Maurice smiled. 'Don't be silly. You can do it while we're at church. If you don't mind being alone in the house. There are no ghosts. I promise you. We had the place exorcised long ago.'

Richard laughed at Maurice's little joke. 'Well, if you're sure you don't mind?'

'Of course not, dear boy! Now, we must be off. You know where the kitchens are... if you feel like a cup of tea.'

'Thank you. Er...the alarms won't go off, will they, if I...?'

'No, no. When someone's in the house we always leave them off.'

'I see.'

'Anyway, the service is in the village, so we should be back in an hour or so. See you later.' And with that Maurice hurried off to join the rest of the staff.

Richard waited until he heard the staff's two cars make their way out of the courtyard and away down the drive. Then, turning to the doll's house, he quickly assembled the pieces. It wasn't difficult. The tricky part had been making it look as though it might be.

(ii)

Sitting in a Ford Focus GT parked in the shade of the cedars, Harry watched as the cars carrying the Creswell Manor staff left the open gates of the estate and turned towards the village of Creswell.

'Bingo!' he breathed.

At his side sat Mr Morrison. The two Ghelanis and Mrs Morrison were squeezed together in the back. None of them had spoken more than a word or two all the way there.

Starting the car, Harry drove swiftly through the gates and down the drive. A Ford Focus GT seemed the right sort of car for someone dodgy in property, Richard had suggested when they'd hired it. That may be so, Harry had thought, but he wished it was his. He looked in the rear-view mirror at his passengers. 'Don't forget, you've all worked here for years. You're comfortable in a grand house.'

Again, nobody spoke.

Harry frowned and considered his passengers. Ted Morrison, who, dressed in an old tweed suit, thick check shirt and woollen tie, was gazing at Creswell Manor. He looked terrified. Sanjeev was in awe.

'At least, they're all Jerricoe's victims and have something to gain if this comes off,' Richard had explained when, in the absence of any real con artists, he'd recruited them.

It was true, but it was no less worrying. They were amateurs. One wrong word and the scam would be void. And he would be running for his life.

(iii)

Just the thought of the country made Craig Hunt itch. It meant flies, mud, cold and smells. The journey from London had seemed interminable, especially once they'd got off the motorway, nothing but up and down and round again, through higgledy-piggledy back lanes, and Angel driving more carefully than Hunt had ever seen him. It was understandable. The last thing Angel wanted was to get sixty thousand pounds worth of BMW bent on some farmyard tractor. He was an Islington boy. He didn't like the country either.

'Here it is.' Jerricoe announced, suddenly leaning forward in his seat as they approached, and then passed through the large open iron gates.

Hunt morbidly took in the Tudor facia and honey-coloured wings of the house at the end of the drive. Whatever it was about history, he just didn't get it. They could bulldoze all this rubble for all he cared. History was damp and dirty and, like the country, bloody snobbish.

For a second, he glanced out at the gardens as they rolled down the drive. Some distance away a silly sod of a gardener in a woolly hat was turned away from them, breaking his back digging muck with a fork on what looked like a dunghill. Jesus, what a life!

Then, even before Angel could bring the car to a halt, the biggest front door in Oxfordshire opened and the tosser from Heyes and Heys was marching across the forecourt as if he owned the place. What was it about estate agents that made them so bloody grand? They were only jumped-up market traders.

'Mr Jerricoe, how are you! Welcome to Creswell Manor. Found it all right, I see.'

Of course, he'd found it. He was here, wasn't he? The dope had his hand out to be shaken. Jerricoe ignored it. That was better, Hunt smirked. He liked it when Jerricoe did that. It put people off balance.

Not that it seemed to dent this idiot's confidence. 'Come and take a look around,' the estate agent schmoozed as he led them into the house.

(iv)

From the compost heap at the end of the rose garden, Richard watched anxiously as the oak doors of Creswell Manor closed.

Thank God for gutsy women, he was thinking. Neither Mr Morrison nor Sanjeev Ghelani had immediately been keen on helping, and it had been left to their wives to persuade them. Both women were homemakers who had been forced from their homes. That made them vengeful. Even so, neither they, nor their husbands, had asked too many questions, presumably thinking that the less they knew the less culpable they'd be if something went wrong.

(v)

Harry had noticed Jerricoe's refusal to shake hands. It amused him. The fellow was putting on an act, just as he was. Everything about Jerricoe was fake and exaggerated, from the built-up shoes to make him look taller, to the dyed blond hair and the sparkle on his wrist, and the suit that was so crisp he could have been wearing it for the first time. Perhaps he was. New money, Harry reflected, could be so unattractive. And he made a mental note to remember that when his big pay day came.

Leading the way across the bare flagstones towards the estate manager's office, which, Richard had told him, was down a corridor to the right of the front porch, he tapped gently on the door. It swung slightly ajar at his touch. 'Oh, Larry, I don't think you've met Mr Jerricoe, have you,' he said entering.

Sitting at the desk in the office, with the *Daily Telegraph* rugby page open in front of him, was Mr Morrison. A cup of coffee and a digestive biscuit were at his side. Behind him on a mantelpiece was a silver framed photograph of a young girl in jodhpurs and a riding hat, sitting on a white pony, the bridle of which was being held by a slightly younger Mr Morrison. Forger Inky had done a good job there.

Mr Morrison began to rise. 'Oh, yes, very pleased to meet you.'

Jerricoe just looked at him, then immediately glanced around the small office, quickly taking in as much as he wanted.

'And his colleague, Mr Hunt.' Harry indicated the glowering lawyer.

Hunt nodded, studying Morrison closely.

Mr Morrison sat down again, trying to avoid more eye contact than was necessary. His hand, Harry noticed, was trembling. Jerricoe had seen it, too.

He quickly stepped forward. 'Larry's the estate manager…the trustee, I mentioned…' he said, drawing attention back to himself. 'I thought I'd show Mr Jerricoe the house, if that's all right, Larry.'

'Of course.' The older man was barely audible.

Outside in the corridor Harry dropped his voice. 'Sadly, old Larry can overdo it a bit sometimes on the malt. It gives him...you know...a touch of the...' And he shook his hand slightly.

'Silly old sod,' Jerricoe smirked.

Affecting not to have heard, Harry strode on into the main hall. 'Well, as I'm sure you can see, this is the oldest wing. Legend says the beams came from Spanish ships sunk in the Armada, so that dates it as late sixteenth century. It had been a monastery before, but there isn't much of that left now, apart from the remains of a chapel in the garden, most of the stone being re-used after the Dissolution to build the house as it is now.'

Ignoring him, Jerricoe was walking the length of the hall, looking up at the murky portraits of long dead members of the Creswell lineage on the walls.

Hunt watched him, his lip curling in disdain.

He's the problem, Harry thought, the bloody lawyer. We'll have to watch him. Then, smiling, he spun around, and held out his arms. 'You know, I always think this would make a splendid banqueting hall for pals in the City. That would put them in their place, show them where wealth really lies...in land and property as it always has done. And, of course, the estate is absolutely marvellous for weekend house parties.' And he clapped the rocking horse on its newly restored rump.

From Jerricoe there was no response.

Serious again, Harry pointed to a high, semi-circular window. 'Oh, yes, and note the Diocletian window...a late classical addition, obviously.' And, with that, he led them from the room. Swotting up on Cotswold country houses had come in handy. But what did it take to make these guys lighten up?

They were now walking past the doll's house in the library. At the end of the room Sanjeev Ghelani, in a black suit, was standing dusting on top of some trestle steps.

'Good morning. Hard at it, I see. Excellent!' Harry beamed.

Sanjeev nodded as they passed.

Jerricoe and Hunt ignored him.

'While along here we have...' And Harry opened a door on to a wide, flag-stoned kitchen, with saucepans and tureens suspended above a vast Aga. Standing at a scrub-topped table, polishing the silver, wearing a black dress and white blouse, was Angela Morrison. With her bonnet of white hair, she looked absolutely the part.

'Ah, good morning. Don't let us interrupt you.'

Mrs Morrison smiled back her greeting.

'And, as you can see, a kitchen big enough to feed half the county... though possibly in need of a little updating, I imagine. The aristocracy do love their traditions, don't they!'

There was an awkward silence.

Mrs Morrison filled it. 'I wonder, would any of you gentlemen like a cup of tea?'

Harry felt a shiver of fear. That hadn't been in the script. She was improvising. There was no time for tea. The real staff would be back in an hour. 'Thank you, but I'm afraid, we must get on,' he said. And, quickly, he marched out of the kitchen. 'Salt of the earth,' he said as they reached the main staircase. 'She's been here for donkey's years, as have nearly all the staff.'

Then, realising that this might conceivably present a difficulty for any purchaser, he hurriedly added. 'Luckily, they're all on short term contracts. So, there won't be any problem there.'

Being an estate agent was getting to be fun, he thought. He would have been brilliant at it.

(vi)

The singing of *Jerusalem* had finished. Now the Creswell Manor staff congregated in the first few rows of the little Norman church, were waiting expectantly.

Slipping from her place in the front pew, Jenny slowly climbed the stone steps into the pulpit. Clearing her throat, she looked around. 'Thank you all very much for coming,' she said. Then realising that her voice wasn't carrying enough, she repeated herself. She tried to wet her lips with the tip of her tongue, then continued. 'My name is Wendy Hornton. But on one side of my family most of my relatives, by blood, anyway, had a name which I think is more familiar to you: Creswell.'

She stopped at the congregation's evident astonishment. Her cheeks were a healthy, outdoor pink from a sunbed in Wandsworth Bridge Road, her hair was in braids, and her accent was Australian, something she'd developed when, as a schoolgirl, she and her whole class had watched *Neighbours*.

If there were any real Australians in the church she might be spotted as a fraud, but, thankfully, all she saw was a puzzled, trusting mist in the expressions of these English country people. As Harry always said: 'People believe what you tell them. If you have a plausible story, why wouldn't they believe you?'

She looked down at the tiny congregation. Apart from Maurice, they were mainly men from the estate and capable looking local women. Jenny's job was to keep them interested in her for at least an hour. She would have to take her time.

Leaning forward on the lectern she began to talk more quietly, confidentially.

'For too long,' she said, 'the circumstances of my birth, which, if you don't mind, I won't go into here, although I want you to know it really was a love match between my father and mother, no matter what people might have thought....'

Every eye was on her. She was beginning to enjoy herself. Once an actor..., she told herself as she continued.

'Yes, for too long those circumstances have kept me apart from the English side of my family. I can understand that. I must have been an embarrassment. The wrong side of the blanket still held a stigma forty odd years ago, even in Australia.'

She let them consider that for a few seconds. A very thin old lady just below the pulpit nodded sadly.

'But, though my very existence, was, I know, a closely kept secret, there was one person who never turned her back on me. And that was an old lady you all knew very well. To me she was just Great Aunt Alice.'

Looks were exchanged around the little church.

'She was probably in her sixties when I last saw her. I was a little girl in Sydney then, and I can remember the day so clearly. She wore a plain pink, belted, sleeveless dress and carried a little navy handbag like a man's wallet. It was a very hot day. Some things you never forget, and that picture of her is so clear in my mind. But what I'll also never forget, is that unlike all the rest of the family, all of whom are now sadly long gone, she didn't make me feel as though I'd been forgotten, that I didn't exist or didn't have the right to exist. She accepted me for what I was, not for the label some members of the family might have put on me.' She paused. 'And it's not a very nice label, I can tell you.'

At that Jenny found herself catching the eyes of a couple of the women staff sitting together, who, their heads up, were listening keenly, as people do when hearing some totally astonishing piece of gossip.

'You see, to me, Aunt Alice wasn't the daughter of a duke who could trace her ancestors back to one of the barons at the signing of Magna Carta. She was just an eccentric old lady, who told very glamorous, thrilling stories of garden parties at Buckingham Palace when she was a girl, and how she used to stay out half the night at dashing debutantes' balls.'

Maurice and the women in the church smiled. They'd heard those stories many times: as had Richard.

'As a little girl I loved all that. It seemed so fairytale romantic, so wonderful, and so different from my own life, growing up in a single storey rented house on Woomera Drive.' She hesitated, not quite suppressing a catch in her voice. How easy it was to become an actor again for an hour, and to experience the power of imagined emotions.

Her gaze found that of Maurice. The letter she'd sent to him introducing herself had brought an immediate response and kind invitation to visit Creswell Manor. That they were preying on his good nature had bothered both Richard and her. But, unable to come up with an alternative plan to get the staff out of the house while Jerricoe was shown around, the best they could do was hope that Maurice would never know.

She was continuing. 'Then, of course, there were those folded twenty-pound notes she'd sometimes send me in those far-off days…such a generous person,' she said.

There was an immediate ripple of surprise. A foot scraped on the stone floor of the church.

Instantly, Jenny realised her mistake. Distracted by a pang of guilt about Maurice, she'd been tempted to add to her story.

Below her the staff were casting little glances from one to the other. Alice Creswell had obviously been anything but generous.

'Or maybe it was just pound notes. Whatever, it seemed an absolute fortune to me then, and I would hurry to the bank to get them changed.' Quickly she reverted to the agreed text. 'But my best memory of Aunt Alice is of her running behind me when I was learning to ride my bike, and her shouting encouragement in that aristocratic English manner "For God's sake, Wendy, bloody pedal, you idiot".'

The faces of the staff relaxed into smiles. That was more like it. Richard must have got that side of the old lady dead right.

Jenny sneaked a look at the clock at the back of the church. She'd been going too quickly. She needed to kill a little more time, or the service would be over too soon.

'But now, before we go on to the next part of our service, perhaps you could all stand and join with me in singing our second hymn today, *I Vow to Thee My Country*, which was always one of Aunt Alice's favourites.'

And as Jenny raised a hand to the local organist in his little gallery, the music began to play.

(vii)

'Sorry! I hope we didn't get you out of bed! Ha ha!' Harry was facing Sarojini Ghelani across the four poster that she was in the process of making. Wearing a little maid's dress, she really looked rather saucy.

From the door Jerricoe was surveying the panelled bedroom.

'Oh, goodness me, no, sir! My bedroom isn't as grand as this,' Sarojini retorted almost cheekily and then giggled.

'Well, I'm sure it's very nice,' Harry smiled and holding out an arm indicated the bathroom to Jerricoe. 'And, of course, the *en suite* bathroom is fully equipped with all Tudor mod cons...ha-ha!' and he held the door open.

Jerricoe didn't bother to look. He and Hunt had spotted something outside.

Striding towards the window, Harry looked down the long avenue of trees. 'Ah, yes, wonderful view ...' He broke off.

A police car was making its way up the drive towards the house.

Jesus! Had he triggered an alarm that Richard hadn't known about?

Sarojini was staring at it, too.

'You've got visitors,' Jerricoe said.

'Ah, at last!' Harry smiled. 'My word, they've taken their time! Would you excuse me for just one moment!'

And, leaving Jerricoe and Hunt to Sarojini, he hurried from the room.

32.

(i)

Richard watched anxiously as the police car drew up outside the main doors of Creswell Manor. Across the drive, he could see Jerricoe's driver in the BMW, watching them from behind his sunglasses. Almost before the two policemen were out of their car, Harry had emerged from the house. He was, of course, smiling.

(ii)

'Good morning, officers! What can we do for you today?' Harry could feel his shirt sticking to his neck.

The elder of the police, a bald sergeant, spoke first. 'I wonder if we might have a few words.'

'Of course?' The sergeant was looking at him uncertainly. 'I don't think I've seen you here before, have I?'

'Ah…you've probably talked to my colleague, Maurice. I'm afraid he isn't here at the moment.'

'Maurice, yes…'

'He'll be back this afternoon. But is there anything I can help you with in the meantime? Or would you rather wait for him?' Over the bonnet of the police car, Harry could see Richard watching.

'Oh, no, sir. It's just about security,' the sergeant replied.

'Security?' Harry looked quizzical.

'Home security,' came in the younger officer.

'Yes, you'd be surprised if you knew just how vulnerable some of these more isolated properties are.' As he spoke the sergeant took a plastic folder from the younger man.

'Really!'

'Oh yes! In fact, the larger the estate the more likely it is to be broken into, and, of course, usually the more to be stolen. I'm sure the main house is well looked after, and I see here…' He'd already opened the folder. '…that the house alarm has a direct connection to Safe-and-Secure.com.'

'That's right, yes.'

'But some of the cottages on the estate might have been overlooked. So, we're calling around the district offering advice on windows, locks, doors...'

Harry cut him off with a smile. 'Splendid! One can never be too careful. And the Duchess was a stickler for security on *all* the buildings. You know how old people are. I must say, she liked to look after her employees, too. We'll miss her, though she ran a tight ship. Maurice will tell you that.'

'If only everyone was so careful, but...'

'If only.' Harry smiled.

(iii)

Jenny could sense the growing impatience of the congregation. She looked again at the clock. She'd stretched the service out for just about as long as she could. There was nothing left to say.

'So, now,' she smiled, 'before we go to our final hymn, I'd just like to say how grateful I am to you all for making this Australian girl so very welcome in Creswell...and to ask you all to join with me in a few minutes of quiet reflection...'

And she closed her eyes.

(iv)

'So, when you have a minute, sir, you might ask the rest of the staff to look over our twenty safety tips.' The sergeant passed Harry a Police Home Security brochure.

'Thank you so much. I will indeed.'

'You never know, but you might be leaving the place wide open and never realise it,' offered the younger officer.

'How very true. Thank you so much for calling.' And with that Harry walked the two policemen back to their car.

(v)

Richard exhaled in relief as the police car drove away down the drive, and he watched as Harry walked swiftly back into the house. The fellow was as slippery as an eel, but sometimes it was difficult not to admire his panache.

(vi)

'Of course, there's a lot of polishing to do, and so many nick-nacks to look after,' Sarojini was saying as Harry rejoined Jerricoe and Hunt in the bedroom. 'But every time I change the sheets on one of these four-posters, I can't help wondering about the famous people from history who might have slept in this very bed…and wonder, you know, who they might have been with.' She giggled naughtily.

Jerricoe and Hunt stared expressionlessly at her.

'Sorry about that,' Harry breezed. 'A slight contretemps with a badger on the road this morning. They're a protected species, so I thought I'd better report it. The police have gone off to locate the beast now. God, he was big blighter! Handsome though!'

'We usually just gas them down here,' Sarojini smiled. 'They spread TB.'

'Yes, well…' Harry turned to Jerricoe. 'Anyway, that's the house. How about a stroll around the gardens?' And he led the way back down the stairs.

But Jerricoe wasn't a gardens man. He was a developer. Acreage was what interested him. And location. So, it was a short tour.

'Well, there we are. Lawns, tennis courts, a maze, stables, two cottages and a hundred acres of England's finest,' Harry chattered as he stopped with Jerricoe and Hunt at their car. 'What do you think?'

For the first time since he'd arrived, Jerricoe smiled. 'What was it that gave you the idea that I was soft in the head?'

'I'm sorry?'

'Ten million for this?' Jerricoe looked around derisively. 'Come off it!'

Angel was already holding the car door open for him.

'But…it's worth at least fifteen,' Harry stammered.

'Not to me it isn't. Nice try.' And, climbing into the back seat of the BMW, he slammed the door.

On the other side of the car, Hunt smiled triumphantly.

Dismay hung from Harry's features as he watched the car slide away down the drive. Then he turned and, reaching the house, he began to smile.

Richard was already waiting for him when he reached the hall. Then the Morrisons and Ghelanis joined them. Richard smiled. 'Well done, everyone.'

(vii)

'Well, then?' Hunt asked as the BMW left the estate and turned back towards London.

Jerricoe was stroking his cheeks. 'They're giving it away at ten million. We could move it on tomorrow for fifteen.'

Inwardly, Hunt cursed. This wasn't what he'd wanted to hear. 'You think? '

'I know.'

'So?'

'Nine would be more like it. He's trying to screw me.'

Hunt swivelled his head and looked back at the house just as it went out of sight behind a bend in the road. 'He's certainly screwing someone.'

33.

(i)

It was a night for celebration in the scaffolding cage that was now the River House. Gathered around Richard's tiny kitchen table, cluttered with flickering candles, an instant meal of a cooked chicken from the grill at Tesco, stir-fried vegetables that Jenny had prepared downstairs in her own kitchen, and much wine, cheese and fruit, the three conspirators regaled each other with their accounts of the day.

They'd wanted the Morrisons and Ghelanis to join them for dinner, but Sanjeev and Sarojini had been anxious to get back to meet their sons out of school, while Mr Morrison was exhausted by the anxiety of it all.

'If you need any further help, just call,' Sarojini had told Richard as the group raced to put away the silver in the Creswell Manor kitchen, remake the four-poster bed and clear Maurice's office of any signs of Mr Morrison. 'We'll be there.'

'When a buyer questions the price of a deal rather than the product, he's hooked,' said Harry as he poured the wine. 'The rest is negotiation. Jerricoe will be back with an offer, you'll see.'

'We'll need a lawyer by then,' said Jenny.

'And we'll have one. A chap called Barney Penn. He's the best lawyer I've met in his line of work, and there are quite a few runners in that race.'

'So, where's this Barney now?' she pursued.

'Abroad, but due back any day. You'll love him.'

Jenny grinned. 'As long as he can do what he has to, I'll leave the loving to you.' More than a little drunk, she was enjoying the fun of having rattled the skeletons in the Creswell family cupboard. 'I think Maurice thought for a minute I was going to claim that I was the rightful heir to the Creswell title,' she giggled.

'You'll have the Creswell staff gossiping about Wendy Hornton for generations,' Harry applauded. 'She'll become a legend.'

Jenny nodded: 'Like that mystery Romanov princess...Anastasia. "Wendy Hornton, the tragic Aussie bastard who British high society disowned". I can see it all now. Extracts in the *Daily Mail*, Keira Knightley playing a younger me in the film. You should have seen me outside the church after the service, playing for time, insisting I shake hands with every member of the staff, like the Queen used to.'

Richard smiled. It had been Jenny's idea, and at her own insistence, that she would be the decoy.

'I hope we haven't permanently damaged your morals,' Harry said as he plucked at a bunch of large black grapes.

Jenny took a grape, too. 'I think my morals can take care of themselves, thank you very much,' in her Australian accent.

There was a moment's silence. Then, reaching for his Figure of Eight board, Richard changed the subject. 'So, anyway, let's see. Now that we've got Jerricoe started as a *buyer* of Creswell Manor, the next step is to get him going as a *seller* of the River House, which, in turn, will get *us* going as *buyers*. And *that* involves...?'

'The heritaging of the River House,' Jenny finished for him.

'So does anyone have any ideas about the sort of historic person who might have lived here, in the River House, in the nineteenth century?'

'Personally, I always felt Guy Fawkes deserved a blue plaque for giving us bonfire night,' Harry offered.

'Possibly,' allowed Richard. 'But as he was about three hundred and fifty hanged, drawn and quartered when the River House was built...'

'Really! Poor chap.'

'Charles Darwin would have been around at the right time,' mused Jenny. 'And Dickens. But they'll already have blue-plaqued houses and societies all over the place.'

'What about Robert Louis Stevenson,' Harry tried again. 'Jekyll and Hyde was a cracking good yarn.'

Jenny turned to him. 'Which are you, Harry? Jekyll or Hyde?'

He turned to her with a smile. 'Which would you prefer?'

For a second, Jenny she'd blushed slightly. Quickly she said: 'Then there's the Lady with the Lamp.'

'The first woman coal miner?' This was Harry, of course.

Shaking with laughter, Jenny put her hands up. 'All right, Richard, come on, tell us. We know you've already got someone in mind.'

Richard acknowledged the implied compliment. 'Well, I did have one idea. Do you remember Elspeth Worsley?' he asked her.

'Er... No.'

'The name on the gravestone we saw along the river on the day it snowed?'

'You mean the one with the angel over it?'

'Yes. There were no details about her, so I looked her up. She's been forgotten now, but, apparently, she made her home a refuge for what they then called "fallen women".'

'She lived here in the River House?' Jenny asked.

'I doubt it. I couldn't find any trace of where she lived. It was probably flattened long ago for a warehouse. But if we can make Jerricoe believe that she *did* live here, and that we're about to make her the most overlooked woman in London's social history, it might be enough.'

'Fallen women. Where would we be without them?' Harry raised his glass. 'To the River House...headquarters-to-be of the Elspeth Worsley Society and fallen women everywhere.'

'To Elspeth Worsley,' agreed Jenny, reaching for a pen and writing the name on the back of an envelope. 'It's very Victorian sounding.' And she quickly drew an outline of a determined looking woman in a shawl with her arms out like the angel on the statue.

'Hey, that's not bad!' Harry complimented.

Jenny dipped her head towards him. 'You should see me draw kittens for the children.'

Richard noticed.

(ii)

He wasn't coming on to her in an over-obvious way, but Jenny saw what was happening. Little by little, Harry was pursuing her. And, step by step, despite herself, she was going along with it. But why, she asked herself, as, too excited to sleep, she later lay in bed and replayed the day? How could she possibly allow herself to be distracted by someone so transparently insincere? She knew the answer, of course. With his compliments and jokes and his little attentions he made her feel good about herself. Whereas Richard…

She stopped. Whereas Richard what? As sleep approached, she pictured him sitting alone, bookish at his worktop, deep into the early hours. There was always a slight wariness about him. As friendly as he was, he never flirted. No matter how much time they spent together, or how close they became, she still didn't really know what he thought of her, or what he wanted her to think of him.

(iii)

She was right about Richard working into the night. Plotting and replotting, it was getting the details right that mattered to him. At three in the morning, he put his notes together and made a list on his sketching pad. It began:

The Elspeth Worsley Society
1. Registered charity, established 1935
2. Stationery (logo)
3. Invent history
4. Name plate by door – weathered

Occasionally, as he worked, he pictured Jerricoe - the blond thug he'd seen from the Creswell Manor rose garden that morning. But mainly he thought about Jenny as she'd been at dinner, pink with excitement and too much wine, and *so* full of life in her shirt and jeans, her hair still in the braids she'd had woven for her appearance as Wendy Hornton.

He'd always thought of her as being pretty, rather than beautiful. Her nose was probably too small, and the frown lines between her eyes often too deeply etched. But her life force and sheer exuberance as she took on all obstacles was dazzling. And, though she'd gone back down to her own flat hours earlier when Harry had left, the ghost of her presence kept him company throughout the night.

Could they really pull off this scam, he still wondered. He'd talked himself into it, more as an exercise than a real plot, and he'd then convinced Jenny. Right from the start, Harry had said it was mad, and that the job was too difficult. And now with every step it became ever more complicated, ever madder.

But having begun, the only way out was to give in, pack their belongings, leave the River House and let Jerricoe have his gymnasium and sauna. They'd tried being honest and reasonable and it hadn't worked. So here they were, being sucked ever deeper into a labyrinth of their own making.

Yes, it was mad. But they couldn't stop now.

(iv)

Jenny woke before the alarm. It was still dark. She'd had a restless, troubled night. Perhaps it was the wine. But by seven thirty she was dressed, and, pushing her bicycle down the garden path to the road, she cycled to the river. Stopping at the slipway, she rested her hands on the handlebars, and, standing for several minutes, watched a River Police launch surge upstream, disturbing two swans which were fishing just below the towpath. The Thames was at its most magnetic early in the morning, which today was steel coloured like the sky.

On an impulse she looked back to the River House and up at Richard's window, remembering the times she'd come home from school in the early evening and seen the light in his window, and been glad to see it there.

Then, getting back on her bike, she set off for school.

34.

(i)

Richard and Harry watched as Jerricoe's secretary made her way along the pavement towards the post box. Reaching it, she took a wad of letters from her satchel bag, patted them together and posted them. Then, turning away, she trudged away and around the corner towards the bus stop.

'Same time as always!' Richard noted from the Volvo, this time parked down the street in the shadow of a former brewery. 'It would be better if we had someone in Jerricoe's post room, but…'

'In this business we work with where we are and what we have, not where we'd like to be,' chided Harry at his side, and went back to looking at his phone.

Richard turned to Inky, who was sitting in the back seat. 'Any thoughts?'

This was the first time Richard had seen the forger outside the darkness of his railway arches studio. He was a taciturn, small man with a constantly pained air. He was also, according to Harry, married to a very attractive, slightly older Italian woman who'd been an artist's model in her younger days, and who was quite devoted to him. 'Women love him,' Harry had confided. 'He makes them look beautiful.'

In the back of the car, Inky grunted. He was staring down the telephoto lens of a camera, focused on the post box.

'Should be easy enough. Standard 1980 Type K Post Office design.' The shutter on his camera clicked and clicked again. 'Quiet street, too. Not overlooked. I'll need to make a mould.'

It was the most Richard had ever heard Inky say. 'Right. Thank you,' he said and turned to Harry, who was scrolling through *Rightmove* on his phone. 'What about you? Find anything?'

'A couple, maybe. This one might be all right: "Smithfield. Two ground floor rooms. Short let."'

With one last glance towards Jerricoe House, Richard started the car. 'Let's take a look.'

They dropped Inky off at his studio and then drove on to Smithfield. If they were to create an Elspeth Worsley Society, they would need a believable base. The first rooms they saw were unsuitable, in that the basement of the building was home for a courier service, with motor bikes revving constantly outside. A better one, on a more sedate Georgian street in nearby Clerkenwell, was quickly viewed and rented.

Portobello Road with its antique shops and market stalls was the next stop.

'We want anything that's Victorian London and shows life as it was on the Thames in the nineteenth century,' Richard instructed as he and Harry split up to search.

An hour later they had their props, old maps of London, an early sepia photograph of a fog shrouded Thames, a faded watercolour of an ancient barge loaded with coal and several prints of poor people. Richard had also come across a slightly crumbling framed portrait of a strict looking woman in her forties, her hair pulled back in a tight bun.

'God! Who's she?' Harry asked as they met. He was also carrying a painting, wrapped in brown paper.

'I've no idea who she *was*, but from now on her name is Elspeth Worsley, and she's about to be hung over the fireplace in our rooms in Clerkenwell.'

'Looks like a battleaxe to me.'

'Battle-axes got things done in the nineteenth century. What about your picture?'

'Well, I like her,' said Harry, and pulled back the brown paper enough to reveal an early photograph of a rather plump, nude model, her modesty preserved by a delicately positioned potted date palm.

'I don't think the Elspeth Worsley Society would be likely to have that on their wall.'

'Oh, no. This is for me, for my flat. Lovely, isn't she! Apparently, her name's Phoebe. See, it says here.' And he pointed to a title under the photograph. 'Good name, Phoebe, don't you think! I think I'll call her Jenny.'

Richard considered him. Was Harry looking for a reaction? If so, he would be disappointed. 'Shall we go?' he said. And, collecting his haul of Victoriana, he set off back to the car.

(ii)

'It's like stepping on to the set of a period movie,' Jenny said as she looked around the Elspeth Worsley Society. She'd cycled to Clerkenwell after school, had pressed the front doorbell alongside the copper name plate, that looked, thanks to Inky, as though it had been there for seventy years gathering rust, and was now peering at the dark walls studded with sepia photographs.

The room had the smell of history, she thought, with the heavy old desk lamp and a stern, elderly armchair picked up in a charity shop.

'So?' Richard asked.

'Perfect. Dry, dusty and very worthy.'

'And what about this?' Turning to the computer, the only twenty-first century item in the room, Richard clicked the mouse.

'"Elspethworsleysociety.com!"' Jenny read. 'Crikey! How long has that been there?'

'Since today. I cribbed the design off an Emily Bronte website, added our girl's portrait, and then nicked a lot of background stuff from a Victorian London organisation. Jerricoe's bound to look us up. And then there's this.' He passed her a sheet of stationery for the Elspeth Worsley Society.

'Hey! My squiggle!' At the top of the sheet of pale cream paper was an embossed letterhead showing the outline of the Victorian woman who Jenny had drawn at dinner.

'Your *design*,' he emphasised. 'It's good. Maybe it's the start of a second career?'

'Third, actually, after I've completed my prison sentence for grand larceny?' she laughed. 'Or would that make it four. I didn't know you'd saved it.'

'I must be learning a few tricks from Harry.'

She pretended to frown. 'Just don't learn too many.'

He turned to the computer and clicked to another page. 'Would you like to check our letter before I send it to Jerricoe.'

Pulling on her glasses, she began to read.

'Dear Sir

Re: The River House, Wharf Lane, London SW23
You may not be aware, but the above building, which I understand Jerricoe Properties now owns, was the last home of Elspeth Worsley, that great British crusader for the moral welfare of poor, young, Victorian women.

In the nineteenth century, Miss Worsley was sometimes known as the Florence Nightingale of the Thames for her saintly work among destitute girls, many of whom were forced, by the circumstance of their poverty, to sell their bodies along the banks and wharves of the river. For them, the River House became a haven where they were safe from violence and disease, and where they could learn a trade that would keep them off the streets.

As the River House is such an historic building, we at the Elspeth Worsley Society are very interested in purchasing the property for use as both our museum and headquarters, because, as you will know, there is always work to be done among the poor.

I would be grateful therefore if we might meet to discuss the future of the River House to what will, I believe, be our mutual benefit.

Yours sincerely
Charles Foster
Chairman, Elspeth Worsley Society'

'Charles Foster?' she smiled as she finished. Charles Foster Kane? As in *Citizen Kane*?'

'Ah! I knew it sounded familiar,' Richard smiled.

'It's an honest sounding name. It suits you.'

'Yes? Is that a compliment?'

'I don't know. But it's the sort of truth.' She then read the letter a second time. 'How do you think Jerricoe will respond?'

Richard shrugged. 'He may ignore it.'

'And if he does?'

'Then we'll make another move that he can't ignore.'

Going to the window, Jenny looked out on the terraced street. 'Do you really think we can beat him?'

He shrugged. 'I can't say for sure. But I do know that if we give in, we're bound to fail, so we might as well get out now. On the other hand, if we stay and fight and keep trying, well…we're in with a chance.'

She laughed. 'You sound like a Third Division football manager talking to his team before they play Liverpool in the Cup Final. How can anyone possibly beat us when we have a philosophy like that?'

'If there were any fairness in the world, they wouldn't!' Richard replied. Then he clicked 'Print' on his computer, and they watched the first letter ever written from the Elspeth Worsley Society unroll from the printer.

For months, Mark Jerricoe had been harassing them. It was now their turn to harass him.

35.

(i)

Jerricoe had been eating his morning pastry, licking the vanilla from between the storeys of a wedge of millefeuilles and now flakes of pastry littered the front of his suit. 'Have you seen this?' he demanded, wandering into Hunt's ground floor office and slapping a letter on his desk. 'Who the hell are the Elspeth Worsley Society?'

Hunt had seen the letter. He'd also taken the precaution of already having looked at the Elspeth Worsley Society website. 'Bloody goody-goodies, aren't they,' he replied. 'They're multiplying. Breeding probably. Every day the world gets more and more full of them. They want to turn everywhere into a bleeding museum.'

He could usually tell what Jerricoe would be thinking, so he said it for him. It made for an easier life.

'Just tell this Elspeth Worsley crowd to get stuffed!' Jerricoe snapped.

Hunt took the letter from him, noticing a sticky patch of vanilla on one corner and avoided touching it. 'Right, Mark!' Then he watched as Jerricoe made his way back to his own office.

Jerricoe had been particularly ratty recently because of the problems with the Greensleeves plans. At least the Elspeth Worsley Society would be easy to squash.

(ii)

The reply from Jerricoe Properties was waiting on the mat in Clerkenwell when Richard got to the Elspeth Worsley Society the following day. At least the bastards were punctual and economical in their straight-talking, he thought, as he read it.

They hadn't chosen to send an email either. In their eyes a letter must have carried more 'old fashioned' weight, which was interesting, too.

His reply was equally direct.

'Dear Mr Hunt,

We are naturally disappointed to receive your negative response to our enquiry. We were hoping that a useful dialogue might have been opened between us.

But as this does not appear likely, and since, as I pointed out in my earlier letter, the River House is a building of significant British cultural history, I'm afraid I have to tell you that we may feel we have no alternative but to make an application to London Heritage to ensure its protection.

Yours sincerely

Charles Foster'

(iii)

'Who does this Charles Foster scumbag think he is!' Jerricoe was raging.

Hunt had hoped that by leaving the reply from the Elspeth Worsley Society until the weekly rentals meeting, Choudhrai's perennial problems with late payers might deflect what would be Jerricoe's inevitable fury. It hadn't worked. All thoughts of late rents went on hold. 'You've got a legal right to do whatever you want with that house,' he replied, which, as leaseholders were still involved, he knew wasn't true.

Jerricoe was out of his chair at that. 'If bloody London Heritage stick their bloody noses in, I'll have sod all. Remember Pepperdome. Months of reports, committee meetings, talks, ulcers. And down two hundred thousand in the end.'

'That was the National Trust. It isn't the same.'

'They're all the same! National Trust, English Heritage, London Heritage. They're all bloody Lefties.'

'Come on, Mark. It's just a try-on. This Foster guy hasn't got a leg to stand on.'

'He bloody won't have. Go and see him. Talk to him. Do whatever it takes. Then tell Vincent to get his boys to sort him out if you have to. He's not going to get bloody London

Heritage involved. If he does, we could be sitting here waiting for a decision for years.'

'Right, Mark!' And, as Choudhrai kept his eyes firmly on his books, Hunt turned towards the door.

'And Craig!' Jerricoe called after him. 'Those two tenants at the River House. They're still there, aren't they!'

'I'm working on it, Mark.'

'Well, perhaps you should try working a bit harder for what I pay you. All right?'

Raw at being humiliated in front of another staff member, Hunt hurried down to his office. The bloody River House! That was all he ever heard. What was it with those two idiot tenants?

(iv)

Jenny looked him up and down.

'Am I fogeyish enough, do you think?' Richard asked.

'Almost nerdyish, I'd say,' Jenny said quietly. 'What do you think, Harry?'

For once, Harry was serious. 'You're quite sure this Hunt guy didn't see you in the garden at Creswell Manor?'

'Not close enough to recognise me.'

'And he hasn't seen you here at the River House, coming and going?'

'I don't think so. And, if he has, I hope I looked nothing like this.' And Richard took a quick glance at himself in the mirror. Wearing horn rimmed glasses, an ancient, pin-striped suit and heavy brown shoes, all of which he'd picked up in an Oxfam shop, and with his wavy hair now slicked back and shining with gel, he certainly looked different; older, too. But could he convince as Charles Foster of the Elspeth Worsley Society?

Harry shrugged. 'All right! But remember, if things go nasty, there's no back-up. You can't run to the police, not unless you want to face three years for attempted fraud, which, when Jerricoe finds out, you might not be in a fit enough shape to serve.'

Jenny bit her lip. Harry was worried. For the first time, she was afraid.

Richard, however, was smiling. 'Anything else?'

'Yes. It's all in the performance. To make the guy believe you are who you say you are, and that you intend to do what you say you'll do, you have to sort of believe it. Right Jenny?'

She nodded. 'Yes, like those Method actors who once they got into a part couldn't stop playing it in the pub afterwards.'

'But did they convince?' Harry asked.

'Oh, yes. But then they would go on and on and get incredibly boring.'

'Which is probably exactly what Charles Foster friends would say about him,' Richard smiled.

'Good luck,' said Harry.

Jenny was surprised. It wasn't exactly a tender moment. There were never such exchanges between these two. But, for just a second, Harry looked as though he might mean it.

Harry, however, hadn't finished. 'Because if you get found out, I'll have wasted an awful lot of time.'

Like boys showing off, she thought, the one not prepared to admit to any fear, the other denying that he had any decent feelings.

36.

(i)

Hunt enjoyed being driven around town in Jerricoe's BMW, even if it did smell of dogs. As the car made its way along Marylebone Road, Smooth FM was playing an old Eagles' favourite that Hunt had listened to when he'd been prison. It had relaxed him. It still did. Especially the line about sleeping with the girl 'in the desert tonight, with a million stars all around'. For a moment he saw himself sitting in his cell with his headphones on thinking about what that song had suggested.

It hurt to remember. He'd done well since he'd been out, and even better since he'd begun working for Jerricoe, spiteful bastard though the guy could be. But grieving over the past made no sense. If he hadn't gone to jail, he'd never have studied law nor made so many useful contacts.

It had been Jerricoe's idea that Angel drive Hunt to Clerkenwell. 'A posh car and driver will make those Elspeth Worsley tossers see they're not dealing with some little fly-by-night firm who are going to roll over for them,' he'd said.

Hunt hadn't disagreed, and, looking out on the new office developments around Kings Cross as the car drove east, he considered the hundreds of millions of pounds contracts that must be involved. One day Jerricoe Properties would be doing deals with top projects like this. Or maybe, just maybe, it would be Craig Hunt Properties that would be throwing them up.

First, however, there was the job ahead. He hoped it wouldn't be difficult. Jerricoe liked 'difficult'. He liked violence. At least, he liked being told about violence, though he made sure he was never there when it happened. Hunt didn't like it. He'd seen it, both out of jail and inside. He'd helped organise it, too. And it had been terrifying, even when it had been necessary. He really hoped this silly sod at the Elspeth Worsley Society wouldn't make it necessary. And turning around he watched the car behind, a grey Renault, as it followed the BMW first into Grays Inn Road, then off again into the side streets of Clerkenwell.

'Just wait here, will you,' Hunt instructed Angel as they reached their destination 'It shouldn't take long.' And, getting out of the car, he made his way up the three steps to the house. As he did, he heard that the Eagles had been replaced in the car with the aggressive bark of hip-hop. Angel wasn't much of a romantic when it came to music.

Hunt glanced down the road. The Renault had stopped about thirty yards away. Turning back to the front door, he examined the faded copper plate. 'The Elspeth Worsley Society,' he read, thinking, 'Jesus, that could do with a polish.' Then he pressed the bell.

(ii)

Richard had been waiting for over an hour and still wasn't sure that he was ready. He'd pulled the blinds halfway down to make the room even gloomier than usual and had fretfully considered his outfit numerous times in the mirror in the little bathroom behind the office. Then there was his voice to worry about. Even if Hunt hadn't seen him before, there was a chance he might recognise his voice from the phone call he'd made to Jerricoe Properties on morning that the Ghelanis had left the River House. He would have to remember to speak in a lower tone.

As the front doorbell rang, he pulled on his new glasses and went out into the hall. He'd chosen the rooms because the rest of the house was sub-divided into flats and would largely be empty during the working day. Now, as he reached the front door, he wondered if that had been such a good idea. The house echoed menacingly in its emptiness. 'Be the part,' he reminded himself. 'Be a method actor.' Then he opened the front door.

'Mr Foster?' Hunt was smiling up at him, an empty business smile on his face.

'Welcome to the Elspeth Worsley Society,' said Richard. Over Hunt's shoulder he could see the BMW parked outside. Then, leading the way into the office, he indicated a chair.

For a moment, as they faced each other across the desk, while Jerricoe's lawyer looked around at the photographs, there was silence.

Richard blinked first. 'Well,' he began, 'our finance committee has met and…'

Hunt interrupted immediately: 'Mr Foster, I have to tell you that the River House is not for sale.'

'Indeed. As you suggested in your letter. But we haven't even begun to discuss it yet. Our society has been very fortunate in receiving a rather large bequest in the will of one of our late members and…'

Hunt interrupted again. 'There's nothing to discuss. Jerricoe Properties bought the house in all good faith and we intend…'

'I'm sure you did. But you didn't know then that it was an historic building.'

'So, you say. But it belongs to Jerricoe Properties and we intend to develop its commercial potential as we see fit. I'm sorry, but that is how it is.'

Richard put his hand to his head. Then, remembering that his hair was greasy with gel, took it away. 'I'm afraid then, we must see what London Heritage have to say about that.'

Hunt's expression hardened as the faint smile of the professional go-between faded. 'Mr Foster, if you take my advice, you won't approach London Heritage.'

Richard pretended not to have heard him. 'I expect they'll take a dim view of a national treasure being vandalised. As will the *The Guardian* when they hear about your company's intentions.'

Hunt's tone stayed perfectly even. 'Mr Foster, I don't think it would be wise for you to approach London Heritage or the newspapers.'

'Oh, but I must. This very day.' Richard didn't know where the 'this very day' phrase suddenly came from, but it seemed suitably Churchillian for a fogey.

'No, you mustn't, Mr Foster. You really mustn't. It could delay our plans by months, and I'm sure you will not get the result you want.' Hunt was staring at him, his eyes unblinking.

And for the first time Richard saw that he had a white scar peeping from his shirt collar at the side of his neck as though someone had once slashed him.

'But I have to do what is right for the society,' Richard said stiffly. 'You must see that! And the River House is absolutely where our society should be.'

(iii)

'The pompous fool,' thought Hunt as, twenty minutes later, he returned to the BMW. 'The dope, the unworldly, little prat, stuck in his bloody Victorian time warp!' He just wouldn't listen. Why did they always have to make it difficult for themselves? Well, no-one could say he hadn't tried. If this was the way the guy wanted it, so be it. And, as the BMW pulled away, he pulled out his phone.

(iv)

Lounging on his couch in his little flat, Harry turned the society pages of *Tatler*, admiring, as he did, the photographs of rich and beautiful women at society parties. Theirs was the class he should have been born into, he told himself. Life as a debs' delight would have suited him perfectly.

His phone rang.

'Hello?'

Down the line he could hear Richard almost chuckling with relief. 'Did it!'

'Really! And everything went according to plan?'

'Everything! I just laid out the situation and let him go back to Jerricoe to think about it.'

'And he believed you were who you said you were?'

'Absolutely. It worked like a dream.'

'There were no threats?'

'No. A lot of pressure, but nothing specific. He made the same points over and over, but no threats…'

Suddenly Richard broke off. His voice now became less distinct, more distant. Harry pushed the phone closer to his ear.

'Excuse me?' he heard Richard ask. 'Are you looking for someone? You can't just come barging in here like...?'

(v)

At first, he'd thought they were just a couple of chancers who'd forced the front door and were trying their luck in the first room they reached. They were young and athletic, one in a black tracksuit, his brown hair just about shaved to his skull, the other with a woollen hat pulled down to his eyes. 'Can I help you....? What d'you...?' Richard was still rising to his feet when a blow to his head sent him smashing down on to the desk, as the phone was snatched from his hand.

That was when he knew why they were there.

(vi)

At the other end of the phone, Harry winced as he heard the cry of pain. 'Richard?' He listened hard. 'Richard!'

The line went dead. He dropped the magazine he'd been reading. Bugger. Hunt *had* made real threats, but Richard just hadn't recognised them.

'Amateurs,' he thought.

(vii)

'Money,' the thug in the tracksuit shouted. 'Money!'

Richard was still at his desk, pinned down across his mouth and jaw by a gloved hand. He tried to stand, but as he did the pressure on his jaw was increased. Pain shot up to his temples. He wanted to cry out, but no sound would come.

In front of him the other intruder lurched around the room smashing the photographs so carefully chosen. The framed portrait of the woman, whom Richard had decided would be Elspeth Worsley, was pulled from the wall, its pane of glass cracked. Almost casually, the computer screen was then tipped off the table and kicked in.

'Money! Money!' the shouting continued, as fingers pushed inside his jacket and pulled out his wallet. He'd left ninety-five pounds inside it, just in case, but there was nothing in it that would identify him.

As the wallet disappeared into the pocket of the guy in the tracksuit his companion was rummaging through his desk. A cardboard box with a few pounds of petty cash caught his attention.

'Money! Cash!' the demands continued, as Richard, no longer struggling, was dragged away from his desk, and pushed on to the carpet, the toe of a shoe going into his solar plexus. Another kick followed and another, until finally one caught the side of his head by his right eye.

At last, the kicking stopped. He could now feel blood running down his chin. The eye that had been kicked was almost closed. He couldn't turn to see what was happening, but then he felt it as he heard the staplegun he'd bought for his desk snap shut. Something had been stapled to his ear. He screamed.

Then his assailants were gone.

For several minutes he lay on the carpeted floor of the office, trying to collect his thoughts. At length, somewhere close by, a mobile phone tune began to play. Then he remembered. He'd hidden his mobile with his usual clothes in a duffel bag between the pipes in the tiny bathroom behind the office.

Crawling into the bathroom, he reached into the bag and found the phone. 'Yes?' he gasped.

'You all right?' It was Harry.

'Never better!' he groaned, pulling himself to a standing position and seeing his reflection in the bathroom mirror. A photograph of Victorian children bathing in the Thames at low tide was attached to his ear, with blood running down it and dripping into the basin.

'That sounds as though you're not so good. You had visitors?'

'Yes!' Richard gasped.

'Ah... It can be a rough business at times. But there's an upside here.'

'Yes?'

'Well, I'd say that you must have been convincing. You've got them worried.'

Richard stared at himself. He was shaking from the shock of the violence. 'Thank you,' he muttered and sank back to his knees. He'd never known anything could hurt so much. But first, somehow, he had to find a way of unclipping the photograph from his ear.

(viii)

The BMW was almost back at Jerricoe House when the call came to tell Hunt that the Clerkenwell job had been satisfactorily completed.

'Well, then, there's the other matter that we talked about. Problem with a tenant. Okay?' As they were paying the guys for the whole day, they might as well get their money's worth.

37.

(i)

Distracted by worries about Richard, Jenny had struggled all day to control her class, with head teacher, Christina, looking in at one point, surprised by the racket the children were making.

Apologising, Jenny had gathered the class around her for a story about a little boy called Sam who wore a chimpanzee suit at a fancy-dress party. But the disguise had gone wrong when he'd been mistaken for a real chimpanzee and found himself carted off to the zoo. The children liked it.

Because of a special needs budgeting meeting after school, it was after six and already dark when she set off for home. She didn't like cycling in a herd through the rush hour traffic and was glad when she got off the busy road and headed alone towards the towpath along the Thames. It was raining now and, with her head down, she crouched over the handlebars.

Reaching the river, she became aware of a car behind her and kept well to the edge of the asphalt so that it might easily pass. There was no pavement here, just an iron fence above the water.

The car didn't pass. At first, she thought it might be the police and she hoped that her rear light was working. She cycled on. The car stayed behind her.

Glancing back but all she could see were two large headlights on full beam. They blinded her, so she pedalled more quickly, hoping to pull away from the car.

But as she quickened her pace, so did the car. When she went more slowly, the car slowed, too.

Fear now began to govern her as she pedalled faster again, holding ever more tightly on to the rubber handlebar grips. The rain stung her eyes. Apart from her and the car, the road was empty on this wet evening. Soon she was approaching the corner before the turn for the River House. Dare she stop when she reached her home, or should she carry on cycling?

The decision was made for her, when, with a loud, prolonging blast of its horn, the car pulled alongside her, then stayed there, running parallel with her, just inches away.

She was afraid to take her eyes off the road. But as she reached the end of the fencing, where the slipway down to the river began, the car suddenly nosed towards her. For a moment, as she struggled to keep her balance, she tried to brake. But it was too late. As the car blocked her way, she careered on to the slipway down to the river.

It was high tide. The water was lapping up the ramp towards the road. Even had she seen the chain, put there to prevent people from wandering into the water by accident, she couldn't have avoided it.

As her front wheel hit it, the chain swung away and upwards, then stopped. The bike bucked, its front wheel twisted sideways, its back wheel reared up behind her. And Jenny felt herself being tossed over the handlebars, and falling forwards, her mouth and nostrils filling with water as her elbow, hip and knee hit the bottom of the slipway.

Almost before she'd realised that she was in the water, she was stumbling to her feet, shocked, spluttering and spitting, standing up, and clutching at the still swinging chain to steady herself.

The car that had pursued her was gone.

(ii)

Richard saw her as he parked the Volvo outside the River House. She looked a slight, waif-like figure. With water drippping from her clothes, she was still wearing her helmet and dragging her bicycle after her. Its front wheel was buckled.

'Jesus!' Richard gasped as he hurried towards her.

She tried to smile. Then she saw the bruises and plasters on his face. 'Oh, my God!' she said.

He put a hand to her. 'But you…what happened?'

'I fell off my bike.'

38.

'We're like a couple of injured soldiers after a battle...showing off our wounds and gloating about our survival,' Jenny said, as she squeezed some antiseptic cream on to a strip of lint. 'Except that you probably had some dishy young nurse at the hospital putting you back together again.'

Richard tried to smile, although his face ached when he stretched the skin. 'Actually, I did.'

'Really?'

'He was from Bratislava.'

Laughing for the first time since she'd cycled into the river, Jenny laid the lint on to her grazed knee.

He watched her. He'd never envisaged violence, although he now knew he should have done. The River House caper had begun almost as a game. He'd always suspected that Jerricoe was capable of violence, but until this afternoon that violence hadn't been visited on either Jenny or himself. Today Jerricoe had shown how far he would go to get his way. But would he go further?

'After what happened to you, I think...' He hesitated. 'I mean, do we really think it's worth the fight? The next time someone tries to run you off the road...who knows what might happen?'

'So, what are you saying?' Jenny sat up. 'That we give in? That Jerricoe gets what he wants and we limp away hurt. No way. Can you just hold the bandage for me, please?'

He reached for the bandage and watched as she wound it around her leg. 'What I was saying is...that car...it could have killed you.'

'Oh, maybe not,' she smiled. 'It was probably just some tearaway out in his dad's car getting a buzz out of trying to frighten a middle-aged woman on a bike.'

'I don't believe that. And nor do you.'

'Okay. No, I don't. But if you put you head in a lion's mouth, you can't really complain if you get bitten now and again, can you?' she laughed.

An hour earlier she'd been shaking, fighting tears, when he'd led her, dripping, back into the River House. He'd wanted her to go to hospital, too, but she wouldn't have it.

'Nothing's broken, apart from my bike,' she'd said as they'd reached her sitting room. 'And I had a tetanus booster last summer, so there's no problem there.'

His own injuries, badly bruised ribs, a cut eye with four stitches and a swollen red ear lobe, had called for a visit to Guy's Hospital A & E department. A doctor there had insisted he report the incident to the police. He'd promised that he would, but he hadn't. He didn't want to have to answer any police questions about the Elspeth Worsley Society. As Harry had warned, he was outside the law now.

As was Jenny. Now fortified by a shower, paracetamol and a change of clothes, her resilience had been strengthened. 'I'll be all right. I used to get worse at school playing hockey against the rough girls from Our Lady of Lourdes. They had some real hooligans on their team.'

They were both in denial, Richard realised, neither being prepared to admit how frightened they'd been. He looked at her. There was no way this slightly eccentric, pretty schoolteacher was going to give in to Jerricoe's bullying. Under siege, she'd grown a new defiance. Jerricoe had no idea what he was now up against.

At nine o'clock, Richard left, and, in some pain, climbed the stairs to his on flat. As he was closed the door, his phone rang. It was Harry.

'So? Back in one piece?'

'Pretty well,' Richard lied.

'Good man. What next?'

'Your turn,' said Richard.

39.

(i)

Sheltering under an umbrella, Harry picked a careful way along the line of planks that cut through the mud of the Greensleeves building site. Small, shallow industrial lagoons and tan puddles of wet concrete lay to either side of him. One false step and he'd ruin his only good pair of shoes. The backs of his trousers were sure to be covered in splashes of cement when he got home. They were already soaked below the knee as the gale blew the rain under his umbrella.

At a portacabin office parked some way ahead, Jerricoe was standing by the door watching him, a white hard hat covering his yellow hair. Nearby the rattle and drop of a vast revolving concrete mixer crunched noisily.

Reaching firmer ground, Harry stepped from the planks on to a small mound. This really wasn't his natural habitat, but he tried to smile.

'Not so cocky today then?' Jerricoe said,

Harry looked puzzled. 'I'm not sure I follow.'

'No? Well, *you* phoned *me*. I didn't phone you. *You* came to *me*. You haven't got any other customer for Creswell Manor, have you?'

'Well...'

'Which leads me to the conclusion that, in your estate agent jargon, it's a buyer's market.'

Jerricoe was obviously enjoying this. And, for the first time, Harry noticed how unnaturally white were his teeth.

'Actually, I didn't want to get into some kind of auction, so I've been holding off showing...' he began.

'Balls!'

'Well, I suppose I had been hoping to hear...'

'Nine million,' Jerricoe interrupted.

'What?'

'Nine million.'

Harry looked appalled.

'For a quick sale, which is what you want. Nine million pounds.'

'But they'd get at least fifteen on the open market. Probably more. Not even these trustees are so stupid. Creswell Manor is a very large and historic...'

Jerricoe shrugged. 'Take it or leave it.'

'They'll leave it. No doubt about that.'

'I don't think so. Not if you sell it to them right, they won't.'

Harry shook his head. 'I'm sorry, Mr Jerricoe. This just isn't going to work. I've wasted your time.' Rain was running down his umbrella and cascading all around him.

Jerricoe grinned. 'What is it? Afraid you'll have to give up too much of your own slice?'

Harry didn't answer.

'You might be able to con them, but you can't con me.'

'There'll be other...other buyers,' Harry mumbled, looking thoroughly dejected.

'Possibly,' Jerricoe conceded. 'But not through you. And not when the trustees discover you're trying to rob the estate blind. Not when Heyes and Heys find out about your little sideline either. And not when the police get wind of it.'

Harry stared at him. 'But you wouldn't do that. We have an understanding.'

'Oh, but I would. Believe me, I would. This is business. And I understand business. Now, shall we say nine million. You know you can do it.' And, without waiting for an answer, he went back inside the portacabin and closed the door.

With extreme care, Harry made his way back along the planks.

(ii)

From a window in the portacabin, Hunt watched the poncy representative from Heyes and Heys leave the site.

'You know, you want to get over that chip on your shoulder,' Jerricoe scoffed as he joined him.

'I don't trust him,' Hunt replied.

'You don't trust anyone who you think is a toff. But you're going to have to get used to them. An attitude like that could hinder your career. If we play this idiot right, he could do us a very big favour. So don't screw it up.'

Hunt didn't reply.

40.

(i)

'It's a man, isn't it?' Sally, who taught Owls, declared. She and Jenny were waiting at the bus stop outside their school. While her bicycle was being repaired, Jenny had been travelling by bus.

'I'm sorry?' Jenny didn't follow. A minute earlier they'd been talking about the nightmare of parents who thought of teaching as a branch of the social services. Now it had become personal, and kind though Sally was their friendship did not include sharing romantic details.

'Well, some of us in the staff room, although mainly me, I suppose, can't help noticing that you seem to have been a bit distracted recently. So, we've decided, at least I have, it must be a man.'

'Actually, it isn't.'

'Oh, come on. Not even that quiet art restorer from the top flat you brought to the New Year's Eve dinner. I thought he looked rather ornamental in an academic sort of way.'

'Absolutely not him or anyone else,' Jenny said. 'Sorry if I've seemed a bit preoccupied. I've had a lot to think about with the harassment by the landlord. It's like living under siege.'

Sally sounded disappointed. 'Ah well. If there's no man, there's no man.' And she stepped forward as her bus arrived first. 'See you tomorrow.'

Jenny watched the bus leave. So, I'm looking distracted, she thought. That was probably true. She *was* distracted. A player in Richard's Figure of Eight meant living a double life, one that she could share only with Richard and Harry.

This must be how it feels to be a spy or if you belong to a terrorist cell, she reflected, as it began to rain and she stepped inside the bus shelter. Trying to keep up a front of normality, while the only people you could really talk to were your partners in crime.

Were she and Richard turning into locked-in co-conspirators who fed off each other's obsession? Not quite.

But the secrecy involved was driving them closer together. Trust Sally to assume there was romance or even sex involved. At least, Jenny had been able to deny that bit honestly. Because, while Harry was now beginning to flirt openly, Richard remained a mystery. An emotional contradiction, he was close yet distant, generous in the giving of affection, but careful in the taking of it. She just didn't understand him. She wished she did.

And then there was Harry. Richard and Harry. Harry and Richard. Chalk and cheese. Cheese and chalk. Sally hadn't got it wrong. There wasn't one man. There were two. It might not be sexual, but she was involved with and distracted by both.

(ii)

Even by his own cheery standards, Harry was in unusually good spirits. 'Splendid news, you two. I've just heard from Barney. Our lawyer will be back in town next week.'

'At last,' Richard sighed. Confined to his studio while his face and body repaired themselves, he'd been beginning to wonder if Barney the lawyer even existed.

Harry's visit to the River House had been unexpected. Bringing with him some London Heritage stationery that Inky had copied and printed, he was now opening a bottle of wine. Providing the wine was rare for Harry.

Jenny, whose fingers were stained with flame red and yellow markers from preparing a lesson on the Great Fire of London, took a glass from him. 'You know, Harry,' she said, 'you've never told us where Barney has been all the time.'

'Yes, I did. Abroad.'

'Right! But abroad is big. Australia, Peru, Kazakhstan? Antarctica? Where abroad?'

Harry looked vague. 'Well…er, Switzerland, I believe.'

'Switzerland.' Jenny paused. 'Doing what?'

'How should I know?'

'*Don't* you know?' Jenny pursued. 'I thought he was a "good friend".'

'All right, as a matter of fact, I do know. He's in…in chambers there.'

'"In chambers?" She looked quizzical. 'I'm not a lawyer, what exactly does that mean in lay terms?'

He looked at her sternly. 'It means that it might be impolite to enquire too deeply.'

There was a moment's silence. Then she suddenly laughed. 'Oh, God, "Chambers!" You mean he's locked up. He's been in jail. And you've been waiting for him to get out.'

'Open prison, if you must know,' Harry snapped.

'*Jail?*' Jenny repeated the word.

Harry turned on her. 'So…?'

She was embarrassed. 'It's just that I never thought…'

'Thought what?'

She didn't answer.

'I think we're surprised, that's all,' Richard pacified.

Harry nodded scornfully. 'Which is exactly why I didn't tell you earlier. For heaven's sake, how long will it take you two to realise that everybody involved in this scam is on the wrong side of the law. Including you. And jail is what happens when it goes wrong. It's a professional hazard that Barney accepts and lives with. And Barney is the best man I know for this. All right?' He looked challengingly at them both.

Harry had seemed impervious to any insult, but now Jenny's teasing had touched a nerve.

Richard defused the situation. 'Well, if Barney's the best you know, we're looking forward to retaining his services.'

Harry turned to Jenny. 'Yes, we are. And if he's looking for an attractive, cross-questioning trainee barrister, we'll know where to find one, won't we!' And he flashed Jenny a smile.

(iii)

Harry didn't stay much longer. He had to meet someone. Further explanation was neither expected nor offered. It never was.

'Sorry, I got to him, didn't I?' Jenny said as she heard Harry's steps retreat down the stairs.

Nodding, Richard poured the last of the wine into their glasses. 'We're just tourists in his world. Conning is Harry's life.'

'It must be a strange…spending your days trying to take advantage of people,' Jenny ruminated.

For a couple of seconds Richard didn't answer. Then he said: 'You used to hate him.'

Jenny laughed. 'Well, he deserved it, didn't he! He robbed us.'

'But you like him now? Right?'

'Don't you?'

'He's a conman. I'm supposed to like him.'

'He's a *rogue*,' she retorted.

Richard glanced up at her. 'I always thought women rather liked rogues.'

'Sometimes they're difficult not to like.'

He hesitated. 'I suppose so.'

Jenny waited, not quite sure where the conversation was leading.

Then, as so often, Richard abruptly changed the subject. Reaching across to his worktop, he picked up a sheet of the London Heritage stationery. 'It seems to me it's almost time to start reeling Jerricoe in. So, how would you like to be the executive director of conservation at London Heritage?'

Jenny beamed. 'Are you offering me a job?'

'In a manner of speaking.'

'When do I start?'

'Just as soon as you've got a new landline phone number.'

'Offer accepted.' Then, finishing her wine, Jenny bade him goodnight, and hurried back to finish painting her version of the conflagration in Pudding Lane for school the next day.

(iv)

When she'd gone, Richard regretted asking her about Harry. Questions could get in the way. The wrong answer could hurt. Sometimes it could destroy a life. He'd learned that lesson.

Getting up, he went to the window and looked sideways at the narrow, shining strip of the river, seeing nothing, remembering everything. When a marriage fails the past is never just the past. Its memories are a paperchase of pain. Dragging his mind into the present, he went into the bathroom and took a couple of paracetamols. Though his eye was healing, his ribs still ached. Then, returning to his worktop, he fed a sheet of the London Heritage stationery into his printer.

(v)

The annoying thing, Harry reflected later that night as he watched the arrivals' board in Terminal Four at Heathrow Airport, was that those two amateurs had no idea of the aggravation he'd been through trying to find a lawyer. By their very nature, lawyers were cautious people, and dodgy lawyers the most cautious of the breed, certainly cautious enough not to want to take on Mark Jerricoe and his associate thugs. The only reason Barney was up for it was because he'd been out of circulation for a while. He needed the work.

A second thing, and it had been mulling in his mind for weeks now, was that Jenny was just the sort of woman he might have gone for had he had a respectable job; had he, in fact, had any kind of job.

He could just picture her there in the kitchen making dinner when he got home from the bank or the office, two good looking children, probably now in their teens, mucking about on the lawn of the pleasant suburban house they would have lived in, the house she would have turned into a comfortable family home.

Sometimes they would have dinner parties for his colleagues and their wives as he continued to rapidly climb the slope of his profession, and he would smile proudly as she was justifiably complimented on her cooking and the décor of their home, all of which she'd organised.

How she found the energy to do everything, in addition to her teaching job and charity work for Age Gap, or whatever it was called, would fill him with admiration. And when their guests had all gone home, he would follow her to the welcoming, sparkling white duvet of their bed where they would have, as always, hours of passionate, creamy sex…

A change of information clicked up on the arrivals board. Passengers from the British Airways flight from Johannesburg were in the luggage reclamation hall.

Putting his thoughts of Jenny aside, he went to join the cab drivers and families at the arrivals gate.

41.

(i)

A letter was lying open on Hunt's desk when he got to the office. It was from London Heritage. Scrawled in capitals in purple felt-tip across the top in Mark Jerricoe's handwriting was the one word: *'SO???'*

Putting on his glasses, Hunt began to read.

Dear Mr Jerricoe

Re The River House, Wharf Lane, London SW23

We at London Heritage have received information from the Elspeth Worsley Society concerning the above property, which, we understand, is registered in the name of your company, Jerricoe Properties. As, I believe, you are aware this house is known to have been the home in the nineteenth century of that great London philanthropist and social reformer Elspeth Worsley.

As the current chairman of the Elspeth Worsley Society, Mr Charles Foster, has written to us expressing worries that the building is in imminent danger of being damaged by out of character renovations, we, too, are now concerned. It is rare that a house of this period, cultural heritage and quality, with so many of its original features intact, comes to our attention before its character is destroyed by modernisation.

We must therefore request that no further changes be made to the structure of this building, according to the provisions laid down by the Historic Buildings Act of 1977, until further investigations can be carried out to see whether it is of sufficient historical interest to warrant a preservation order.

I'm sure you will understand our concern and we look forward to your co-operation in this matter. If, however, we are given reason to believe that your company is not complying with the provisions of the Act, we must warn you that, as the house was built before 1840, it is within our regulatory rights to immediately apply to the High Court for an emergency injunction.

We will be in touch in due course to inform you of the date that we intend to begin our research on this building, although, I must warn you, we do have a current backlog. Should you perhaps wish to discuss this matter with me further, please feel free to telephone me on my direct line during normal office hours.

Yours sincerely

Tessa Patricks
Executive Director, Conservation
London Heritage

Hunt put the letter down. *Tessa Patricks*. Tessa! Why were these bossy bitches always called Tessa? Jesus!

A peripheral movement, as first one then the other Rhodesian ridgeback pushed his office door open, prompted him to look around.

Jerricoe was watching him. 'Well,' he rasped, 'you certainly put the frighteners on Mr Elspeth Worsley Society, didn't you! You put him off going to London Heritage all right! He must have been bloody terrified.'

'I don't get it…'

Jerricoe cut him off. 'Neither do I. But, he went, didn't he! And they're only about to put the block on us!'

'Vincent's boys said they gave him a good smacking.'

'It obviously wasn't good enough, was it! What's going on with you? No one's taking you seriously anymore. First the River House, and now this. You're supposed to fix these things.'

'I'll go and talk to them…to London Heritage. I'll sort it out. Nothing's gonna get blocked…'

Jerricoe snatched the letter up. 'Don't bother. I think you've sorted enough!'

And, with the dogs following, he left the room.

(ii)

It was the half-term holiday. In normal circumstances Jenny would have been enjoying a lie-in. But today she was at her desk, dressed, alert and nervous, with the din of an excavator in her ears as it levelled the garden wall at the side of the house.

She'd been trying to write mid-term reports on her class but had been finding it increasingly difficult to keep her mind focused. Looking away from her list of children, she picked up her phone to reassure herself that the new business number she'd added to her line was working.

'How can we be sure Jerricoe will phone and not write back to London Heritage?' she'd worried when she and Richard had composed Tessa Patricks' letter to Jerricoe Properties.

He'd had no doubts. 'Everything we know about Jerricoe tells us that when it comes to greed, he's dead rational. He's impulsive in everything he does, and he believes in the personal touch. So, the offer of Tessa Patricks' private line will be a hook he won't be able to resist.'

After writing the letter, he'd driven at night over to Jerricoe House to deliver it in one of Inky's London Heritage franked envelopes. When the staff arrived the following morning, which was always after the normal post had been delivered, it would have looked like any other letter.

Now, in the daylight gloom of her partly boarded-up basement flat, Jenny was nervous. If Richard was right, at some time in the next couple of days Jerricoe or Hunt would phone. She half wished Richard could be with her, but they'd agreed his presence would only make her self-conscious.

She was struggling to find a kind comment for a report on an unpromising little boy called Carl, when the klaxon blast of a barge on the river broke her concentration once again. It was close and long and quite deafening. But, when the noise suddenly ended, she found herself surprised by the quiet.

Then she realised. The diesel engine of the excavator, which had been rattling away in the garden all morning, had stopped. Crossing to the window, she peered through the gap that Richard had made for her in the boarding. The workmen were sitting down. The foreman was taking a call on his mobile. Abruptly, he put his phone away, and, after a short conversation, a cover was pulled over the seat and controls of the excavator. Casually, the workmen made their way from the site.

For a few moments the significance didn't hit her. Then her new phone number rang.

She settled herself and, on the fifth ring, she answered. 'Tessa Patricks!' she said abruptly.

There was a slightly awkward hesitation, and then: 'Er, Miss Patricks. My name's Jerricoe. Mark Jerricoe of Jerricoe Properties. You wrote to me about a property my company owns...the River House...'

The voice was softer, pitched higher, more boyish than she'd imagined. It didn't sound like the voice of a tyrant. 'Could you give me the reference number, please?' she asked curtly.

There was the sound of paper crackling, then: 'VHT-RH1000-TW' Jerricoe read out very carefully.

'Just a minute, please.' Putting the phone closer to her keyboard she began to type, paused, then typed some more. Then she picked up the phone again. 'Ah, yes. That would be the River House, Wharf Lane, London SW23?'

'That's right.'

'So, how can I help you, Mr Jerricoe?'

'Well, Jerricoe Properties, my company, has a lot of money tied up in this development, and, as you will appreciate, any delays can be very expensive.'

'I'm sorry. London Heritage can't be held responsible for any costs which might be incurred because of necessary investigations. You should have checked with us before you made any plans.'

'You and I need to meet,' Jerricoe came back bluntly. 'To talk.'

'At the moment, I'm afraid there's nothing for us to talk about. My office has only just become aware of the situation concerning this house. We will, of course, be in touch with you when a report has been made.'

'Just a few minutes! That's all I want. It really would help. If I could just explain the situation that we find ourselves in...'

'I'm sorry...'

'I'd be really very grateful.'

Could this wimpish, pleading voice belong to the man who'd terrorised them for months? 'Well...unfortunately, I'm afraid I'm completely blocked this week, and I'm going on leave for three weeks on Friday...' She liked that phrase. '*Going on leave*'. You only heard that in the armed services and from civil servants.

'That's okay, I'll come in today. What time would suit you?' he persisted.

'I'm sorry, I can't...'

'I'm sure there must be a way.' He wasn't giving in.

'Well, perhaps at the end of the day, it might...?'

'Perfect. What time?'

'Er, well... How does six-thirty sound?' she said.

'Six-thirty it is. I'll be there. St James's, right?'

'Yes. That's right. Just ask for me at reception. I'll see you at half past six, Mr Jerricoe.'

'I'll be there.'

The line went dead.

(iii)

'Bloody woman!' Jerricoe spat to himself. And stupid, bloody Hunt! What a waste of space he was! It was always the same. If you want something doing, do it yourself.

(iv)

'So, how do I look?' Jenny asked as she emerged from her bedroom.

A woman asking how she looked was a question that Richard hadn't faced in some time, but what Tessa Patricks of London Heritage would wear to work had been worrying Jenny all day. 'It can't be anything that's too glamorous or pretty,' she'd told him. 'And I don't want one of those power suits that women execs always wear in television series to show how tough they are. I haven't got one, anyway. On the other hand, it can't be too dowdy, and probably not anything too ethnic.'

In the end, she'd settled for the fitted bottle green jacket, loose skirt and white sneakers, with her hair clipped back by some old fashioned green and red butterfly clips.

Richard smiled. 'Perfect. Tessa Patricks looks the earnest-but-fun sort.'

'But as subtle as a tank when it comes to a bullying property developer!' she snapped.

He looked at her. She was an actress again.

The London Heritage offices were in a five storey Queen Anne house around the back of Green Park, opposite an equally ancient pub, the Unicorn, and next door to a wine bar.

Richard knew the Unicorn. 'I'll keep watch from across the street,' he told her as they drove there. 'Just in case.'

'In case of what?' she asked.

'In case I get thirsty.' And he passed her a leather document case stuffed with downloaded London Heritage documents. 'Enjoy your first day in your new job.'

They then parked several blocks away in an underground car park near Victoria Station and walked to St James's separately.

At just before six twenty-five, as Richard went into the pub, he looked over his shoulder and watched Jenny enter the London Heritage building.

42.

(i)

The reception area of London Heritage was a wide, darkly lacquered panelled room, on the walls of which hung photographs of old buildings saved from destruction by the efforts of the organisation, and a Fifties watercolour of the Festival of Britain. The place had, Jenny thought, the slightly faded atmosphere of the gritty worthwhile. While English Heritage and the National Trust did all the glamorous work, London Heritage took on the jobs which slipped between their various radars.

At the far end of the room, a middle-aged, uniformed porter with a grey ponytail was sitting at a desk reading *Uncut* magazine.

Jenny approached him. 'Excuse me, I wonder if Mr Jerricoe is still here?' she said quietly.

The porter looked up from his magazine. 'Jerricoe…? Jerricoe did you say?'

'That's right.'

'I don't think we've got a Jerricoe here. What department does he work in?'

'I'm afraid I can't say. Something to do with preservation, I believe.'

The porter laughed. 'Ah, well now, that could be just about anywhere in this place. Let's see now James…Jenner…Jones…' And he scrolled down a list of names on his computer screen.

Jenny looked at a clock over his head. It was six-thirty.

'No, I'm afraid there's no Jerricoe,' the porter said finally. 'Are you sure you weren't thinking of English Heritage? People often confuse the two.'

'Perhaps I was…'

But, as she spoke, she felt the sudden draught of the door opening. She turned around.

Mark Jerricoe was looking at her.

'Mr Jerricoe? Tessa Patricks! You're bang on time!' she said approvingly, marching towards him.

'Miss Patricks!'

She'd known he was a dyed blond, but he was also plump in his navy-blue suit with the delicate pin stripe. At his wrist was a clutch of jewels which she took to be a watch.

Half-turning, she threw a line back to the porter. 'It's all right. Problem solved. Thank you.'

And immediately she began to walk Jerricoe towards the door. 'I haven't got much time, but let's go next door to the wine bar, shall we? They're closing up here. You know how we civil servants are about time keeping.' Then, looking back at the porter, she called fondly: 'Good night, George.'

And before the puzzled chap, whose name was not George, could react to the unexpected familiarity, she'd led Jerricoe from the building.

(ii)

This heritage cow wasn't that bad looking for a civil servant, Jerricoe conceded, though typically dull looking clothes. Sitting at a table in the far corner of the wine bar, obviously well away from the prying ears of any of her colleagues who might have decided to have a drink before going home, he watched her taste the white wine. Yes, she wasn't bad, but she also had that holier-than-thou look that all these self-appointed guardians of the nation's traditions wore, the people who, because they couldn't do anything useful themselves, just wanted to stop everybody else.

'It's very kind of you to see me at such short notice…' he began after a cosy meander about what he suspected must be the great convenience of working in a place as central as St James's.

'Yes, well,' she nodded, with an expression that conveyed that she would like to get to the point quickly.

He did. 'You see, the property in question, the River House, was just about derelict when we bought it. It had been neglected for years by the previous owner, while all around that stretch of the river was being developed…'

'So, it was empty when you bought it…?'

'Oh, yes. There'd been tenants in the place, although God knows how they'd managed to survive there with the rats and dirt. But they'd all left by the time we got the place...'

'I see,' she said thoughtfully. 'But, of course, none of that affects our interest. Our responsibility is towards the house itself and its cultural heritage.'

Heritage! That bloody word that was ruining London. He wanted to snarl, but he said: 'Oh course. And I do understand your situation, Tessa, I honestly do. You don't mind if I call you Tessa, do you?' He dropped his voice for her first name.

She didn't look delighted. 'Well...' she murmured without encouragement.

He hurried on. 'But you must see our point. The fact is, as I told you, any delay resulting from your need to investigate and have a report drawn up will be very expensive for my company.'

'We have to follow procedure.'

'Oh, absolutely! I couldn't agree more. But, you know, when you've made your investigation, and the report has been written and everyone involved has read it and it's been through all the relevant committees, you'll find in our favour in the end. I'm sure of that. I mean, the local authority, Riverbank, had no problem.'

'I'm afraid London Heritage, and, as you know, we report directly to the mayor's office, have a different set of criteria from that of Riverbank. I only wish we'd been alerted rather more quickly to some of the abominations they allow. Tory council, of course.'

Jerricoe could feel his stomach buckling with frustration. What a sanctimonious, bloody Leftie she was! 'Let me get you another drink,' he said, although there was still some wine in her glass. And, without waiting for an answer, he headed to the bar to rethink his strategy.

(iii)

Jenny watched him go. There was something definitely porcine about him. All he needed was a trough. The Ghelanis and the Morrisons would have been interested to hear that the River House had been unoccupied when he'd bought it.

By the time Jerricoe returned with the drinks, he was smiling again. He continued smiling and staring at her as he sat down. It was unnerving.

'Yes?' she asked. 'Is there something wrong?'

'Well, it's just that…I'm sure I've seen you somewhere before.'

She felt the thump of fear. Had he been sneaking near the River House and spotted her? 'I don't think so,' she said quietly.

'Oh, yes. I never forget a face.' He examined her more closely. 'Perhaps we've passed on the street, or live near each other? Where do you live?'

'I…er…' Her mind blanked. 'Er…Hackney,' she said.

'Oh, trendy.'

The idiot was still staring at her.

'I'm sure I've seen you somewhere…Or is it just that you're a dead ringer for a young Cameron Diaz?' And he grinned widely.

She spluttered angrily on her drink. 'Oh, for heaven's sake!'

He realised his mistake instantly. The smile vanished. 'Ten thousand pounds.'

She didn't follow. 'I'm sorry?'

He took a quick look around: 'You just close your file on the property and…ten thousand pounds. What do you say? A nice little commission.'

She was astonished. 'I say we end this conversation.'

Jerricoe sighed, world wearily. 'Fifteen thousand.'

She shook her head, anger was bubbling. 'I don't think you…'

His face turned mean. 'How much then? Name your price.'

Fury now bit. 'Price? *Price?* I'm not for sale, Mr Jerricoe.'

'Oh, come on now.'

'No. *You* come on. You can't buy me just so that you can get your own way. Houses aren't just property, just bricks and mortar to be magicked into money. They're about history and culture and homes and people, people who've lived in them, and people who still live in them.' She realised she was raising her voice. That hadn't been the plan. She was supposed to be behaving professionally. But she was letting her anger get in the way.

His expression never changed. 'Twenty thousand.'

'Mr Jerricoe…'

'Twenty. Final offer. What do you say?'

She stood up, rigid with anger. 'Mr Jerricoe, London Heritage does not take bribes.' And, with that, she got up and left.

(iv)

From the window of the Unicorn, Richard saw Jenny leave the wine bar. Jerricoe left immediately after her, his BMW driving swiftly away in the opposite direction. Richard finished his drink.

'All right?' he asked, as he caught up with Jenny at the underground car park.

She pulled a face, then smiled. 'He's worried.'

(v)

Jerricoe didn't go back to the office. He had Angel drive him home to Notting Hill Gate. He was sticky with humiliation.

Same time tomorrow, Mr Jerricoe?' Angel asked as he dropped his boss off at his apartment block.

'And don't be late!' snapped Jerricoe. Then, crossing the forecourt and lobby, he stepped into the express lift to the penthouse suite.

How dare the bloody cow walk out on him, he was still ranting to himself as he closed his front door. Didn't she know who he was? Of course, she bloody did!

Pulling off his jacket, he threw it on to a white leather sofa and stared across the road at Kensington Gardens. Where did *she* live? Hackney. Typical! Probably she was in some former council house that she'd got her purer-than-pure hands on. And where did *he* live? In a penthouse in a brand-new apartment block. Jesus, it had to be one of the best sites in West London. And how had he got here? By bloody hard work.

Feeling in his top pocket he searched for the 5mm yellow Valium he always kept there for stressful times and quickly swallowed it.

He wished now he'd sent Hunt to meet her. First Greensleeves and now this blasted River House. It was never ending. He'd have to spend the next six months being humiliated behind his back by this goody-goody socialist. By tomorrow she'd be blagging all round London Heritage about how she'd turned down a bribe from Mark Jerricoe. He'd deny it, of course.

He stared out across Kensington Gardens. It was dark, but he could just make out the chimneys of Kensington Palace behind the trees. That wasn't a bad address; not a bad freehold. It was smarter than Buckingham Palace, really, which he always thought looked like a museum. Kensington Palace had class.

Turning around, he considered his sitting room. His mother always complained that it looked bare and empty when she came to visit. That was because it was new. He hesitated in his train of thought. It would always be *new*, always be modern. New was where the money was these days: but old, like Kensington Palace, was *class*.

He thought about that for a while, then, turning back, he looked at the lights of the cars making their way to and from the West End. How old had the guy said Creswell Manor was?

Then, going through into his kitchen, he looked in the fridge for a packet of pasta for his dinner.

43.

Barney, the lawyer, was a surprise. A moth-eaten sort of chap, he was sitting enjoying the February sunshine on a bench in Middle Temple Gardens, while barristers scurried past to the Inns of Court just across the Strand.

'Hello, Barney,' Harry said gently.

The lawyer looked up from his *Racing Post* and smiled fondly through thick-lensed glasses. 'Harry, old boy. Good to see you again.'

'This is Richard, Barney, the lunatic I spoke to you about,' Harry introduced, as the other man put his sandwiches and newspapers away in a battered black briefcase. 'And this, Richard, is the famous Barney Penn.'

Barney stood politely to shake hands. He must have been in his mid-sixties, his thick, iron-grey hair rebelliously tufting at the sides, his double-breasted suit shining with age, a college tie faded. What must once have been a handsome face was now a *vin rosé* delta of broken veins.

At Barney's suggestion, they went to a wine bar in Fleet Street. It being too early to pretend that a drink was lunch, they found a corner table where he ordered an expensive claret. 'So, this conveyancing caper you mentioned,' he began. 'Are we buying or selling?'

'Both, actually,' Harry answered.

'Jolly good.'

'Well, not exactly,' Richard cautioned.

'You said it's a big job?' Barney looked back at Harry.

'Very big,' Harry confirmed.

'Tell me.'

Carefully Richard explained the situation with Jerricoe Properties as Barney listened, breaking in occasionally to elicit more information.

'Ah, the classic doubles games?' he said as Richard finished.

'But buying and selling on the same day.'

'Trickier, of course,' Barney said.

Richard agreed. 'It seems to me that to make it work we need to create what look like two law firms, one representing the sellers of Creswell Manor and the other representing the buyers of the River House.'

Barney nodded agreement. 'And you're certain that Jerricoe will agree to sell the River House?'

'Not yet. But if he doesn't the whole con is off. The River House is the entire point. We don't want Jerricoe's money if we can't buy the River House with it.'

Barney looked at Harry, a glaze of confusion in his eyes.

Harry shrugged. 'Tell me about it. I've had months of this.'

The lawyer refilled his glass. 'Unorthodox. But… all right, we'll just have to make jolly sure he does sell the River House, won't we! Go on.'

'We'll also need two new bank accounts…'

'Richard knows about finance,' Harry interrupted.

'Handy,' approved Barney. Then, getting into the spirit of it all, he continued: 'You'll also need two sets of new identities for you and the schoolteacher, which means false passports, addresses, birth certificates and utility bills.'

Richard was nodding in agreement. 'Inky's already on to that,' Richard said. The ease with which Inky had been able to create false identities had astonished him.

'Very good. Inky's no fool.' Suddenly Barney hesitated.

'Yes?' Richard asked.

'There's just one other thing. If I am to become involved, I'm going to need an advance to pay for various sundries.'

'Sundries?'

'An office, computers, phones, a telecoms expert who understands the value of silence….'

'And you're sure you can get one?'

Barney smiled. 'There's nothing in this world that you can't get, if you know where to look and can come up with appropriate financial inducement. Isn't that right, Harry.'

The two men chuckled.

'How much do you need?' Richard asked.

'Twenty thousand pounds.'

Richard was surprised. 'So much?'

'So much!' was the take-it-or-leave-it reply.

Richard looked from Barney to Harry. Could he trust these people? Why should he? Sitting here, one on either side of him, they were smiling, but they were crooks. Criminals. He could find the money, but if he paid Barney this twenty thousand, he would, with Inky's and Harry's advances, already have spent more than the scam's entire budget.

Jerricoe was his target. But how did he know that Harry and his friends hadn't made Jenny and him their targets in a con of their own?

Across the table Harry was playing nonchalantly with a lock of hair, as if reading Richard's thoughts.

Richard still pondered. On the other hand, would they throw up the chance of a very big pay day with a long con with Jerricoe the mark, by settling for a much smaller amount if he was the mark?

Well, they might, he heard himself answer as he watched Barney refilling his glass. In the end, the decision was easy. Having come so far, he had no alternative.

'All right! Twenty thousand pounds advance against 4 per cent,' he agreed. He wouldn't tell Jenny the figures. She would only want to contribute more, and she couldn't afford it. He was glad that she was at school today and not around to argue. She had a habit of winning arguments.

Barney's watery eyes seemed to flush over as the arrangement was agreed. 'Splendid. Leave it to me, old boy. And now what about another bottle?' And, without waiting for an answer, he held up his hand to the waiter.

'Yes, he's a drunk,' Harry admitted as he and Richard left Charing Cross Station at the end of the afternoon, having helped Barney on to his train to Purley.

'You should have told me,' Richard worried. After an encouraging start, the afternoon had achieved less and less.

'No, I shouldn't. If I had, you'd have wanted someone else. Barney won't let us down.'

'What was he in jail for?'

'For getting caught…as everybody in jail always is,' Harry retorted irritably as they crossed the cobbles of the station forecourt. 'And you can bet he won't do that again in a hurry.'

He stopped by a waiting taxi on a rank. 'Now, if you'll excuse me, I have to leave you.'

'Can I give you a lift anywhere?' Richard's car was parked in the multi-storey at Trafalgar Square. 'I'm going over to see Inky.'

Harry shook his head. 'No thanks. I'm off to catch up with an old friend. See you tomorrow. My love to the lovely Jenny!' And, with a sly tick of a smile, he climbed into the cab and slammed the door.

Richard watched the cab pull out of the forecourt and head away towards the West End. Who exactly was Harry, he wondered, as he often did. Where did he come from? Where did he go? Who did he see? Was Harry even his real name? He didn't know any more about him now than he did when they'd met on that carol singing day.

Inky was at his desk when Richard reached the railway arches. Glueing a light cotton bag to the back of a rectangular shaped mouth of sheer transparent plastic, he was, as usual, in no mood for conversation.

A large photograph of the red post box that stood down the street from the Jerricoe Properties headquarters was pinned to a cork wall in front of him.

'I brought our passport photographs,' Richard said, passing the forger an envelope.

Inky nodded. There was another silence.

'You've known Harry a long time, haven't you?'

Still nothing.

'He's quite a character. A real enigma! I mean, he never says very much about himself.'

'She's a bit of a looker, isn't she?'

'Sorry?' He turned towards Inky, who, had now opened the envelope and was looking at the photographs of Jenny and Richard.

'Interesting bones. Ever do any modelling? Life class, sort of thing?'

'Er...not that I know.'

'No? Well, just a thought.' Then Inky returned to the cotton bag. 'This looks about right. It'll be ready when you are.'

Yes, Jenny was a bit of a looker, Richard thought, as he made his way back to his car. But irrational though it was, Inky's comment bothered him. Should he be amused that Inky had imagined Jenny nude modelling for him, instead of being jealous that the forger had even imagined it.

He drove home via South Kensington. An advertisement in the classified advertisements at the back of *Private Eye* had caught his attention. It was for a shop called Best Address in the Old Brompton Road, a one room poste restante. There for £200 a month, paid in advance in cash, he rented a letter box under the name Lathom and Greenaway.

An up-market address was important in the property game, even when it consisted only of a locked metal box and a key.

44.

(i)

The arrival of Barney had changed everything, Jenny felt as she looked around the white-walled office over a kebab shop that the lawyer had rented in Bayswater's Westbourne Grove. She and Richard were now completely in the hands of professional criminals.

By degrees, they had both become part of a criminal fraternity, and she wondered if that was how a life of crime started.

Barney, gentlemanly and calm, was accompanied by a silent young technician in a very old Radiohead T-shirt, as he oversaw the installation of two computers and two phone lines.

'This is Barney at his best,' Harry whispered as he stood very close to Jenny. 'He's setting up a couple of virtual legal practices. It'll all disappear just as quickly when it's no longer needed. You'll see. Magic!'

From the shop below came the smell of sizzling lamb. Reminded of food, Jenny, in a blouse and tweed jacket, wondered whether the young student on teaching practice would be able to cope without her. She'd never taken the afternoon off school before.

On the other side of the office, Richard was leaning over a desk examining a folder of documents that Inky had brought in. Other than when he'd worn his young fogey Elspeth Worsley outfit, it was the first time Jenny had seen him in a suit and tie.

'Okay, here you go,' Richard said, handing her a passport and a sheaf of documents. 'Birth certificate, gas bill, tax demand from HMRC, a bank account number and an RBK&C council tax bill all for Jessica Anne Lathom. That's you. I'm Michael Paul Greenaway and we live together, unmarried, in the Old Brompton Road, South Kensington, London SW10.'

Jenny nodded, as she looked at the photograph of herself in the back of the passport. Seeing it alongside the name of Jessica Anne Lathom was unnerving.

'Or, to put it another way,' Richard continued, 'together we're Lathom and Greenaway, the names of our imaginary legal firm who will be representing the imaginary trustees in the sale of Creswell Manor.'

Jenny nodded. She knew the plan by heart. Richard had been working at his computer for weeks, drawing on his banking knowledge of offshore facilities.

'It's like looking at life from the opposite side. I was a fireman when I worked in the City,' he liked to joke. 'Now I'm planning to light a fire that no-one else will be able to see.'

'And you're sure you can do it?' she'd asked.

'Yes,' he'd said.

Barney was watching her. 'Just look at it this way,' he began softly. 'Lathom and Greenaway is the name of the law firm to whom the money will be sent when Jerricoe buys Creswell Manor. That's you and Richard, aka Lathom and Greenaway. We could hardly use your real names. And, despite our long-standing friendship, Richard didn't want the money sent to Harry, Inky and me!'

Even Inky half managed a smile at that.

'Right,' she nodded.

Harry smiled. 'It has to be complicated, or everyone would be selling houses they don't own, and then where would we be?'

'Unemployed,' chimed Barney.

Apart from Richard, who was anxiously looking at his watch, everyone laughed. 'I think it's about time,' he said. 'Are you ready?'

Jenny nodded.

'Good luck,' Barney smiled.

Harry caught Jenny's eye. He was smiling at her.

(ii)

Richard didn't feel like talking as the taxi made its way past St Paul's Cathedral and on through the City. At his side, Jenny was silently watching workers hurrying between the towers of finance. Was she finally having regrets about taking on Jerricoe, he worried.

So far, the biggest crimes they'd committed had been a few fibs and a couple of cases of impersonation; nothing very serious. But if they went any further, they would, in the eyes of the law, be serious criminals. Was that what he still wanted: what Jenny wanted? Because Jerricoe was morally wrong in trying to force them out of their homes, did it make them morally right to try to swindle him? He knew it didn't. But…their anger and emotions had told them something different.

The taxi was already drawing into a lane off Bishopsgate. It stopped outside a narrow Georgian building that looked as if it had been squeezed between two much bigger financial giants. A discreet plaque on the wall told of a 200-year banking legend: Cornish-Callendar. Inside the bank, a junior manager would be waiting to greet them as Michael Paul Greenaway and Jessica Anne Lathom. When he'd worked in banking, part of Richard's job had been spotting fraudsters…people like the man he now found himself to be.

He looked at Jenny. 'All right?'

'You mean, am I still sure I want to go on with this?' she asked.

'Well...' he hesitated.

'Come on. Let's just do it.'

Then, climbing out of the taxi, she waited as Richard paid the driver and joined her outside the bank's reinforced glass doors.

(iii)

'So, that's Michael Paul Greenaway and Jessica Anne Lathom…' A ginger haired, junior banker nodded, as he read out their application forms, simultaneously checking their names on the documents they'd given him.

Jenny glanced around the room as she sipped her tea. She'd never been in a merchant bank before, but clearly the rich got a lot more attention than she did with her online account.

The young banker, meanwhile, was going through the paperwork that Inky had provided. 'Let's see now…passports, birth certificates… utilities… more utilities…splendid…splendid! So much paperwork and security checks these days. Government regulations to prevent money laundering and all that. But you don't look like a couple of terrorist or drug barons to me. Ha! Ha!'

Jenny and Richard smiled dutifully.

'As I told you on the phone, Jessica's…my partner's grandmother died recently and…' Richard began, indicating Jenny.

'Yes, I'm so sorry,' replied the banker.

'Thank you,' Jenny returned with a sad little smile. 'We've sold her house in the country, and we're waiting for a rather large sum of money.'

'Yes! So, I understand. And you're wanting to open a joint account…as Lathom and Greenaway. You almost sound like a firm of solicitors.' The young banker laughed again.

'Don't we!' agreed Jenny.

So, it went politely on, until at last the young banker said: 'Now, let's see…what else can we do for you?' the banker wanted to know.

'Er…the availability of electronic same-day facilities. I mentioned it in my letter,' Richard reminded.

'Of course, of course. No problem there…'

Jenny smiled and wondered whether she and Richard had struck the young banker as a pleasant middle-aged couple. She hoped so.

It was an ordeal, but an hour and fifteen minutes later, after completing innumerable forms and identity checks that was it. They had a joint account in the name of Lathom and Greenaway with the Cornish-Callendar Bank.

'You'll be hearing from us within the next few days when the checks have gone through,' the banker said, 'officially informing you that the account is open and providing you with details of your online status, and all the other safeguards you'll be needing. Welcome to Cornish-Callendar. I hope you enjoy doing business with us.'

'I'm sure we will,' thanked Jenny.

(iv)

They were both giddy with relief as they emerged back into the street. 'There you go, all those years working in banking turned out useful after all,' Jenny said, digging Richard playfully in the ribs as they walked back towards Bishopsgate.

'The one useful thing you learn when you work in any institution is how to subvert the system,' Richard agreed. 'And banks are greedy. Promise them a big deposit, speak nicely and snow them with information and the hint of more money, and they usually give you an easy time. Hence the welcome mat for the dodgy Russian oligarchs and their warrens of offshore accounts.'

'And our checks…the ones we gave him?'

'They'll all be fine. Banks usually only start getting jumpy when you turn up with a suitcase full of readies.'

'I'll remember that next time a Vladimir gives me a suitcase full of roubles!' Jenny laughed.

It was a sunny, if cold and windy day, so at Richard's suggestion they decided to go home by river taxi from the little jetty at Blackfriars. The boat was stuffed with tourists which meant they couldn't sit together as it chopped its way up the Thames, past the London Eye and Westminster, and then on upstream.

Richard was disappointed. He'd wanted these moments to relax and just enjoy being together with Jenny. Instead, they gazed out separately across the water at the tranquil grandeur of London, hundreds of years of history in property, arranged, as if for their inspection, along either bank.

Just past Chelsea Harbour, as the boat crossed from the north side of the Thames to the south and pushed on towards Wandsworth pier, he caught Jenny looking at him. He'd seen that look before at New Year. But what her expression said…he couldn't be sure, and, he was reminded of a sudden thought he'd had while the junior banker had been looking at the passports of Michael Paul Greenaway and Jessica Anne Lathom. Had the guy thought they suited each other as a couple, he'd asked himself, and, for a moment, he glanced away from Jenny, reflecting on that. Had she thought that, too?

When he looked back, Jenny had turned away and was watching the gulls swooping over the boat.

She went to collect her bicycle from the repair shop when they got home. Richard telephoned Harry. It was time to jerk the Creswell Manor bait.

45.

(i)

Harry stopped walking when he reached the copse of trees. Somewhere above him in the branch of an oak a blackbird was protesting his invasion of its territory. Perfect. Taking out his phone, he pressed for Jerricoe's private line.

'Hello!'

'Good morning, Mr Jerricoe. Harry Culshaw. How are you today!' His voice sang with confidence.

'Get to the point,' Jerricoe snapped.

'I'm down here at Creswell Manor and I believe I have some very good news for you.'

'I'm waiting.'

'Well, my clients have accepted your offer of nine million pounds for the property.'

There was at first a silence down the phone. Then: 'Didn't I say you could do it?' Jerricoe laughed.

'It was a tricky business. There was some other interest, I believe, but…'

'Bollocks!'

'Yes, well…' Harry changed the subject. 'You know, it's lovely down here in the Cotswolds this afternoon. Absolutely beautiful spot. It's a little late in the day now, but I'll get on to the vendors' lawyers, Lathom and Greenaway, right away and ask them to get in touch with you.'

'You do that.'

'Absolutely. Anyway, congratulations. Bye for….'

But Jerricoe had already hung up.

Putting his phone in his pocket, Harry began the quarter of a mile trek from the birdsong of Battersea Park to the rush hour racket of a South London main road.

He hoped Jerricoe had heard the blackbird. It had been quite a trudge for a bit of rustic background sound.

(ii)

Jerricoe pushed his head around Hunt's door, one of the dogs behind him.

'What did I say! Nine million for Creswell Manor. Accepted!'

'They agreed?' Hunt was astonished.

'Of course, they agreed. That Harry Culshaw's a greedy little bugger, but no fool. So, let's nail it down before word leaks out.'

Hunt grimaced. 'I'm not sure about this, Mark. Maybe we should...'

He didn't get any further. 'You're not sure! You're never damn well sure!' Jerricoe snapped. 'That's why you'll always be an overpaid dogsbody because you're never bloody sure of anything. How anyone who pretends to be in property can't be sure when we're snapping up a fifteen million pound property for less than two-thirds of that, I don't know. Didn't they teach sums at your school? Add-ups and take-aways? Obviously not. So, I'll tell you. Fifteen million minus nine million means we're six million up on the deal. Right? Now just bloody well do what I pay you to do and get on to it.' And he banged out of the room. The dog followed.

Hunt's eyes went to the drip of saliva on the floor that the dog had left. Disgusting! He'd been on the end of a Jerricoe tongue lashing before, far worse than this. But the guy was getting nastier. The chance of getting his hands on a posh piece of English history was going to his head.

Ah, well, sod him! This overpaid dogsbody would do what he was paid to do. And leaning forward he left a message for his secretary: 'Can we draw up the usual correspondence for searches on Creswell Manor, Creswell, Oxfordshire.'

Hopefully the searches would unearth something that would put Jerricoe off the bloody place. Then they could get back to the bricks and mortar London they knew about.

46.

(i)

'What is it you always say about a scam?' Richard asked. He was sitting in a hired van, staring fifty yards down the road at the brick block that was the counting house of Jerricoe Properties.

'Lots of things,' replied Harry. 'Some of them I even believe. But you probably mean the bit about scams succeeding when the predictable occurs…'

'And failing when it doesn't,' came in Barney.

'Predictability over probability,' Richard murmured to himself, and looked at his watch.

Harry noticed. 'It's only just half past five. She'll show. She always does.'

As if she'd heard, at that moment the front door of Jerricoe House opened and the secretary began to trudge, head down behind a brown umbrella, into the rain.

'There's our girl,' cheered Harry. 'Loyal as a leach and a brilliant timekeeper. Fifty quid says that she likes Quality Street chocolates and goes to Saturday matinees of West End musicals.'

Richard ignored him. The secretary was now approaching the corner, where she stopped, opened her large handbag, took out a wad of letters and popped them into the post-box. Closing her bag, she then continued up the adjoining road towards the bus stop.

Richard waited until her view was obscured by the bend in the road, then pulled the car forward to the corner.

Harry was ready. Climbing out, he swiftly put his hands to the mouth of the post-box, lifted sharply and tugged. As he did, the see-through mould of the post-box's lips came away, pulling with them Inky's attached white cotton bag. In seconds he was back in the car.

'Neat job, Inky!' Harry complimented as Richard accelerated away.

In the back seat, Inky grunted a vague acknowledgment.

'Anything there?' Richard asked.

Opening the cotton bag, Harry riffled through the day's outgoing mail from Jerricoe Properties. 'No…no…no…no… Ah, yes. Here we are. This looks like it, Oxfordshire County Council…and another…to….' He pulled out two envelopes, opened them and passed them to Barney.

Putting on his glasses, Barney began to read the first letter. *"Dear Sir, re Creswell Manor…"* It's from their lawyer, Craig Hunt. He wants to know about…let's see…boundaries, utilities, history of any flooding, drainage, proposed developments, ancient titles, any restrictive covenants, rights of way, roads, restrictions on use, all the usual.' He turned to the second letter. 'And this one's addressed to the District Land Registry, asking, as the estate has never been registered, if there are any cautions against first registrations. I'll give Jerricoe Properties one thing. They're quick off the mark.'

'Ancient titles? D'you think you could manage those, Inky?' said Richard.

'Give me the words and I'll give you the Dead Sea Scrolls,' he replied.

A half mile down the road, Richard stopped the car at another post-box and Harry reposted the rest of Jerricoe Properties' outgoing mail. Only two letters interested them.

Jerricoe was being gently drawn in, but it was only now that Richard appreciated the skills of his new colleagues. Harry might be a smooth front man, but the legal confidence of Barney and artistic wizardry of Inky equally dazzled. In his studio in the railway arches, surrounded by ordnance survey maps and examples of Oxfordshire County Council and utility company letterheads, Inky set about creating the searches for Creswell Manor, together with deeds and scrolls, and letters of authority for the sale from the other two trustees. While, in his instant office above the kebab shop, Barney began a legal correspondence with Jerricoe Properties on Lathom and Greenaway stationery, using the poste restante address Richard had acquired in South Kensington.

Nothing fazed them. Quite why they hadn't pursued honest careers, Richard didn't understand. In honest careers they would have done well.

With little to offer at this stage, Richard retreated to his worktop at the River House. A couple of eighteenth-century miniature portraits needed some delicate restoration, and just to be doing something that he loved relaxed him. This was how it had been when Jenny had first come knocking on his door.

Jenny! Each day when she got home from school, she would come to see how he was, and he would wait for the light tap of her footsteps on the stairs. He thought about her as he worked, remembering her composure at the bank, and wondering about that look she'd given him on the river taxi. Then he pictured her in class with the children, and how, on her bike, she'd caught up with him while he'd been out running along the river, her face, pink and determined in the cold.

Exactly when had he fallen in love with her? Not when they'd first met, for sure. He'd been determined not to fall in love with anyone ever again then. Not when she'd worried about Jerricoe's threats, either. He'd thought she was just being difficult.

Somewhere along the way, though, they'd begun to get along, and gradually they'd become friendly as housemates. Then friends. And over the months he'd begun to look forward to seeing her every evening. The River House, with its scaffolding and blocked windows, didn't look much like a home, but her presence in it had made it feel like one.

And now? How do you go about telling a friend that you're in love with her? What if that wasn't what she wanted to hear? He'd got it wrong once before. Badly wrong. What if he were to make a sudden declaration, and she replied along the lines of, 'That's very sweet, Richard, but....'

He couldn't have taken it. Yet, alone with his work, the compulsion to do something remained. He eventually chose a mild, sunny evening. But when, for once, Jenny didn't come up to see him after school, he phoned down to her flat.

'I was just wondering,' he said, 'if you've nothing planned for tonight, no lesson to prepare or anything, perhaps the chairman of the Elspeth Worsley Society might take the executive in charge of conservation at London Heritage out to dinner.'

As soon as he'd spoken, he felt a fool. Why had he said all that nonsense? Why make such a big deal out of asking for a date, if that was even what it was?

He recognised the catch in her voice immediately. 'Richard, that would be lovely... But... I just can't tonight. Any other night, yes. But I...er... I mean, just not tonight.' She was stammering with embarrassment.

Immediately, he withdrew. 'Oh, that's all right. It was just a thought...'

'It's a nice thought. Really nice!'

'Right.' He hesitated. 'We'll do it another night.'

'Yes.'

47.

(i)

Harry was on the phone when she arrived at his flat, opening the door to her at the same time as saying goodbye to a caller. 'Jenny!' he beamed. 'More beautiful than ever! Just one second!' Then, turning back to the phone as he closed the front door, he said: 'I have to go, Roger. Something wonderful just turned up. Call you tomorrow. Okay?' And he hung up.

She felt awkward. She'd got there slightly early.

'Sorry, an old friend,' he apologised as he showed her into his living room. Taking her coat, he looked at her mischievously. 'You're different tonight. What is it? New dress? No. I know. It's the Alice band in your hair. I've never seen that before.'

She was sure she blushed. 'It isn't a new dress,' she said, quickly. The smell of roast duck was coming from the kitchen.

It was the first time she'd been to Harry's place. A small table was set for two. None of the glasses, or knives and forks matched, but the cutlery was bone handled. A bottle of Sancerre was already open. Paper napkins with 'Savoy' inscribed on them lay on side plates. Two candles glowed. The only other light was coming from a 40-watt standard lamp.

Stepping towards the mantelpiece, her eyes were drawn to the nude painting above it.

Harry passed her a glass of wine. 'What do you reckon?'

'Very nice.'

'I call her Jenny.

'Really!' She turned away. She knew she shouldn't be, but she was almost flattered. That was why she'd come, why, when he'd phoned, two days earlier, she'd been aware, despite herself, of a ripple of excitement. She'd wanted to tell Richard, but she hadn't. She hadn't known how to, although she was pretty sure he wouldn't have cared. That was just the way he was.

Harry was talking. 'Anyway, make yourself at home. How was your day at school?'

She sat on the only armchair. 'You don't really want to know about school.'

'I do if you want to tell me. Do you want to tell me?'

She shook her head. 'Why don't you tell me something about yourself instead? You never have done.'

'You wouldn't be interested?'

'Why not?'

He shrugged, in a gesture of self-deprecation. 'Well…I'm a crook, aren't I!'

'You weren't always a crook. What about your childhood, for instance? What was that like?'

'Childhood, wow! Let's see. I suppose I was from an ordinary family. An only child in a happy home.' He paused. 'Until I was eleven.'

'Only until then?'

'Well, yes. My parents died, you see.'

'*Both* your parents died?'

'Sadly. In a car crash. It was terrible. Then I was farmed out to an aunt and uncle who had this appalling son. It was all rather gruesome, until I was suddenly packed off to a sort of gothic boarding school. Actually, that was all right. I made a couple of pals there, a boy and a girl, and we had loads of adventures and…'

'Were you any good at Quidditch?'

'I'm sorry?'

'You've just borrowed Harry Potter's childhood.'

'Ah…have I! Oh, well, he must have gone to the same school.'

She had to smile. Harry was a rascal, but he never failed to amuse. 'Do you *ever* tell the truth about *anything*?' she asked.

He gave her a sly grin. 'Do you always tell the truth about everything?'

She hesitated. 'Perhaps not quite always.'

'Not quite always…' he echoed. 'Well, now…'

(ii)

He was surprised that she'd agreed to come. But, where women were concerned, you never could tell, he'd been thinking, as he'd put the duck into the oven to keep it warm. He had no idea what might happen this evening, but, as with everything, romance and sex was a percentages game. Just getting her to his place was a ninety per cent step forward.

He'd been pursuing her for weeks, flattering, paying her little attentions. Sometimes, he hardly knew when he was doing it. He could see that Richard, on the other hand, found it more difficult, although it was clear to him, if not to Jenny, that he was crazy about her. That, though, was Richard's problem.

The fact was, she was a very attractive woman, and, as so often happened, the better he'd got to know her, the prettier she'd become.

'I'm sorry that I don't have any chopsticks for the rice. Like most of my belongings they're in storage,' he apologised as he served the duck and wild rice on to their two plates and brought them from the kitchen.

'I'm rubbish with chopsticks anyway,' Jenny said with such disarming honesty that for a moment he almost regretted the lie about the storage.

So, their dinner for two began in a jolly way as he told her about his time in Vietnam, where he'd learned to cook while working as a sous-chef in Hanoi, before the conversation moved on to the kind of geography she taught at school. Normally in these situations, that is, dinner with a pretty woman, he would have been wondering at what point he could work the conversation around to sex. But Jenny always seemed to block that route. What she wanted to talk about was Jerricoe.

'You know, if...*when*...all this works out, Jerricoe will be after you as the front man,' she said, as they moved on to the grapes. 'I mean, you're the only one of us he knows.'

'Do we have to talk shop tonight?'

'But it's true,' she persisted. 'You must have considered it. You'll be in real danger.'

This was getting better. 'You're worried for me!'

'Not worried, just curious as to what your plans are for staying in one piece. I'd be worried if you haven't made any plans, because, when he catches up with you and tortures you horribly, you might reveal the identities of Richard and me.'

He laughed at that. 'Well, let's put it this way: I've always fancied Brazil.' And, getting up, he began to clear the plates. 'Coffee?' he called from the tiny kitchen.

But she was already beside him, holding the remainder of the plates, and smiling now at the Restaurant de Saigon packets from Putney High Street. They must have arrived by Deliveroo before she got there and were now lying on top of the waste bin.

'With milk,' she said. 'And I didn't for one minute believe you'd cooked dinner or ever been to Vietnam or worked as a sous-chef.'

'Well spotted,' he said, not at all abashed, and, filling the kettle, he leant across to open the tiny fridge, accidentally trapping her against a wall. 'But have *you* ever been to Rio?' And he reached for the milk.

'No.'

'It'll be Carnival soon.' And putting the milk on to the Formica work surface, he leaned back to her and kissed her on the cheek.

'Er, Harry.' She moved from one foot to the other, but there was no way past him.

He didn't move. 'Yes?' And he kissed her again, this time his lips brushing the side of her neck.

She looked at her wrist. 'You know, I think it would be better if…'

'We went somewhere more…comfortable? Good idea! I was wondering when you were going to suggest that.'

'If I went home.'

'It's comfortable here, too, you know. Modest, I admit, but comfortable.'

'It's very late. I have to be up for school tomorrow.'

'Ah, you schoolteachers! Did I ever tell you how I fell in love with my teacher when I was seven. Or was she in love with me? She certainly behaved as though she was. I think I told her I was too young to go-steady.'

And this time he kissed her on her lips.

She didn't pull back. 'No,' she replied when they parted, 'you didn't tell me that. And if you had, I wouldn't have believed that either.'

He now had his arms around her, his hands resting on the small of her back. 'I'll tell you one thing you can believe,' he murmured in her ear.

'Which is?'

'You've got lovely little ear lobes.'

She smiled. 'Your problem, Harry, isn't just that you con everyone, you con yourself as well.'

'Which only goes to show how good I am,' he said and kissed her again.

48.

Richard heard the taxi as it brought her home. It was just getting light. He didn't want to, but he couldn't help looking at his watch. It was ten past six in the morning. He'd worked right through the night.

He sat quite still for some time. He'd guessed where she'd been; whom she'd been seeing. Had it been anyone other than Harry, she would have told him. It hurt.

Why hadn't he told her, or somehow shown her how he felt about her, weeks ago, months earlier?

Shortly after eight he heard her leave for school. The house felt empty without her.

49.

Jerricoe viewed the correspondence that was spread across Hunt's desk. 'Tell me,' he said.

'The searches on Creswell Manor. They came this morning.'

'And?'

Hunt adjusted his glasses and began to read through the main points. 'Grade 1 listed, one hundred and five acres…three cottages… no motorways planned or extensions to airport runways… unregistered as built before the 1925 Land Registration Act…considerably before…buyer will be the first person to register it. Utilities… electricity, gas, water and sewage services… they're all here. Town And Country Planning Act…greenbelt protection Act 2005… Some special provisions under Wildlife and Countryside Act… But, other than that, all the usual. No problems I can see.'

'In other words, clean as a Muslim bride.'

Hunt flinched at the simile. 'Apparently. A prompt reply, too.'

Jerricoe picked up the covering letter on the Oxfordshire County Council notepaper. 'That's because they know who they're dealing with. Okay. Let's get back on to the trustees' lawyers. What's their name…?'

'Lathom and Greenaway.'

'Right. Hurry this one through! Okay!'

'Don't you think we should take another look at it, Mark? It's a lot of money we're talking here.'

'And worth much more.'

'All the same…'

'For Christ's sake, just do it!' Jerricoe was irritated. 'Exchange the bloody contracts! Haven't we got enough to worry about with that Greensleeves cock-up, rent arrears, and London Heritage now poking their noses into our affairs. I know what I saw. A fifteen-million-pound estate available at nine million. That, to me, is a good deal. We could move it on next week. Just bloody well buy it.' And, with that, he stomped off back upstairs.

Hunt sighed. The guy had bought on sight dozens of times before, trusting his instinct, and he'd invariably done well out of his deals. Why should he pay attention to anyone else when he was always right?

Turning to his Creswell Manor file, he looked through his correspondence for Lathom and Greenaway. If Jerricoe wanted to buy a poncy, country estate, he'd get it for him.

50.

(i)

Richard's car wasn't outside the River House when Jenny got back from school. She was relieved. She'd seen his light on when she'd got back that morning, and had felt a stab of...

What was it? Guilt? No, it wasn't guilt. She had nothing to be guilty about. Not regret either. There was nothing to regret.

Was there?

Duplicity, perhaps. By seeing Harry alone, had she risked the balance of the relationships between the three of them? Or was it something deeper, the betrayal of her friendship with Richard? Or something deeper still?

When Harry had asked her to dinner, had she considered that the evening might end in sex? And, if it had, why not? She was a single woman. She'd had one-night-stands before and enjoyed them. She had no commitment to Richard. He'd never shown any romantic interest in her. Had he?

She was watching the six o'clock news when her phone rang.

It was Harry. 'I just wanted to say...I hope you got home safely and that you weren't too tired at school today.'

'I was fine.' She couldn't think what to say. 'Thank you for...for dinner. You don't know where Richard is, do you?'

He didn't. But he would have picked up the anxiety in her voice, she knew that. They didn't say much more.

She heard Richard return at around midnight, listened to his footsteps on the garden path, and his key in the door. This time it was her light that was on. He must have seen it. But he didn't come down.

The following day was Saturday. She'd become used to Richard wandering down in the mid-morning for coffee. She waited for him. He didn't come. At mid-day she heard him go out. After that the afternoon passed slowly.

Harry phoned again in the evening, inviting her to the cinema

'Thanks for the thought, but I'm really busy tonight,' she told him.

'What about tomorrow then?'

'Tomorrow's difficult, too, Harry.'

'Ah.' She could hear disappointment in his voice. 'You know, I really enjoyed the other night. I mean…I really did. The whole evening. It was…good.' His tone surprised her. He sounded as though he meant it.

'I enjoyed it, too,' she said. 'Speak to you next week.'

It was the Sunday evening before she and Richard met. She'd just put the newspapers out for recycling when she saw the Volvo draw up outside. He'd been out all day again.

She waited nervously for him at the gap in the boarding by the front door. 'Hello. You've been very busy this weekend.' She could hear the struggle to sound casual in her voice.

Avoiding eye contact, he looked down at some documents he was holding as he entered the flat. 'Helping Inky with a few historical details. He has a lot to do.'

She looked at him. Hurt was etched in his expression.

'I was just about to make some tea…' she began.

But already he was crossing the hall. 'Thanks, but I must get on. Busy week coming up.' And he hurried up the stairs.

She watched him until he went out of sight around the bend in the staircase. For months she'd wondered how he felt about her. Now, as he retreated into an internal space that only he inhabited, she knew. And she knew, too, how she felt about him. She'd spoiled everything.

51.

(i)

A silence hung over the River House. From her basement, Jenny heard Richard come and go, as, again and then again, he went out running. They didn't meet or speak as he avoided any situation in which they might be together, but she didn't know what to do about it. So, she went to and from school, planned her classes and watched the river.

Harry phoned her a couple more times. She put him off.

Only when Richard couldn't avoid her did they meet again, not at home in the River House, but in Barney's office. She'd come from school, and now she and Richard were armed with more of Inky's phony documents and a new poste restante address in The Strand. For this, their names were James Cassidy and Sarah Buchanan, or, for Barney's purposes, the legal partnership of Cassidy and Buchanan.

Then the two of them went back to the City to open another bank account for the buying of the River House for the Elspeth Worsley Society.

Barney accompanied them in the taxi, but, as Richard listened intently while the lawyer went over the details of how the Cassidy and Buchanan sting would operate, Jenny was now an observer more than a partner.

The interminable interview in the private bank that followed held no fear for her. She was now an actress again, just playing a part.

(ii)

As he waited for negotiations over the sale of Creswell Manor to go through, Richard spent much of the time at Barney's office. His online preparations had been intense, but it all now depended on two computers and two phones, one on either side of Barney's desk. Next to each was a small stack of stationery, one in heavy cream paper for the smart South Kensington partnership of Lathom and Greenaway for the sale of Creswell Manor, and the other in more functional hi-white for the

Buchanan and Cassidy firm on The Strand for the purchase of the River House.

'The trick is...' Barney said one day, as he considered a message from Jerricoe Properties, 'not to reply too quickly. Lathom and Greenaway are a small, old fashioned South Kensington firm that deals in weeks rather than days. If we respond too quickly Jerricoe might become suspicious. A few more days, I think.'

One morning, Harry arrived at Barney's office. 'Richard, good man!' he greeted. 'I thought I might drag Barney off for a spot of lunch. Fancy joining us?'

It was the first time he'd seen Harry in a couple of weeks. If Harry had any sense of awkwardness, he didn't show it.

Richard declined the offer. 'There's still some tidying up to do in Clerkenwell,' he excused himself. 'Besides, I think it's time the Elizabeth Worsley Society put in a silly offer for the River House.'

Harry was gleeful. '*Yes!* Terrific! How much were you thinking of?'

'Two million.'

Harry's face opened in shock. '*What?* Two million! As an opening offer?'

'Yes.'

Harry frowned. 'That's' insane. Why so much? He'll only want more.'

'That's okay. It'll be his money we'll be giving him back.'

'Yes, but...' Harry stopped speaking, and became thoughtful. Then said: 'But that really is a silly offer.'

(iii)

Harry enjoyed his lunch with Barney. With the lawyer he could be himself. Being a conman was a lonely life. Most of the time this didn't bother him, but something Jenny had said about conning himself did.

He'd laughed it off at the time. Jenny's openness was part of what made her so attractive. But she'd made him question himself, which was uncomfortable. And now, when he phoned her, she chatted happily but always found an excuse not to see him again. He tried not to show it, but he was disappointed. Actually, it hurt a little. For a while he'd let himself imagine a different life. But that had been a mistake.

In Barney's company, his life was simpler. With Barney, Harry knew who he was, and why he did what he did.

52.

'Charities! Don't you just love 'em!' Jerricoe cackled as Hunt entered his office. 'Never happy unless they're throwing away our donations.'

'Donations?' Neither Hunt nor Jerricoe were much involved in giving to charities.

Jerricoe shoved an email into the lawyer's hand. 'Your mate from the Elspeth Worsley Society only wants to give us two million for that River House heap of aggravation.'

'No?' Hunt looked at the letter. 'Well, well. You can't put some people off, can you! What did we pay for it? A million, wasn't it?'

'Nine seven fifty. I beat the old bastard down. The place was almost derelict.'

As Hunt recalled, he was the one who'd done most of the negotiating over the price of the River House, which, although neglected, had hardly been derelict. But he let it pass. Jerricoe was in a sunny mood; it was wise to keep him that way. 'It was a good buy,' he said. 'It's a nice location there on Wharf Lane. We'll do well with it.'

Jerricoe shook his head. 'It was a good buy then. But nine hundred and seventy-five thousand for a house that might now be stuck in development never-never-land with London Heritage, where two of the bloody tenants seem to have nailed their feet to the floorboards so that we can't even drag them out... it could be more like a liability.'

Hunt was indignant. 'Oh, come on! This is just a blip. That Elspeth Worsley lot are too small. London Heritage are right out of order. We'll fight it.'

Jerricoe snorted. 'Yes, right! And you know what? Every day you fight, I lose money.'

Hunt hesitated. 'You're not thinking of selling, are you?'

Jerricoe chuckled. 'Not at two million, I'm not. It's worth at least two and a half. I'm not a complete idiot, not like all those who've spent years giving money to that whinging prat at the Elspeth Worsley Society so that he can chuck it away on a property deal.'

53.

(i)

Richard had bought a house before, so he knew the ritual. When the Elspeth Worsley Society's first offer for the River House was rejected by Jerricoe Properties, he waited a couple of days. Then he increased the price that 'the Society was prepared to pay' by a hundred thousand pounds. As expected, that, too, was rejected.

Sitting alone in his Clerkenwell office, he waited a further few days and then increased the offer by another hundred thousand. Another rejection followed.

This time he hesitated even longer before upping the offer once more. It was an elaborate dance, each rejection of his offer by Jerricoe Properties being just a little less final, each gap before the next offer always a little bit longer. At two million, three hundred and ninety thousand pounds he stuck and waited. Finally, after five days, he moved with the 'Society's final offer of two and a half million pounds…after discussion with the trustees.' It was, as Harry had said, 'silly money'. But, because it was silly money, Jerricoe accepted.

Now it was down to the Elspeth Worsley Society's lawyers, Cassidy and Buchanan, in the shape of Barney Penn, to do the conveyancing on the River House, using their poste restante address in the Strand.

'Did you ever think about going into conveyancing professionally?' Richard asked one day as, sitting at Barney's side, he watched the lawyer's smooth confidence as he wrote answers to the various questions that Jerricoe Properties posed.

'Did it for years, old boy,' Barney smiled. 'Before I turned pro.'

One lunchtime, Richard drove him over to Inky's studio. As usual Inky was in a sulking mood. His work surface was littered with stacks of ancient deeds, fading letters, quill pens and various little dishes of home-made inks.

'Everything all right?' Richard asked.

Without speaking the forger passed him a roll of white parchment.

Richard opened it. Written in spidery, faint, italic handwriting in Elizabethan English it detailed the rights of the owner of *'the estate and chattels of the House in the Manor of Creswelle, in the county of Oxfordshyre'* detailing the numbers of rooms, stables, cottages, acres for pasture, as well as hunting rights and approximations of *'livestocke, swine and fowle'*.

Richard frowned. 'This is terrific,' he worried. 'Except that it was supposed to have been written in 1599 and it looks brand new.'

Taking the scroll back, Inky walked across the little studio to a small, much stained sink beside which was a teapot. Then holding out the parchment he doused it in cold tea. The white paper turned an ancient yellow colour. 'That'll look old enough when it's dry.'

Watching, Barney smiled: 'Waitrose Essentials?'

'Waitrose? This is Aldi, mate!' replied Inky.

Richard almost smiled, too. It would have made Jenny laugh, he thought, in the days when they'd talked and laughed together in the evenings.

(ii)

Who said there was no God in heaven, Jerricoe was thinking as Angel drove him to work. There surely must be, and it was one who rewarded those with guts and who got things done. 'God helps those who help themselves,' his mother had always told him. Never had a truer word been spoken.

How quickly things could change. A few weeks earlier there'd been nothing but aggravation on the horizon, with the Greensleeves situation becoming a real pain and the cultural commissars of Soviet London Heritage poking their noses into what didn't concern them over the River House. Now, thanks to a little greasing of the wheels, Greensleeves was back on track, and he was getting shot of the River House and its problems for a million and a half more that he'd paid for it.

The staff were all at their desks when he reached Jerricoe House, accountant Whiley and rents manager Choudhrai, and the assistant Mira, computing away in their little hutches; his own secretary, Thelma, opening the post.

'Morning, Mark,' Hunt nodded, as the lawyer arrived.

'So, what crises have you got for me today then?' Jerricoe smiled.

'No crises, Mark. Everything's fine. We've had a slight tug of war with the River House. We wanted to complete on the twenty-third but apparently the Elspeth Worsley Society funds won't be available until the day after when we were due to complete on Creswell Manor. So, we'll do it after we buy Creswell Manor. That all right? I would have preferred it the other way round, but…'

'That's fine. The sooner we get Creswell Manor the better. Well done.'

Hunt was surprised. He wasn't used to being praised. 'But…Mark?'

Jerricoe stopped as he was about to go into office. 'Yes?'

'Creswell Manor. I thought I'd nip down and take another look at it. Just to be on the safe side. You don't need to come.'

Jerricoe looked at him. 'You're betraying your working class prejudices again, you know, Craig,' he mocked.

'Yes, well, maybe, but the deal's got under my skin a bit, and…'

'It's because of that chip on your shoulder, Craig. That's what's under your skin. A chip. Very uncomfortable, I would have thought. You don't want to dirty your hands by buying from the land-owning aristocracy. You didn't keep banging on about wanting to see that brown field site in Croydon we turned round. I could hardly drag you down there.'

Hunt didn't answer.

Jerricoe shrugged. 'All right. You go.' Then, he stopped again. 'No, I tell you what, I'll come with you. I fancy a day out. Get that prat from Heyes and Heys to arrange it for tomorrow afternoon. We can take one of the dogs. It'll give him a chance to get used to worrying the odd sheep.'

54.

(i)

'He wants to see it *tomorrow*?' Richard gasped. He was standing in Barney's office.

'Sorry. Bit of a problem, yes?' Down the phone, Harry nursed the understatement.

'Jesus!'

'Absolutely. Hunt just called. I had to agree.'

Barney was watching from his desk.

'Do you think Jerricoe's having second thoughts?' Richard asked.

'Not Jerricoe,' Harry came back. 'But Hunt's never been keen on the deal. He's a suspicious bugger, that one.'

Richard swore softly to himself. 'And you can't talk him out of it?'

Harry sounded irritated. 'If I had been able to, don't you think I would have done? And it's hardly my idea of a nice day out in the country to go to the Cotswolds with Jerricoe and Hunt, only for them to discover that I've been conning them.'

Richard was hardly listening. Despite Jerricoe's reputation for making snap decisions, he wasn't surprised that he might want another viewing. But now, with only two days to go, it would be impossible to get Maurice and the staff out of Creswell Manor again so quickly. Set-ups needed time. 'I'll get back to you,' he said, and hung up.

There was a silence in the little office.

At last Barney cleared his throat. 'I don't know whether this helps or not, old boy, but in my day when we found we couldn't provide our clients with the impossible, we usually tried some kind of distraction manoeuvre. Though, in this case, exactly what that might be…' His voice faded.

Richard nodded his thanks. He had no idea either.

(ii)

It was the Easter school holidays and Jenny spent the afternoon swimming. In term time she was too busy for introspection during the day. But it was difficult to hide from oneself during holidays. Bleak in her loneliness, she'd pushed herself on, length after length. The extra reading classes she'd organised for the children who were struggling to keep up had been the only respite of the week.

With her hair still wet, she cycled home. A couple of envelopes addressed to her were lying on the mat. Nothing much of interest, she thought: a credit card offer from Capital One, and a circular from the National Union of Teachers. Richard's post looked, if anything, even duller, just a brochure from Christie's, the auctioneers, and a brown envelope from HM Revenue and Customs.

Usually, she left his letters on the settle in the hall, but she and Richard couldn't go on avoiding each other. Picking up his mail, she went up the stairs.

'Oh, hello,' he said, surprised as he opened his door to her knock. Then, awkward, his eyes fell to the envelopes in her hand.

'I thought I'd be the postman today.' She forced a smile.

'Thank you.' He took the letters.

'Yes, well…it looks like a tax demand or something…but…' She felt awkward and turned to leave, but then hesitated, and, on the top step, turned back to him. 'Richard…'

But he was staring at one of the envelopes. 'Revenue and Customs.' he murmured, then spelled out the letters. 'V.A.T.'

55.

(i)

The car was going too fast, Harry worried, as they careered around another tight bend in the road. At this rate they'd get to Creswell Manor too soon. At his side, in the back of the BMW, one of the dogs lay panting. Beyond the dog sat Jerricoe. How strange, Harry had been reflecting all the way from London, that a man who spent so much on his suits was so careless as to whether they got covered in dog hairs. Harry would be sending his to the cleaners the minute he got back. If he got back! Usually, he quite liked dogs, friendly collies and spaniels, anyway. They were good for starting conversations with pretty little dog owners in the park. But this slavering great beast belonged in a horror film.

He looked out of the window at the passing countryside. This was his second journey with Jerricoe, and again there was no conversation. Hunt, who was sitting in the front with the driver, seemed to be making a deliberate effort to ignore him.

Perhaps, as an estate agent, he ought to be trying a little bit harder. 'You know, the thing I like most about this part of the world is the colours,' he mused aloud, 'especially at this time of year. They make it all so... so English... The honey-coloured stone of the houses, and the wisteria buds just beginning to show around the eves. And yet, you know, we're only forty miles from Oxford and academia and all those...'

'Tossers,' Jerricoe spat.

'Er, yes, well...quite!' Harry agreed. So much for conversation.

The dog turned its massive head towards him, its spit dripping on to the seat.

Harry edged closer to the door.

Jerricoe noticed. 'Do you know, the Nazis bred this type of dog as a killing machine,' he said.

Harry considered the dog. Its purple tongue was hanging between its white fangs. 'No, I didn't know that,' he said.

And, as the BMW began to slow as Creswell Manor came into view, he wondered how efficient this jaw-dripping killing machine would be. Then he checked his watch. It was only two forty-five. They were going to be too early.

(ii)

Climbing out of the hired blue Ford Focus, Jenny, in large round glasses, her hair tied back off her face, wearing a sensible navy-blue jacket, and matching skirt, and with a briefcase under her arm, led Sarojini and Sanjeev Ghelani along the pavement to Jerricoe House. Then she stopped at the front door for one final inspection. Both Ghelanis were wearing sober, high-street suits they'd bought just an hour ago. 'Perfect,' she murmured, then pressed the bell.

'Yes?' came a woman's voice over the Entryphone.

'Good morning!' Jenny said firmly into the speaker. 'Revenue and Customs.'

(iii)

'What about that! Fallow deer in the meadow, trotting around like half a dozen Bambis! Aren't they beautiful! There are red deer, too, I believe. Perhaps you'd like to see the estate first. It's such a lovely day.' Harry was beginning to blabber as the BMW drove through the gates.

'I can see it from here,' Jerricoe snapped.

'Of course, you can,' Harry came back. 'Ah, look, and here's Mrs...er...you remember the lady from the kitchen. She must be going shopping.' And he raised his hand as the car swept past Mrs Morrison who, carrying a basket, was walking down the long drive towards the gates.

She waved back.

'Wonderful woman.' He was panicking. They were virtually at the house. This wasn't going to work.

At his side, Jerricoe was gazing at the house as they approached.

'Did I tell you that it's thought Charles II may have stayed here when he was escaping from Oliver Cromwell? That was before the oak tree escapade, of course. I wonder which bedroom was his.' And he looked up at the windows of the house as the car came to a halt.

Jerricoe wasn't even listening. He opened his car door. Harry opened his,

As he did, an irritatingly tinny Big Ben chimed in the front of the car.

With a curse Hunt answered his mobile. 'Yes. What? *What?'*

Jerricoe was now out of the car. Harry opened his door.

'Mark, we weren't expecting a visit from Revenue and Customs, were we?' Hunt called to him.

Jerricoe had stepped a couple of paces towards the great oak doors of the house. He stopped. 'What?'

'It's Ella. She says a VAT team have turned up for a spot check. Choudhrai and Mira are getting the books out for them.'

For a moment Jerricoe's features appeared to ossify in non-comprehension. Then they shattered. 'Jesus Christ!' And, heaving himself back into the car, he grabbed the phone. 'Tell, Choudhrai not to show them the Greensleeves accounts, no matter what, nor the Croydon ones. He has to fob them off. Keep them talking. We're coming back. Jesus!' Then hitting Angel on the shoulder, he bellowed. 'You heard me! 'Get going! Back to London! Drive!'

As Harry hurriedly closed his door again, the car came back to life. And, as a man with bright chestnut hair emerged from the side courtyard, it swung around and began to accelerate down the drive away from the house.

'But I thought you wanted to see the house!' Harry protested. 'Just a brief look, perhaps... Such a shame after coming all this way.'

Jerricoe ignored him. 'If those bloody VAT people spot anything, I'll kill you,' he rasped at Hunt as the car raced towards the gates.

Hunt didn't answer.

Harry relaxed and looked out at the estate, putting a hand up to Mrs Morrison as they rocketed past her again. If Jerricoe remembered anything else about this day, it would be that the woman from the kitchens had been there.

(iv)

Jenny had played bigger parts in her career. But seated now at the Jerricoe Properties boardroom table, sifting through lists of figures on a computer screen under the worried eye of Jerricoe Properties' rentals manager, Mr Choudhrai, she was the leading lady. Acting and teaching had prepared her for learning things quickly before pretending to be an expert in them. An evening's googling and a few pointers from Richard on what to expect from a visit by a tax inspector had given her enough words and phrases to sound knowledgeable.

Also at the table were Sarojini and Sanjeev Ghelani.

'Hmmm...' Sarojini murmured sternly from time to time, before making a note on a yellow foolscap pad. She was a natural at improvisation.

'So, what about rentals for the previous quarter?' Jenny asked, taking off her reading glasses.

'Oh yes. Let me show you,' said Mr Choudhrai keenly, and, as Jenny closed her documents, he opened another file on the computer she was using.

Across the table, Sanjeev Ghelani had paused to take a sip of tea and a digestive biscuit, but as Jenny glanced firmly at him, he quickly went back to work at his screen.

Jenny looked at her watch. If Jerricoe and Hunt had left Creswell Manor at three o'clock, the earliest they could be back in London would be four thirty.

'Are you sure these are *all* the rentals?' she asked the accountant. As VAT inspectors they had to appear to be thorough.

And, as Mr Choudhrai hurriedly showed her another file, she took a biscuit and went back to examining the books. They had nearly an hour and a half still to fill.

(v)

Jenny had wanted to talk last night when she'd come up to his flat, Richard was reflecting, as he sat at his worktop in the River House and waited for news. There'd been another occasion when someone else he'd loved had wanted to talk.

Hunt's stomach was clenching with anger. It was always his fault. Whatever went wrong, he was blamed. Now he'd been humiliated in front of that fop of an estate agent. Was that a smirk he'd noticed as the guy had asked to be dropped off at Northfields Underground station? A smirk would have been typical of his type. Posh accent, easy job, he'd never known what it was to live on his wits.

The BMW was now rocketing through the commercial estate towards Jerricoe House. If Angel hadn't been caught by half a dozen speed cameras on the way back it would be a miracle. The boy didn't realise that when he got too many points on his license because Jerricoe always wanted to go faster, he would be banned from driving, and Jerricoe would sack him.

Jerricoe House was now in sight. Whatever those VAT snoopers had found could be damning. What a bloody cock-up!

'*Jesus!*' Suddenly he was thrown forward in his seat as Angel braked violently.

A blue Ford had pulled out from the kerb without warning and driven away.

'Watch out, for Christ's sake!' Jerricoe was bollocking Angel now. It made a change.

Climbing from the car, Hunt followed his boss into Jerricoe House, and quickly into the boardroom.

'Where are they?' Jerricoe demanded.

Choudhrai and Mira were shutting down the computers. 'They've gone, Mr Jerricoe,' Choudhrai said. 'You just missed them. They seemed very happy with what we showed them. No complaints at all.'

'What? *None?* No complaints?'

'They just told me to make sure we got our VAT returns in on time, because it caused undue work when they were late.'You didn't show them the Greensleeves file?'

'Oh, no. Ella warned us about that. Nor Croydon.'

Jerricoe sighed. 'Well…' Then suddenly he threw his head back and laughed in relief.

Hunt didn't see anything to laugh at. 'Every day this bloody country gets more totalitarian,' he swore. 'Spot checks now. It's outrageous. I'm going to lodge a complaint.'

Jerricoe shook his head. 'Or maybe not,' he said. 'At least these functionaries of your totalitarian state were incompetent. If you complain, Customs and Excise might send some people round who know what to look for. We got lucky there.'

And he buzzed Thelma to fetch him a cup of tea.

(vii)

Jenny took the Ghelanis home in the hire car. Harry's message from Northfields that Jerricoe was already back in London had prompted an early end to their investigation.

'I have to say you were both brilliant,' she said as she drove. 'You should both have been actors.'

'Thank you very much,' replied Sanjeev Ghelani, pleased with himself, although he hadn't said a word inside Jerricoe House. 'Bollywood would be kicking themselves if they knew.'

From the back seat there was just a thoughtful silence. Then Sarojini leant forward to her husband. 'Did you see all the money they make in there, Sanjeev? Perhaps we should encourage our boys to become property developers. It's a very profitable business.'

Jenny had to bite her lip.

(viii)

Love wasn't a concept for which Harry had ever had much time. Romance was fine, and when it was combined with sex, and, in his case, it always was, it was great fun. But *love,* that fabled commitment to honesty and fidelity, could ruin a happy life, never mind screwing up an exciting profession.

Watching the soot-covered cables rocket past in the tunnel as he travelled back into Central London, he pictured Jenny across the table from him in his flat, with that teasing little smile of hers. 'I know very well what you're up to, Harry,' she'd said.

And he'd remembered again the thrill of anticipation. Was this love, he asked himself as the train pulled into Green Park? It had better not be. It could seriously get in a chap's way.

56.

It was the end of a topsy-turvy day, Jerricoe was thinking as he fed the dogs. He liked to feed them himself last thing at night: always half a pound each of rump steak. That should keep them alert overnight in case any poxy VAT inspectors decided to try a moonlight raid. And then he smirked as he recalled Hunt's fury at the Customs and Excise visit.

Poor Craig, always missing the point, trying to fight the wrong battle, unable to see the wood for the trees. Maybe he'd outlived his usefulness. His contacts were helpful, but perhaps Jerricoe Properties needed someone smoother these days. He really wasn't classy enough for a company that was into buying, and soon selling, a country estate. He'd been useful as an enforcer, both legal and otherwise, but…

'Mr Jerricoe!' Mira, Choudhrai's assistant, was at the rear door of Jerricoe House, cowering, well away from the dogs. 'There's a Mr Sullivan on the line. He says he needs to talk to you.'

'What? No. I'm going now. Tell him to call back tomorrow and speak to Craig,' Jerricoe replied, his hands smeared with blood and grease from the steaks.

'He says it's very important. It's about the River House. Very urgent.'

Jerricoe hesitated. Did he want to discuss the bloody River House? No. He did not. It had been nothing but a pain in the backside. The sooner they'd got rid of it, the better.

But, in the property game, you never knew how much a missed call could cost you. 'Tell him to wait a minute…' he shouted back.

57.

She recognized his tap on the door.

'I just came down to say thank you for everything you did today,' he said as he stood outside her door. 'You were…valiant.'

'Not really,' she joked. 'The monsters were out of their cave. Jerricoe's staff seemed more frightened of us than we were of them.'

'I don't suppose he's an easy man to work for.'

'No.'

'Well, anyway…' He was about to leave.

She stopped him. 'Richard, can we go for a walk?'

They weren't going anywhere in particular, just making their way along the river, taking their time, warm in their anoraks, because, although it was fine, the spring evening was cool.

At first, he said little, other than awkwardly drawing her attention to the squadrons of ducks as they skimmed the surface of the water.

But there was something she had to ask him. 'You know, you never told me…you never said why you got divorced. Am I allowed to ask? I'd like to know.'

He didn't meet her gaze but looked instead at a piece of driftwood that was stuck in the mud of low tide. 'It's difficult…' he murmured.

She waited as they walked on.

'We were married for five years. She was…she *is*, an academic. Meg… Her name is Meg. She's a history lecturer. We'd been together before that for about three years. We bought a house in Kingston, Selwyn Avenue, very nice. Quite a big garden, not far from Richmond Park.'

He looked up as a helicopter interrupted loudly as it passed overhead.

She didn't say anything.

'Anyway, eventually, Meg got pregnant. I was very happy. Excited! We'd had our differences, but, at that moment, my life seemed just about perfect. But, well... Meg...wasn't happy. I didn't know why. So, I just went ahead preparing the spare room for our baby. Decorating. As the weeks went by, though, things between us just got worse and worse. Everything I did or said seemed to irritate her. I kept asking why. In the end I told Meg we just had to talk for our baby's sake. She agreed. She had something to tell me.'

Jenny watched him as he considered what he was about to say.

'She said...Meg said.... that it wouldn't be *our* baby. Not my baby, anyway. I wasn't the father. She'd been having an affair with a chap at college. Another historian. She wanted a divorce so that she could marry him.' He stopped talking, stopped walking.

Jenny didn't speak.

'At first, I couldn't take it on board. I tried to talk her out of it, saying that it would be all right. We could start again. It would be my baby, too, because I would bring him up and love him just the same. We already knew it was a boy. I said that we could put the past behind us. I suppose I must have tried too hard. Because suddenly she just snapped and said, "Don't you understand? I don't love you. I don't want to be with you. It's finished."'

They were standing by the railing now, watching the river.

'I moved out that night, only going back when I knew Meg was out to pick up my clothes and books and stuff. I gave up my job in banking at the same time. I left everything else from the marriage behind.

'The divorce was quick. I...*we*... both made it easy. The lawyers were very efficient. Meg remarried as soon as she could. She kept the house. An arrangement was made. They're still there. I haven't heard from her in a while. There's nothing for us to say to each other. The little boy will be getting on for four now. I don't even know his name.'

He faded, distracted by an image Jenny couldn't see. Then he returned to his story. 'After that I began to pick up more work as a restorer. I'd been doing it on the side, a sort of hobby, since I'd been in my teens. It now became more of an obsession, I suppose. And one day I fetched up at the River

House. The attic has a great light for working. My family and some friends told me I should get other interests to take my mind off things, that I should meet new people. But I didn't want to get my mind off things or meet new people.

'So, instead, I played games by myself. I told you that when we first met, didn't I! Another hobby, but it was something I was good at, something I could do alone. I'd loved chess at school, winning prizes, that sort of thing. And I liked doing puzzles, working things out. I became a real nerd… as I'm sure you noticed.'

He half-smiled as he said that, and she felt herself trying not to nod.

'I imagine some people saw me retreat into myself and decide I'd had a breakdown. Mrs Morrison probably thought I had.'

'Did you?' The question came before she'd realised. She regretted it immediately, because it sounded so blunt.

But he answered as though he'd already given much thought to the possibility. 'Breakdown is too glib a word. I was certainly broken. Broken down. Broken in two. And it took a while, no, much longer than a while, it took months…years for me to mend and to realise that the perfect life I'd thought I had was something I'd only imagined. It hadn't been real. I'd been…' He paused. 'I'd been fooling myself. The signs had all been there. I just hadn't seen them.

'The trouble is, I was…well, frightened, I suppose, in a locked-in kind of way. I felt as though I just didn't want to be involved, or to invest too much of myself in anything. I suppose it just made me…well, blind.'

He smiled wryly at her, as they now resumed their walk. 'And that's more or less where you came in and found this hermit in his attic, who didn't know what to do with himself anymore and just wanted a quiet life without complications.'

'Is that what you still want?'

'I don't think a life without complications exists. Not a full, proper life. Not a life worth living, anyway.'

58.

(i)

They all met at Barney's office at eight thirty the following day. It was a sunny May morning as, on Queensway, office workers hurried to Bayswater Underground Station, greengrocers set out their stalls, and from the kebab shop below the office came the sounds of Turkish voices and music. How bizarre, Jenny mused as she watched the activity from the window. For everybody else it would be just a normal day. For them it was *the* day, the moment when they would discover if the little people really could defeat the bullies.

She and Richard had been the second arrivals, Barney being already at his desk having thoughtfully bought coffees for everyone on his way in. Next came Inky. Harry got there last. He surprised her. For the first time since she'd known him, he looked edgy, subdued even. And, although he made a point of quietly telling her how attractive she looked, his flattering was on automatic.

'Right!' Richard said and opened the Figure of Eight board on his desk for the last time.

Jenny stared at how Richard had visualised everything as a mosaic of drawings and cartoons. There at the top was the river and the River House, then a comb and scissors for where Jerricoe got his hair cut. Creswell Manor was at the bottom but in between was a brass plate outside the Elspeth Worsley Society, then came a sketch of her as Wendy Hornton from Sydney, and another of her as Tessa, the London Heritage executive. There was even a last-minute scribble of a drawbridge in a square representing HM Revenue and Customs. Altogether it represented a map of hope, creativity and not a little cunning as they'd climbed the property ladders, and Jerricoe, though he didn't yet know it, had been, hopefully, sliding down the drainpipes.

'If the Fraud Squad ever sees this, we'll all be jailed,' Richard joked. Then, putting his Figure of Eight board inside a metal paper basket, he lit a match and set fire to it.

Jenny watched it burn.

As the flames went out, Richard looked around the room. 'Anyone got anything to say before we start?' he asked

Barney shook his head. Inky just stared into the flames.

Harry cleared his throat. 'Yes. I do. On behalf of conmen everywhere, Richard, I'd just like to say that considering the aptitude you've shown, it'll be a terrible loss to the profession when you go back to your day job.'

'Hear-hear!' murmured Barney.

Even Inky seemed to agree.

Jenny smiled to herself. The con hadn't yet worked. But it was the first time she'd heard Harry say anything nice about Richard, even if he had been teasing.

'Praise indeed!' thanked Richard quietly, then looked at his watch. 'So, are we ready?'

Barney picked up his briefcase.

'Never more,' said Harry. And, with a brief, almost sheepish grin to Jenny, he and Barney were gone.

A thoughtful haze now filled the little office, as, crossing to Barney's chair, Richard sat down at the computer screen. 'All we can do now is wait,' he said, and reached for his coffee.

(ii)

'Don't worry about the dogs,' laughed Harry as the cab drew up outside Jerricoe House. 'They aren't half as scary as he is.' Then, leaving Barney to negotiate a waiting time with the cab driver, he pressed the bell.

Hunt was ready for them in reception, his expression an undisguised sour mask of derision. 'You're early,' he said.

'Well, you know what they say about the early bird,' Harry breezed.

'Yes. He gets worms,' came the reply.

Harry smiled his most vacuous grin. 'I suppose that's an interesting variation.' And then, with Barney a step behind, he followed Hunt up the staircase.

(iii)

At just after ten thirty Richard logged on to the Lathom and Greenaway account which he and Jenny had set up at the Cornish-Callender Bank. 'When that screen changes...' He didn't finish. Talking at all, seemed to be tempting fate.

(iv)

Seated at Jerricoe's oval table, Harry was in full flow. 'And it wasn't until almost the end of Elizabeth I's reign, over sixty years later, that one of her court favourites, a chap who'd apparently done sterling work against the Armada, was given permission to turn the priory into the fine Tudor mansion we have today. Of course, since then countless changes have been...'

'Do you want me to buy the place or write a book about it?' Jerricoe interrupted.

Harry stopped. Maybe he had been overdoing his estate agent bit. 'Sorry. But one doesn't often get the chance to represent the vendors for a house with so much...*history*.' He turned to Barney. 'Er, Mr Penn...'

At his side, Barney's hands lay on an open cardboard box, stuffed with Inky's yellow, curling documents. 'Thank you. It is indeed an interesting building, as you gentlemen have no doubt been able to see from the photocopies of these documents that I've already sent you...' And he tapped the ancient looking stack of papers.

Jerricoe's eyes were on the pile of papers.

'It's all here,' went on Barney. 'Seventeenth and eighteenth century conveyances establishing a very long chain of title, deeds, wills, bequests, as well as that final trust set up in 1847.'

Impatiently, Jerricoe leant forward, snatched up a deed, unrolled it and began to examine the parchment. Hunt, meanwhile, passed a set of land transfer documents to Barney, who began to peruse them carefully.

Suddenly, Barney's studied look turned into a frown. 'Er...!'

Jerricoe and Hunt stopped reading.

'I hate to be a bore but there seems to be a mistake here.'

'Mistake?' Hunt looked worried.

Jerricoe glared at him.

'Yes, you see the middle initial of one of my clients, the trustee John Rimmer, he's the chap in Africa, should be *H* not *A*. As in John Henry Rimmer.'

'Jesus!' Jerricoe swore and put a hand to his dyed blond hair.

Then Barney smiled. 'But I suppose we can agree on a lawyer's initial, don't you, Mr Hunt?'

'Yes, he does agree,' barked Jerricoe.

Hunt nodded his assent.

Smiling his thanks, Barney made the change on the document, initialled it and passed it back to Hunt.

Harry stifled a sigh of relief as Hunt added his initials. Barney hadn't told him he was going to pull that old stunt.

Jerricoe noticed. 'Close call there, eh!' he jeered. 'Saw your slice slipping away, didn't you?' Then he turned back to Hunt. 'Let's just sign the bloody transfers and get this over.'

Quickly signatures were applied and the documents exchanged again.

'Well, that seems to be about it...' Barney exclaimed. 'It only remains now for the transfer of funds and ...'

'Do the money, Craig,' Jerricoe snapped.

Obediently, Hunt left the room.

Beaming, Harry stood up and leant across the table to shake Jerricoe's hand. 'Congratulations, Mr Jerricoe. You're buying yourself a splendid property. You'll be able to take possession just as soon as the funds are cleared. I hope you enjoy many happy years there.'

Jerricoe ignored the proffered handshake. He was busy gloating over Inky's tea-stained deeds.

(v)

'It's there!' Richard's voice was so quiet that at first Jenny almost missed the moment.

In an instant, she was behind him, staring with Inky at the computer screen. The deposit in the Lathom and Greenaway account had indeed changed. £9 million had been added to it. 'Oh, my God!' she gasped. 'Nine million pounds!'

Richard's expression didn't change. It's only half-time. We haven't got the River House yet.'

That was Richard, Jenny thought, always focused, as he went back to work at the computers.

'But…as Harry and Inky have now fulfilled their parts on Creswell Manor…' he continued.

'It's pay day,' Inky grinned.

'Exactly.' Reaching into an inside pocket, Richard took out a sheet of paper. 'Let's see…bank accounts.' He peered closely at the list of numbers on the paper. Everything had already been calculated, taking in percentages and advances. 'First you, Inky. You want your share to go to an account in…the Cayman Islands.' He smiled. Keying in a series of numbers and passwords, he clicked on *'submit'*.

A moment later the screen changed again. £179,000 had gone to the Cayman Islands.

'There you go, Inky,' he indicated. 'Your money's waiting for you in the sunshine.'

Inky looked almost pleased. 'Thank you very much. I think I might go and get some baklava.' And he went down the stairs.

'There's a man who knows how to celebrate,' Jenny smiled.

Richard was staring at his sheet of paper. 'Now for Barney.'

And a further £160,000 went into the offshore account that Barney had named.

'As for Harry…? Richard hesitated.

'Yes?' Jenny asked.

'I don't know.'

'Don't know what?' Was this something to do with her, Jenny wondered.

'Well, he never did return all the money he stole from Age Gap at Christmas. We got maybe ten per cent at the most off him. Perhaps we should deduct five hundred pounds before we give him his share. That might teach him that dishonesty doesn't pay.'

'Except, in this case, it seems to pay very well. Maybe let him off with a warning.'

'Well, okay. Just this once,' said Richard. And, consulting his sheet of paper, which took into account the funds that Harry had been paid while setting up the scam, he keyed in another series of numbers and passwords, and then entered £4,495,000 into the transfer funds box.

There it goes, Jenny thought as Richard pressed 'submit'. The mountain of money that Harry had always dreamed of having, but which he would never have got without Richard. 'I only hope he doesn't blow it all on something stupid,' she said.

Richard didn't answer. He was busy transferring the remaining £4,135,000 to the Elspeth Worsley account at their Cassidy and Buchanan bank, the one he and Jenny would be using to buy the River House.

(vi)

Sitting in his little flat, Harry was mesmerized by a computer screen, too. He'd finally done it, he told himself, as he stared at his laptop and counted and recounted the zeros on the figure in his Liechtenstein bank account. He'd pulled off the long con. He was rich. He was a millionaire. Four times over. No longer small time.

'Thank you, Mr Jerricoe! Thank you very much!' he said aloud to himself. Then, sagging back into his armchair, he closed his eyes for a few seconds to allow the change in his fortunes to sink in.

Opening them, he looked around. He'd packed the previous night. His old much bruised two suitcases were waiting by the door. He was leaving the nude painting for the next tenant. It had served its purpose as a conversational gambit with Jenny. He smiled at the recollection.

Now, there was just one more thing he had to do. Then he'd be off. He pulled out his phone.

59.

(i)

'Firstly. we'll have a new conservatory built for the Morrisons,' Jenny was musing. 'Not a cheap one, but one of those beautifully curved, white Victorian ones. Then we'll fill it with hanging baskets of fuchsia, forget-me-nots, marigolds and …'

'Wild orchids?' Inky contributed. 'They're very pretty.'

'Perfect!'

Richard watched Jenny from across the little office. She'd always been full of vitality, but now she was shining and joyful.

Barney had arrived back just before noon and was already shredding all the legal correspondence regarding Creswell Manor. Soon the guy with the Radiohead T-shirt would be there, the phones, computers, desk and chair would be gone and the bare room handed back to the owners of the kebab shop, with no record of who'd occupied it.

Richard looked at his watch. It was already nearly three. The leather clad courier, another of Barney's colleagues, anonymous behind his helmet, who'd taken the transfer documents for the River House would, by arrangement, have been at Jerricoe House forty-five minutes ago. He should be back soon with the title deeds and the documents completed, ready for posting, complete with stamp duty, to the Land Registration Department.

He looked again at Jenny and Inky. In all the months he'd known the forger he'd scarcely been able to get two words out of him. Now, with Jenny, the guy was almost garrulous.

'I knew when I first saw a photograph of you that you'd make a great subject,' he was telling her. 'Some artists don't care what shape their models are, in that they see everybody as interesting…emaciated, Rubenesque, elongated, grotesque. You name it. But I like mine to be…you know, just that bit over ripe. So, if ever you're interested…'

'Thank you. I'll think about it.' Jenny was smiling at her evident over-ripeness. 'And what happens to you, now that you've finished here?'

'Well, I usually go to Florence in the summer months. There's an art history course I've been taking for some time.'

'Oh, lovely, you're studying art history.'

Inky looked confused. 'I don't *study* it. I teach it.'

'Oh!'

Behind Richard came a low chuckle from Barney. 'Nothing and no-one ever quite what we seem.'

Richard had realised that at Christmas in the shopping mall. 'It's a shame Harry isn't here to celebrate, isn't it,' he said. 'Did he say why he didn't come back with you after seeing Jerricoe?' he asked.

'Just something about wanting to pack his things. I'm sure he won't leave without saying goodbye,' Barney replied.

The phone, on the right-hand side of Barney's desk, rang at three-thirty. Jenny looked at Richard. He turned towards Barney.

Very carefully, Barney sat down, waited, gathered himself, and then finally answered the ringing. 'Hello.' He paused. 'Oh hello, Mr Hunt.'

Richard was surprised. Barney was speaking with an educated Irish accent. He'd needed two separate voices for each of the two legal firms he was pretending to represent.

'Actually, this is Jerry Cassidy speaking,' Barney was saying. 'That's right. For some reason you came straight through to me. Our receptionist isn't back from lunch yet. Getting married tomorrow, so… You know how it is.'

By the window, Inky put down a cardboard cup of tea as he listened.

Jenny moved a step closer.

Suddenly, Barney frowned. 'Really? That's a very unusual request from a vendor. Very unusual.' He listened again and then began scribbling notes on a pad. 'Is there any particular reason for this?' His expression was becoming more troubled with every word.

'Well, I'll have to put it to my client, of course. Let me get in touch with him, and I'll get back to you. Goodbye now.' Barney put the phone down.

'Tell me,' Richard said quietly.

'Hunt says that Mark Jerricoe has decided he wants Charles Foster of the Elspeth Worsley Society to complete in person on the River House.'

Richard froze. 'What? Why?'

'He wouldn't say. They're waiting for you now, Richard.'

(ii)

Barney and Inky shook hands and said their goodbyes before they left. They'd done their jobs and there was nothing more a lawyer and a forger could now do. They would now disappear. That had been the plan. Richard and Jenny were on their own.

Jenny was very quiet.

All the way over to Clerkenwell in the Volvo, where he'd left the suit that he'd worn as Charles Foster, Richard wracked his brains. Why did Jerricoe want to see him? Something must have gone wrong. But what?

He'd tidied the Elspeth Worsley office in the days after he'd been beaten up there, but there was still a broken picture frame and signs of the assault. He caught Jenny staring at a trace of blood on the carpet.

Taking off his clothes in the little bathroom, then gelling his hair and pulling on his young fogey Charles Foster suit and glasses, he recalled Harry's advice the last time he'd dressed for this part. 'Remember, Richard, it's all in the performance.' And, for a second, he almost wished Harry was with him at that moment. Whatever else he might do, Harry never failed to instil confidence.

Jenny's expression was grave when he came out of the bathroom.

'Come on, I can't look that bad,' he tried to joke.

'Richard, if I asked you not to go...' Her eyes were wet.

'So don't ask me,' he said.

'But the last time...'

He stopped her. 'Don't worry. Just tell me how convincing I am as Charles Foster.'

'Better than Orson Welles could ever have been. And he probably won an Oscar.'

'Actually, he didn't. But I might.'

She tried to smile. Then, going to him, she straightened his tie, and pushed a lock of hair back behind his ear. It had grown since he'd met Hunt in this room. 'You make a brilliant nerd, you know. The best.'

60.

(i)

It wasn't the welcome he'd expected. 'Ah, Mr Foster! Thank you for coming to see us.' Standing at the top of the stairs, Mark Jerricoe, his dyed blond backlit by a circular skylight, was almost laughing as, holding out his arms, he beckoned Richard to join him. 'Please come up.'

Richard looked behind him nervously as Hunt, who'd answered the door, nodded towards the staircase. He was in the lion's den, and as he climbed the stairs, his eyes flicked between the suspiciously grinning Jerricoe and the enlarged photographs of building developments that studded the walls.

At the top of the stairs, Jerricoe guided him into his office. Hunt followed, closed the doors behind them and remained standing by it.

Richard considered Jerricoe. For months he'd hated him, seeing him only from a distance. But now on his home territory, sitting there in his shirtsleeves and red braces, it struck him that this vicious, vain man was also rather fey.

'Well, Mr Foster, it's so good to meet you at last,' Jerricoe was grinning.

'And you too, Mr Jerricoe.'

'Mr Hunt has told me so much about you.'

Richard twisted round in his chair to look at Hunt. The man's face was expressionless. 'You received the transfer documents, I believe,' Richard said, turning back to Jerricoe. 'Was there some problem?'

Jerricoe ignored the question. 'You and your Elspeth Worsley Society... you have a very cosy relationship with London Heritage, haven't you!'

'I wouldn't say cosy,' Richard replied casually.

'But they've done you a favour. You must admit that.'

'They've done the nation a favour, Mr Jerricoe.'

'Ah yes! The nation. We must save our historic buildings for the nation, no matter what the cost to business.'

Richard pushed the horn-rimmed glasses he was wearing more securely on to the bridge of his nose. They didn't fit very well.

Jerricoe leaned back. 'You know, Mr Foster, there aren't many people who beat me in business. I pride myself on that. But…hats off to you…! You outmanoeuvred me into agreeing to sell a property for which I had great plans…!'

'I'm sorry if you see it that way, but…'

Jerricoe wasn't listening. 'Yes, you were very clever, I'll admit that.' Then his smile snapped shut. 'But if you think I'm going to sell the River House to a snivelling, little wanker like you…!'

Richard blinked. 'What?'

Jerricoe turned to Hunt. 'Craig…!'

Hunt nodded and opened the door.

'I don't understand…' Richard started to say.

But as he began speaking, a large, tanned, fair-haired man entered the room, smiling.

'Mr Foster, may I introduce Mr Sullivan. I'm afraid Mr Sullivan beat you to the punch over the River House, Mr Foster. The same price, two point five million pounds. So, you can't complain that you were gazumped. But Mr Sullivan comes without the sanctimonious, pious, heritage bollocks that you pulled on me.'

'But…' Richard stammered. 'We…we had an agreement.'

Jerricoe smirked. 'Did we? I don't remember. Tell you what, sue me! Take me to court. I think you'll find my lawyer, Mr Hunt here, will very quickly find a loophole in any agreement you say we had.'

Richard was on his feet now, shouting. 'You can't do this! You bastard! You *agreed* to sell the River House to us! It should be ours!'

'Can't do it? But I've already done it. You're too bloody late! Now sod off, Mr Elspeth Worsley Society. The River House has been sold.'

(ii)

Craig Hunt had rarely seen Jerricoe in such good spirits, as together they watched Sullivan driven away in a taxi. He'd come up with a matching offer of two and a half million pounds for the River House! The idiot must have money to burn. It wasn't worth anything like that. Not to worry, it was his mistake. Perhaps he'd be more successful in persuading those two obstinate bloody tenants to leave than he'd been. What that wally from the Elspeth Worsley Society had overlooked was that if there was one thing Mark Jerricoe enjoyed more than making money, it was doing down a competitor who tried to outwit him.

Quite how Sullivan had heard about the problem with London Heritage he didn't know. He must have caught the whispers on the property grapevine and made his move. His money had been good, too. It had gone through without a question.

Closing the door, Hunt was going back into his office when Jerricoe appeared on the stairs. He was still laughing.

'What about you and me going out to Creswell Manor to have a look at our new acquisition!' his boss suggested.

Hunt looked at his watch. 'Today?'

'Why not? We may get a good offer and sell it on tomorrow the way business is going.'

Why not, thought Hunt. At least they wouldn't have to put up with that winsome jerk of an estate agent in the car this time.

61.

(i)

They'd failed. He'd failed. Right at the end, Richard's scheme hadn't worked. All the planning and preparations of the scam had been for nothing. Somewhere he'd made a mistake. Something had happened that he hadn't factored in. He'd assumed that greed would be enough. It hadn't been. Spite had played a bigger part. The River House was lost after all.

Richard stared into space in the taxi on the way back to Clerkenwell. 'Does market theory ever not work,' he remembered Jenny had once asked.

'Only when people act irrationally,' he'd told her. 'But everything we know about Jerricoe tells us that when it comes to greed, he's dead rational.'

What he hadn't factored in was the possibility of another bidder.

But something else was troubling him, something he couldn't quite fathom. Had he made another mistake, too?

Jenny was waiting for him in the Elspeth Worsley Society's office. Her smile of relief greeted him, and she watched as he changed back into his usual clothes. 'But they didn't hurt you,' was all she kept saying. 'Nothing else matters. Thank God, they didn't hurt you.'

He continued to shake his head. 'I should have seen it coming,' he fretted. 'I should have been waiting for the unexpected. I thought I'd covered everything. Jerricoe outwitted me. I've let everyone down. I've let you down.'

'No,' she insisted. 'No. You didn't let anyone down. And you've never let me down. It was only ever a game. Just a game of Figure of Eight. Besides, we did beat Jerricoe. We got the money if not the house.'

He looked at her. She was smiling at him, the tough little resilient actress who'd become a teacher, and who wasn't ever going to let anything get in her way. And Richard found himself smiling in return.

A knock on the door broke into the moment as a grinning Harry put his head inside the Elspeth Worsley Society office.

'Hello, you two. You want to make sure you get that front door fixed, Richard. Anyone could get in. Mind if we join you?' And, without waiting for an answer, he entered the room.

We?

From the twilight of the Clerkenwell corridor, a large, tanned, well-dressed man carrying a briefcase followed Harry into the room, smiling.

Richard stared in recognition.

'I believe you've already met my friend Roger, haven't you, Richard,' Harry was beaming. 'Jenny, this is Roger Sullivan. An old pal from South Africa.'

The newcomer grinned. 'Ah, the lovely Jenny. I've heard a lot about you. All good!' He turned back to Richard. 'I almost didn't know you out of your grandad's suit. Good look. Nice to see you again so soon!'

Richard's thoughts were cartwheeling. 'But…you?' Then he realised. 'Oh, Christ no!'

'Richard…?' Jenny's eyes were going from one to the other of the three men.

Richard shook his head. How could he have been so stupid? He saw now the extra factor that he hadn't been able to fathom. He saw his mistake. It had been to pay Harry his share of the Creswell Manor sale before he'd bought the River House.

Harry was laughing, ahead of him. 'I did warn you, Richard. Life isn't fair. Sometimes you have to bend the rules a bit. What did you expect?'

Aghast, Jenny turned from the newcomer to Richard. 'He's the one who…?'

Harry grinned. 'The world of finance is brilliant these days, isn't it! In one bank account and out the other somewhere across the world before you can blink. Of course, the bankers take their slice every time. I've often thought I should have been a banker…'

'But we were partners! Friends!' Richard's face spelled incomprehension.

'Exactly!' Harry beamed. 'Which is why I'm going to offer you a terrific deal. Two point seven million and the River House is yours.'

Richard slumped down bitterly on the edge of his desk. 'You bastard! You rotten, cheating…!'

'Oh, come on. This is business. We're all cheats now, you just as much as me. And I've done you a favour. If I hadn't taught you a lesson by nicking the Age Gap tins, you'd never have been able to buy the River House. So, come on, two point seven and it's yours. I know you have the money.'

(ii)

Jenny felt numb. Harry must have been planning this for months, almost as long as Richard had been working on his scheme. He'd known he was going to do it even when they'd had dinner together: even when she'd spent the night with him. How could he?

But of course, he could. He was a conman.

She looked at Richard. He was now suddenly thoughtful. Standing up, he leant back on his desk.

'Well?' Harry pursued.

Richard didn't answer.

'Come on,' Harry ginned.

'Forget it,' Richard said.

'What?'

'We're not buying it.'

Harry looked pained. 'Don't be silly. It's what you want, what this whole caper has been about.'

'That was before we were rich.'

'Richard, this isn't one of your games. Two point seven million and it's yours.'

'No.'

'Jenny, talk some sense into him.'

She shook her head. 'No. Richard's right. We don't want it.'

For the first time, doubt crossed Harry's face. 'But I *want* to sell it to you.'

'And we don't want to buy it.' This was Richard. 'You'll have to sell it to someone else. Right, Mr Sullivan?' And he looked at Sullivan, who didn't look quite as amused any more. 'I'm sure if you wait long enough a buyer will turn up.'

'Richard!' Harry was exasperated. 'Don't be an idiot.'

Richard turned the screw. 'It's a rising market, they say. I suppose you'll just have to hang around a year or two and hope Jerricoe doesn't find you when he discovers how you conned him over Creswell Manor...you being the guy who sold it to him. It wasn't me.'

Jenny found herself fighting a smile.

Suddenly, Harry grinned. 'Ah! I get it. Clever! Okay, tell you what, I don't want to fall out with you. As we're all friends, you can have it for two point five...the amount I paid for it through Roger here...the sum you agreed to pay Jerricoe!'

Jenny looked to Richard.

He was pursing his lips doubtfully. 'Sorry. It's a buyer's market, Harry,' he said.

'You rat!'

'Probably. You taught me.'

Harry spun away from him. 'Jenny, what about you?'

She shook her head.

'Oh, come on...after everything we shared...' His voice had dropped. He was flirting with her again.

Richard looked away.

'Sorry, Harry. As you said, this is business,' she smiled.

For a fraction she thought she saw a shadow of disappointment in Harry's eyes. Then, instantly resilient, he smiled. 'Okay. Two point four million.'

Richard shook his head.

'Two point three. That's a good deal.'

'Two point two,' countered Richard.

'Done!' And Harry clapped his hands with glee. 'Get them the transfer documents to sign, Roger.'

What a strange fellow he was, Jenny was thinking. By double-crossing them, and gambling that they would pay more, he'd just thrown away three hundred thousand pounds. Yet now he was as cheery as ever.

'Anyway, I only popped in for a minute. I ought to be making myself scarce. I'm on my way to Heathrow. I've signed everything in advance. Roger will take care of it.'

Sullivan was already opening his briefcase and taking out the documents.

Harry turned towards the door, then stopped, and looked Jenny firmly in the eyes. 'I did mean what I said on the phone the other day, Jenny…what I told you the other night.'

She smiled.

'Why don't you come with me? Rio's a hell of a place. You'll love it. Come on! Say you will.'

Jenny looked at him. He really did sound as though he meant it. She was aware of Richard watching. She smiled. 'I'll settle for a postcard, Harry. You know the address.'

(iii)

A minicab was outside in the street ready to take Harry to the airport.

'Watch out, Jenny. Beautiful, rich girls like you can attract the wrong sort of man,' Harry smiled as his lips brushed her cheek.

'I'll keep my eyes peeled for them. Promise,' she laughed.

'And you, Richard. It's been fun. If ever you fancy a career change, I'll be waiting. I mean it. Just imagine, you and me as a team. We could take on the world together. We'd be brilliant. Billionaires.'

Richard shook his hand. 'Stay out of trouble.'

Harry laughed and climbed into the car. 'What else would I do?' And with that he slammed the car door.

Richard watched the minicab pull away down the street. When it was gone, he turned towards Jenny. She was waiting.

62.

(i)

'Slow down, Angel, I want to enjoy this,' Jerricoe called as the BMW raced towards the gates of Creswell Manor.

Obediently, Angel raised his foot off the accelerator, the car sedately entered the estate, and Jerricoe settled back in his seat, gloating as he looked out across the green acres of English history. At the top of the long drive, the timber and brick façade of Creswell Manor seemed to welcome them.

'Who'd have thought that Mark Jerricoe would one day own a place like this,' he chuckled. 'I mean, me, the kid from the damp North Kensington basement who got an asthma attack every time the guy with the Alsatian came when my Mum was late with the rent.' And he patted the dog that sat between them.

'I thought you told me you grew up in Wimbledon, Mark,' Hunt queried. 'In a big house by the Common.'

'Well, I lied, didn't I!' Jerricoe grinned. And turning, he watched a herd of deer grazing by a stretching, old oak tree. 'You know, maybe we'll hang on to this place for a while before moving it on. Get to know what it's really like living like a toff.' And he smiled as he noticed Hunt wince.

The BMW was now drawing up in front of the house. Nearby a minibus was parked against the mullioned windows of one wing. Several cars were alongside it.

'They're bloody untidy,' Jerricoe grumbled as he got out of the car and made towards the massive wooden front door. 'They spoil the look of the place. They should be round the back somewhere, out of sight.'

At that moment an elderly gentleman with bright, chestnut coloured hair, appeared around the corner of the house.

'Who's in charge here?' Jerricoe rapped.

'Er, well, I suppose I am,' the man came back politely. 'Can I help you?'

'Yes, you can. I'm the new owner. I want that lot cleared away.'

'I'm sorry?' The man didn't seem to understand.

'I said, I'm Mark Jerricoe. Your new boss. I don't want a bus and a lot of tatty cars spoiling the view in front of my house.'

The man looked from Jerricoe to Hunt and smiled. 'This is a joke, isn't it?'

Jerricoe glared at him. 'Do I look like a joker? What's your name?'

'Everyone knows me as Maurice, but I don't see…'

Jerricoe wasn't listening. 'Well, listen, Maurice. I like tidiness. That bus and those cars are untidy. Get them moved.'

The man suddenly smiled. 'If you'd like to go on a tour, I'm afraid you've missed the last one. Perhaps you could come back tomorrow. We'll have the signs out then. I'm sorry about that. This is the first open day of our new season. We've been a little bit tardy.'

Jerricoe's patience was exhausted. 'I don't want to go on a bloody tour. Don't you understand? This is my house. I just bought it. Today! And you're sacked.'

'I don't think so,' the elderly man replied, with a quiet dignity.

'What?' bawled Jerricoe.

'You can't *buy* Creswell Manor.'

'I told you, I just have.'

'Oh, no. I'm sorry!'

'*No', No!*' So, who do *you* think owns it?'

'Well…theoretically speaking, I suppose…it must be the King.'

The King!' Jerricoe brayed.

'Well ….as Creswell Manor is Crown Property it must, I suppose, in a legal sense at least, belong to His Majesty the King…King Charles.'

'King!!' Jerricoe stopped. 'The *King?*' Suddenly he couldn't move. His mouth opened, then closed again. At last, a murmur broke through. 'Crown Property…?' His voice had dropped to a whisper.

Then, as full realization seeped in, he exploded. 'Find him! Find him! Find that posh cheating estate agent bastard. FIND HIM!'

(ii)

The best thing about being rich, Harry reflected, as he stood with his glass of champagne in the British Airways first class lounge at Terminal 5, waiting for his flight to be called, was the company you got to keep. It was like joining a club, because no matter how casually the rich dressed to travel, it was still a uniform that you could spot at twenty paces. The two guys by the window, for instance, Brazilian bankers or financiers, obviously, in their crisp, lightweight suits; or the plump matron with the snakeskin handbag and her fat businessman husband reading the *Wall Street Journal*. Business wealthy. Then there was the young athletic looking chap with the tattoos, terrible haircut and Armani jeans: obviously a footballer.

Money was everywhere you looked when you had some of your own, and right now he was enjoying looking at a cool, blondish, expensively streaked, late forties elegant lady in a silk shirt, scarf and trousers that a thousand pounds couldn't have bought.

'So, you live in London?' she was asking. Even her South American accent sounded rich.

'Not all the time,' he answered. 'I've just been here selling a place I owned. In Oxfordshire. Very nice. Sixteenth century. Lots of land. But what do I need with an English estate that I'll never live in!' And he realized that, for probably the first time in his life, he'd used a more or less truthful chat-up line. Jenny would have been proud of him.

The woman smiled.

'And you?'

'Just a little vacation.' She paused: then confided. 'I'm just getting over a divorce.'

'Ah! I see!' said Harry. And he settled his very best smile on her. This looked as though it might be a very promising flight.

(iii)

'I want him killed. I want him dead.' Now hysterical, Jerricoe was screaming. 'I want his balls cut off and shoved them down his thieving throat. Just get him for me. I'll kill him myself.'

'Come on, Mark, just get in the car. People are watching,' Hunt urged as he and Angel struggled to push Jerricoe back towards the BMW.

A group of middle-aged German tourists was filing out of Creswell Manor, staring and listening in non-comprehension as they stopped by their minibus. The elderly man with the chestnut hair just shook his head in non-comprehension.

'I don't care. Just find him,' Jerricoe screamed. 'I'll feed him to the bloody dogs myself.'

If he'd only listened, Hunt was thinking as he steered his boss into the BMW. If he'd only been prepared to take advice. No doubt, the bastard would blame him for missing something in the paperwork. Perhaps he had done. But property greed was the real culprit. He'd gone for a dodgy deal. And because it was dodgy he couldn't now go to the police.

'Nine bloody million. Nine million he took,' Jerricoe was gasping asthmatically as he was pushed into the back seat with the dog. 'Nine million!'

Hunt climbed into the front passenger seat and slammed the door. Quickly, Angel turned the BMW around, passing the watching Germans, and headed back down the drive.

As the car pulled through the gates of Creswell Manor and headed back towards London and a world they both knew, Hunt felt himself smiling. He'd been right and Jerricoe had been wrong. It was a good feeling.

'It's only money, Mark,' he said. 'Think how well we did on the River House.'

63.

(i)

Sarojini was making tea for her sons when the phone rang. It was Jenny, wanting to know if she and Sanjeev were free for dinner.

'*Tonight?*'

'It's very important. We must all be there,' Jenny insisted. 'Everyone from the River House. Richard, me, the Morrisons, and both of you. You *must* come.'

This wasn't so much an invitation as a demand. 'Well, Sanjeev has a cousin who lives near here. She sometimes baby-sits,' Sarojini ventured uncertainly.

'Perfect,' Jenny encouraged. 'We're all going to a restaurant in Chelsea. Very smart. Dress up.'

(ii)

It was the only restaurant Jenny knew where a small private room could be booked for dinner. It didn't matter what it cost; for the first time in her life, it really didn't. It just had to be private.

She and Richard got there first. She'd dressed up for the occasion in a new skirt and blouse she'd bought over Easter, together with a blue silk scarf, silver earrings and a matching bracelet. There would never be another night like this one. She had to look her best. Even Richard looked semi-smart, in his black corduroy jacket.

Mr Morrison looked slightly unnerved when shown into the private room, which was arabesque in design, but Mrs Morrison could scarcely contain her delight. She always liked going to fancy places. The Ghelanis were the last to arrive.

'So, this is all very nice, but why are we here?' Sarojini enquired as they took their seats at the table.

Jenny just smiled.

(iii)

Richard waited until the main course was served and eaten, the waiters had temporarily left the room and the doors were closed before he began to speak.

'As you know,' he began, 'Jenny and I, with your help, have been involved in a kind of game to correct a wrong these past few months, and, well …. today we won that game.'

At his side Jenny nodded her head.

'In simple terms,' he continued, 'that means there are now two new landlords at the River House, Jenny and me. And the new landlords would like it very much if the former tenants, who were forced to leave the house, now return as co-owners of the house with them.' He smiled around at the guests.

There was silence. Instead of breaking into applause the two Morrisons and the Ghelanis just stared at him.

Perhaps they didn't understand, Richard thought. 'Don't you see?' he tried again. 'This means that we'll all own the house together and we'll be able to have our flats for as long as we want them. No-one can push any of us out ever again. We'll share the freehold and be owner occupiers, and instead of having to pay rent or a mortgage we'll even have some money left over to renovate the house the way we want it.'

Once again nobody spoke.

Jenny looked anxiously around. 'Richard planned this for all of us,' she urged. 'He didn't do it for the money. He did it for us. To stop Jerricoe forcing us out.'

The two couples looked from one to the other. At last, Mrs Morrison spoke. 'And we're very grateful to you, Richard. But, and I don't know about Sarojini and Sanjeev, if you don't mind, we won't be coming back to the River House. It was your plan. You did it. Not us. We only helped a tiny bit. We just wanted to have our little bit of revenge.'

At her side her husband nodded.

Richard didn't speak. He suddenly felt emotional. Jenny's hand was on his arm.

There was a long, empty silence, broken only as the Ghelanis murmured to each other at the other side of the table.

At last, Sarojini spoke for them. 'Would it be rude to ask exactly how much extra money there is left over after buying the River House?'

'Well...over a million pounds.'

Eyes opened wide in astonishment. 'So much?'

'So much,' repeated Jenny.

Richard looked around. A new idea was forming. 'Look, Jenny and I, we'd really like you to come back. We always thought of the River House as your home as much as ours. But if you don't want to come back and share the house with us, what would you say if we divided the extra money between you so that you can buy the houses you do want to live in?'

(iv)

They'd taken a taxi to Chelsea, but, as it was a mild evening, they asked to be dropped off down the towpath so that they could make the rest of their way home on foot. As they walked and looked across the river and its flecks of mirrored lights, Jenny put her arm through Richard's. She didn't even realise that she'd done it, until he looked at her in evident pleasure, and, tightening his elbow, cuddled her closer against his body.

The evening hadn't turned out the way they'd expected. But, in the end, it had been agreed. The money from Jerricoe would be divided equally four ways. As they'd been parting, Angela Morrison had already been talking about buying a flat 'somewhere nice, further up the river, near Maidenhead'. Her daughter's family lived there. Ted Morrison's eyes had been wet with happiness.

For her part, Sarojini Ghelani had mentioned Rickmansworth, a garden big enough for a decent football pitch for the boys, and good schools. Sanjeev had agreed, of course.

Richard and Jenny didn't talk as they walked along the towpath. There was too much in this moment to enjoy: too much to anticipate. Only as they turned the corner and stood in the lane, gazing over the wall and looking at the River House was the silence broken.

'So....?' Jenny asked as they hesitated at the garden gate, like a couple viewing a potential new home for the first time. 'What do you think?'

Richard shook his head. 'It needs a lot of work. Redecorating, replumbing, a new roof, repointing. And a new garden needs laying. Altogether I'd say it's pretty decrepit.'

'This is true. But I'll paint and I'll polish and I'll work my fingers to the bone...'

He looked at her. 'You know, for a moment today, I was half afraid you might decide to go off to Rio with Harry.'

'What?' She pulled a face at the idea.

'Well...for a second it seemed a possibility.'

She smiled. 'Why would I do a thing like that, when I've got everything I want here?'

'Everything?'

'Everyone.'

For a long moment they smiled at each other. Then, hand in hand, they walked up the garden path and into their home.

AFTERWORD

In years to come, Richard and Jenny would sometimes ask themselves whether their Figure of Eight game, their conning of Jerricoe, had been evidence of a serious moral failing. Certainly, they had committed a criminal act by stealing a fortune. But, as time passed, they realised that they felt absolutely no guilt. Jerricoe's greed had brought it on himself. Besides, something positive had come out of it.

The River House Children's Stage School hadn't been in the original plan. But it was such a big house it seemed perfect for a place where local children who showed an interest in drama could be taken after school and in the holidays. It was Jenny's idea. Maxwell was among her first pupils.

She and Richard could have afforded to have builders turn the River House into both a home and a school. But Richard was useful with his hands and Jenny enjoyed decorating. So, they had begun doing it themselves. There was no hurry. They had the second half of their lives in which to build their home together.

On sunny afternoons Jenny and Richard would often get out their bikes and go cycling along the river towpath. But they never saw anywhere they liked as much as they liked the River House.

Also by Ray Connolly

SUNDAY MORNING

'A model of its kind…one of the factors that makes *Sunday Morning* remarkable is Ray Connolly's ability not just to endow his secondary characters with distinct and unmistakeable personalities, but also the understated genius with which he modulates and develops the voices of his pivotal quartet' - *Sunday Times*

'Action packed and original…a terrific read' - *Daily Mail*

'A quality read…well researched, stylishly written' - *Daily Telegraph*

'A novel that gloriously captures Sixties London…You feel you know and care about each person. A highly recommended read' - *South Africa Star*

SHADOWS ON A WALL

'Bright and blackly funny…the War and Peace of Hollywood novels' - *New York Library Journal*

'Satire…with a couple of black comedy surprises that would have delighted Alfred Hitchcock' - *San Francisco Chronicle*

'Belongs on that shelf of good literature about Hollywood' - *Washington Post*

'Probably the best novel about movie making ever written' - *Sunday Express*

LOVE OUT OF SEASON

'Funny, charming and compassionate, successfully transposing the conventions of Shakespearian comedy to the 21st Century' - *Mail On Sunday* ****

'The perfect book to give someone who's feeling a bit down… Funny, fun and fundamentally wise, this is a cracker of a book' - *Dublin Evening Herald* *****

'SORRY, BOYS, YOU FAILED THE AUDITION'

On January 30th, 1969, John Lennon ended the Beatles' filmed concert on the roof of their Apple headquarters in London by joking: 'Thank you very much. We hope we passed the audition.' It was the last time the four would be seen playing together.

But what would have happened if in the summer of 1962, the Beatles hadn't impressed at their last chance to sign a record deal? What would the future have held for John, Paul, George and Ringo if producer George Martin had said 'No'?
(Adapted from Ray Connolly's BBC radio play)

BEING ELVIS - A LONELY LIFE

'Connolly carefully and sympathetically paints the many faces of Presley, faces eventually shrouded in despair' - *Kirkus Reviews*

'A sympathetic and exceptionally well written account' - *USA Today*

BEING JOHN LENNON - A RESTLESS LIFE

'Excellent... Connolly draws on his archive conversations with the Beatles to give a superb portrait of a dissatisfied star who couldn't stop reinventing himself' - *Daily Telegraph*

'This careful, thoughtful biography... For Connolly it is Lennon's insecurities that are ultimately most revealing' - *Sunday Times*

'Brisk and eminently readable' - *The Times*

THE RAY CONNOLLY BEATLES ARCHIVE

'Most books about the Beatles are by writers who never met them. I was lucky. I was a journalist. and I was there.' - *Ray Connolly on this anthology of his many newspaper articles about, and interviews with, the Beatles.*

Printed in Dunstable, United Kingdom